...husband, daughter, and two pups. When
she's not writing, Kelly enjoys reading and spending time with her family.
She is down to earth and very in touch with her readers, both on social
media and at signings.

Visit Kelly Elliott online:

www.kellyelliottauthor.com
@author_kelly
www.facebook.com/KellyElliottAuthor/

Also by Kelly Elliott (published by Piatkus)

The Love Wanted in Texas series

Lost Love

COWBOYS & ANGELS
Book 1

NEW YORK TIMES & USA TODAY BESTSELLING AUTHOR

KELLY ELLIOTT

Piatkus
An imprint of
Little, Brown Book Group
Carmelite House
50 Victoria Embankment
London EC4Y 0DZ

An Hachette UK Company
www.hachette.co.uk

www.littlebrown.co.uk

piatkus

PIATKUS

First published in Great Britain in 2017 by Piatkus

1 3 5 7 9 10 8 6 4 2

Copyright © Kelly Elliott 2017

The moral right of the author has been asserted.

A CIP catalogue record for this book
is available from the British Library.

ISBN 978-0-349-41840-7

Printed and bound in Great Britain by
Clays Ltd, St Ives plc

Cover photo and designer: Sara Eirew Photography
Editor: Cori McCarthy, Yellowbird Editing
Proofer: Amy Rose Capetta, Yellowbird Editing
Interior Designer: JT Formatting

Papers used by Piatkus are from well-managed forests
and other responsible sources.

PROLOGUE

The rushing water of the Frio River wasn't enough to drown out the sound of Paxton's tears. They replayed in my head, and nothing would ever be able to erase them.

Lifting the beer to my lips, I took a long drink. My brother Cord sat next to me. He was the only one who knew the terrible secret that would haunt me forever.

"She hates me," I mumbled.

"Right now she does. She won't always."

I finished the bottle and set it next to me. It was the night of my high school graduation and one of the worst days of my life.

"I left her. She told me she was pregnant, and I freaked out and left her. The only thing I could think of was how our lives would be ruined."

"You came back, Steed."

Letting out a gruff laugh, I shook my head before dragging my hands down my face.

"I came back too late. I'll never forget the look in her eyes when she told me she lost the baby and I breathed out a sigh of relief. I've never seen her so gutted." My head dropped, and I felt the tears build in my eyes. "She told me she never wanted to see me again."

Peering up, I turned to my brother. "What do I do, Cord? I love her more than the air I breathe and she can't stand the sight of me."

He shook his head then shrugged. "Give her time. That's all you can do."

My heart told me to run after her. To pull her into my arms and show her how sorry I was. Beg her to forgive me.

If only I'd listened to my heart and not my head.

Steed

Ten years later

I pulled up to the gate and grinned. Ten years ago, I left Texas after graduation and made my way to Oregon. I hadn't seen home since.

With a quick peek up, I passed under the driveway sign that led to my father's cattle ranch.

Frio Cattle Company

"Is this it, Daddy?"

Glancing down to the beautiful blonde hair and blue-eyed girl in the front seat, I nodded. "This is it, pumpkin."

Her smile grew bigger. "I can't wait to see everyone! Do you think they'll be excited to see me?"

My chest tightened. "Of course they will, Chloe. They're family."

Chloe frowned. "Mommy was never happy to see me."

That's because your mommy was a fucking bitch.

I'd met Kim, Chloe's mother and the first woman I'd dated since Paxton, towards the end of my senior year of college.

"Mommy had problems. Loving herself was hard, pumpkin, so it made it even harder for her to love anyone else."

Chloe nodded. Like she always did when I told her the same answer about her worthless mother.

When both of Kim's parents died, she fell into a serious funk. The only way I knew how to pull her out of it was ask her to marry me. It was stupid. *I* was stupid. When I realized I had made a huge mistake, she begged me not to leave. The night I told her I wanted a divorce she told me she was pregnant. Nine months later Chloe arrived and Kim turned into a completely different person. Her thirst for my family's money was the only thing that drove her to stay in the marriage. For some insane reason, she thought she could get her hands on my parents' wealth through me. It took years of fighting, keeping visits with my family a secret.

Finally, I played off a lie that my parents had disowned me. Kim gave up and divorced me. I'd asked her for a divorce so many times her hate for me grew after each attempt, making my life, and unfortunately Chloe's, miserable.

"Daddy, am I a bad girl if I don't miss mommy?" Chloe asked, staring at her little feet.

I took her hand in mine.

"No, pumpkin. I don't miss her either. I wish we could have come to Texas a long time ago, and I'm sorry I wasn't able to make it happen sooner."

She smiled. "We're here now! And I know I'm gonna love it! It's our new home."

"It's always been home."

Home.

The one place I longed to be, but was also scared to death of. Memories of this place were dangerously strong, but Chloe and I needed family. She needed a sense of normal after five years of utter crazy. And I needed to right a wrong that was long overdue.

Paxton.

I wasn't even sure she still lived in town. For all I knew she was married to Joe asshole Miller. I pushed the thought from my mind.

"Let's go see Granddaddy and Grammy," I said.

Chloe fist pumped. "Yes! I'm so excited. Can I ride a horse?"

"Yes," I replied.

"What about a cow?"

"If you want."

Her eyes lit up as the gate swung open. "Really? I can ride a cow?"

Laughing, I nodded.

"Does Granddaddy have goats?"

"Yep."

Chloe's head dropped back in the seat. "I'm so happy, Daddy!"

I'd told Chloe stories about how I grew up on a cattle ranch with my six brothers and sisters. Each night when she went to bed, she'd ask for a story, especially if she was able to talk to my parents over Skype that evening. It had been hard keeping her from everyone. The memories of Paxton kept me from returning to Texas for the first four years after I left and then the nightmare called Kim was the next roadblock. But that was the past. I was looking to the future not only for me, but for Chloe.

"Is Texas like Oregon, Daddy?"

"No, baby. It's a lot hotter and it doesn't rain so much."

She smiled. "More time to play outside! With my new goat!"

I chuckled. My father had told Chloe over Skype a few days back that he was going to buy her a pet goat. She had the name picked out already. Patches.

We drove down the drive, and Chloe took it all in. "Where's the house?"

"Your grandparents own a lot of land, pumpkin. The house is pretty far back."

With a nod, she turned and stared out the window. A little girl shriek came from her lips. "Cows! Daddy, look at all the cows!"

Even though I was queasy from the idea of being back home and the chance of running into Paxton, I was glad to see Chloe's excitement. She was finally going to understand what normal was.

She gasped. "Is that our new house?"

I braked and stared at the house I'd grown up in. So many memories. All of them good. I couldn't think of one bad memory I had growing up here on the ranch. Maybe Tripp putting that scorpion in my bed. Or Cord dropping the bale of hay on my head. I smiled. Yeah. That was what I wanted for my daughter. To grow up with family in the greatest place on earth.

My parents' ranch.

The two-story sandstone house sat among live oak and pecan trees. Throw in a few magnolia trees my father had planted for my mother and it was the perfect setting. It wasn't a small house by any means. Over ten thousand square feet.

"That's the main house, pumpkin. We're going to be living in the guesthouse."

She studied me and I couldn't help but be left breathless by the sight of my own daughter. Those bright blue eyes held so much hope in them. "How many houses do Granddaddy and Grammy have?" she asked, her blonde pony swinging as her head tilted in confusion.

Chuckling, I said, "One main house, two ranch hand houses, and two guest houses."

Her eyes widened. "Wow."

"Yeah, wow."

"How many bedrooms does this house have?"

I laughed. "Ten."

Her eyes widened in surprise. "That's a lot of places to play hide and seek."

"It sure is, pumpkin."

Chloe's life was about to change drastically. We had lived in a nice house in Oregon, but it was nothing like this. It was more your typical middle class twenty-three hundred square foot house. I worked for an investment firm right out of college. The only good part of that job was working from home, which allowed me to care for Chloe since Kim was pretty much gone every single day. Sometimes for days at a time on what she called her "spa trips."

I lightly pressed the gas and we made our way up to the front of the house. I parked and got out. Chloe jumped out of the car, unbuckling her dolls from the back seat.

"We're at our new home! Look how beautiful it is!" Chloe said while showing her dolls the house.

My chest ached as I smiled. I'd heard her so many times telling her dolls how much she would always love them and be the best mommy. Unlike her own mother who hardly ever sat down and played with Chloe.

I shut the car door and took everything in. Nothing had changed in the ten years since I'd been gone. The house still had fresh flowers hanging from pots across the front porch. The four black rocking chairs still sat in what appeared to be the same spots. My stomach dropped as a memory hit me of Paxton sitting on my lap as we talked about our future.

Chloe pulled my hand. "Daddy, why do you look so sad?"

I squatted down and placed my hand on the side of her face. "I'm not sad, pumpkin."

She shook her head. "Your eyes are sad."

I let out a soft breath. This little girl had a window into my soul, always had. For as long as I could remember, when I was feeling down, she would tell me my eyes looked sad. Never could hide anything from this one. "I love you, Chloe Lynn. All I want is for us both to be happy."

She smiled, then frowned, her little eyes growing wet with tears. "Mommy won't be coming to live with us, will she?"

Swallowing hard, I fought to take a breath. This was my karma. The pain I had to suffer for the action I took ten years ago. I shook my head and pulled her in for a hug. "No, baby. Mommy is no longer a part of our lives, and I promise she will never hurt you. Never."

Chloe patted my back, as if she was trying to console me at the same time. When she pulled away, her grin was back, along with the light in her eyes.

"Maybe we can find me a new mommy!"

My eyes widened. My daughter had longed for a mother to love her and I had tried my best to make up for the lack of love from Kim. It was beginning to hit me how much Chloe had longed for the connection I wasn't able to give her. "Um… well… let's not worry about that right now."

She grinned and nodded. "Okay. We'll wait a week."

I was about to reply when two loud screams came from the front porch. Chloe turned and let out a little scream of her own.

Yep. My daughter is a Parker woman. They like to scream.

"Grammy! Aunt Meli!" She took off running and I was spared the new mommy ordeal—at least for a week.

My sister Amelia dropped to her knees and caught Chloe as she barreled into her.

My mother made a beeline straight to me. Her brown hair was pulled up, leaving me a clear view of her gray eyes, which danced with happiness. The bits of red that ran through her hair seemed to glow in the sun. "Steed, darling I'm so happy to have you home."

Holding out my arms, I held my mother tightly. "It's good to be home, Mom."

"Your things came two days ago. I hope you don't mind, but Amelia and I took to placing everything in the house. If you don't like it, you and your brothers can change it up."

"I'm sure it's fine."

She pinched her brows together. "Steed, I know the house is fully furnished and that's why you didn't have any furniture, but there's no bedroom set for Chloe. Of course you're more than welcome to keep the furniture that's in the house, but I thought you might want something a little more kid friendly."

I shook my head. "I want to start fresh. The fewer memories of Kim...the better. We stopped at Haverty's Furniture on the way here and Chloe picked out a brand-new bedroom set. It will be delivered on Saturday."

My mother smiled. "Oh, she'll love that! I'm sorry you couldn't bring your things."

With a weak smile, I replied, "It's not a big deal."

Kim had never physically abused Chloe, but mentally she had done a number on both of us. Her constant screaming had grown worse as the years ticked by. But she also stayed away more, giving both Chloe and me a much-needed break. I was having a private detective follow Kim in the hopes of catching her in an affair.

When she showed up to my job one day with divorce papers and legal paperwork signing all parental rights over to me, I wanted to jump for joy. Once she figured she wasn't getting a dime of money from my family, she realized she had better things to do with her life. Chloe and I weren't part of the plan and that was fine by me. I'd wasted over six years of my life on a relationship that had started out as a desperate attempt to fuck Paxton out of my mind. Look where that shit got me.

My mother shook her head as we walked toward the front door where Amelia and Chloe had disappeared. "I still don't understand how a mother could walk away from her child."

"It was easy. She never wanted a daughter. Chloe was a bargaining tool to Kim, not a child."

We entered the large foyer, my heart about to burst because my father was holding up Chloe as she laughed. My whole family had flown out to Oregon right after Chloe was born, unfortunately giving Kim ideas about my family's money. My parents had come to visit twice a year the first few years of Chloe's life and never questioned why I couldn't bring Chloe to Texas. Then when Kim went full force bat-shit crazy, I had to get creative with my parents' trips. We had gone on a few weekend camping trips where my folks had met up with us. Chloe had been old enough to know it had to be kept a secret from Kim. I hated making Chloe keep such a secret, but it was necessary if I wanted to keep her in my parents' life and get us away from Kim. Other than the few visits, only Skype calls kept Chloe involved in their world. She had loved calling my brothers and sisters and was so excited to finally meet them all.

"The princess is finally home!" my father said, beaming.

I'd never seen Chloe look so happy. "Where are all my uncles?"

Everyone laughed.

My father spun his granddaughter around and set her on the large table that stood in the middle of the foyer. "Tonight, princess. You'll see them all tonight at dinner."

It was my mother's turn to shower Chloe with attention. "Oh, we are going to have so much fun! I think you should have your own area of the garden, Chloe."

With a gasp, Chloe nodded in excitement then did some sort of happy dance while my parents took it all in. My little sister Amelia gave me a sweet smile. I stood back and took her in. Pictures of her over the years didn't do her beauty justice.

"Holy shit. You're a grown woman."

She blushed. "Well, I *was* only twelve when you left."

My heart dropped. "I'm sorry, Meli. I'm sorry I left you."

Tilting her head, the grin grew wider. "I had four other brothers to take care of me."

I shook my head as I brushed her strawberry blonde hair from her face. "My little sister. A New York Times bestselling author." She blushed again, and I kissed her on the forehead. "I'm so proud of you."

"Aunt Meli! Will you read me one of your books tonight before bedtime?"

Amelia laughed. "How about we read one of my favorite bedtime stories instead?"

Chloe pouted then smiled. "Is it about horses? Or cows? Or goats?"

Turning to give me a questioning look, I replied, "Chloe is somewhat obsessed with the idea of living amongst the cows, horses, and goats."

Amelia walked up to Chloe and picked her up off the table. "Then I suggest we head down to the horse barn. I'll introduce you to my favorite pony on the ranch. Stanley."

Jumping with excitement, Chloe turned to me. "May I go, Daddy? Please?"

"Of course you can."

My mother kissed Chloe on the cheek. "Have fun and remember, Amelia, back to school night is tonight, and we're heading there before dinner."

Amelia was about to say something when my mother shook her head. Frowning, Amelia glanced between our mom and me.

Chloe broke out into a dance. "I'm startin' kindergarten. I'm a big girl! I'm gonna go to school!"

Everyone chuckled at Chloe's outburst, everyone except for me. I groaned and shook my head. I wasn't ready for any of this.

"Amelia, why don't you take Chloe to the barn," my mother said.

My sister took Chloe's hand. "We'll take a little tour and then head to the barn."

"Okay!" Chloe said as she turned back and waved to me. "Later, Dad."

I stumbled back and clutched my chest. "She called me … Dad. What in the hell? We're hear five minutes and she's grown up enough she thinks she can call me Dad?"

My father hit me on the back. "Come on, let's go make a drink and you call tell us all about your trip down from Oregon."

"Better make it a strong one," I mumbled.

I followed my father into the den as my mother wrapped her arm around me. "I've already registered Chloe at the school. They only need you to sign a few things and provide a copy of her birth certificate and proof of immunizations."

I hadn't given my parents much notice before moving back to Texas. The divorce was quick and easy, and I'd gotten an offer on the house within three days of listing it. I'd given Kim half of the money I made on the house, even though she never put a dime of her money into it; it felt like the right thing to do.

Kissing my mother on the cheek, I said, "Thanks, Mom. I appreciate you taking care of all of that."

She grinned. "I'm just so happy you're home. Now if we can only get your sister Waylynn to move back."

Dad handed me a rum and coke, and I asked my mother, "Is everything okay between her and Jack?"

My parents both frowned. Neither of them had liked Jack Wilson. In their eyes, he stole their oldest child away and forced her to give up her dreams. "She's unhappy. I hear it in her voice when I talk to her. Amelia is going to New York in the spring. She'll let me know if our Waylynn is happy or not."

I took a drink and laughed. "Sending in the spy, huh?"

Mom lifted her brow and gave me an inquisitive look. My parents had seven kids. Each of us meant the world to them. If they had it their way, we'd all live on the ranch. Under one roof.

Waylynn, my oldest sister, was supposed to be a boy. Dad was certain of it and had planned on naming his first son after his favorite country singer, Waylon Jennings. When the baby came out a girl, he insisted on keeping the name Waylon. Mom agreed to it but changed the spelling. After Waylynn came my brother Tripp. As a kid, he took everything seriously. One reason he makes a good lawyer. Next came my brother Mitchell and me. The twins in the family. The only thing we ever had in common was looking like each other and even then, there were differences. While he always does the right thing, I seem to be the polar opposite. My mother stresses day in and day out over his job as a Texas Ranger. Mitchell loves being a cop though.

Then you have Cord. My bar owning, rebel brother. And the one person who knows my deepest, darkest secret. Cord's dream was to open a bar and, to my father's disapproval, he owns a country western bar in town. Of course, he still works the ranch when needed. It's in all our blood and none of us could ever walk away from it.

The baby boy in the family was Trevor. He grew up to be one hundred percent my father's son. Loves the ranch. Loves being on top of a horse...and a woman.

Last but not least, Amelia, the baby in the family and what my father likes to call his gift from God. My mother was told she wouldn't have any more kids after a hard pregnancy and delivery with Trevor. But two years later, our baby sister was here. She is the apple of my parents' eye.

"Steed, did you hear anything I just said?"

My eyes lifted to my mother. "What was that, Mom?"

"Is Chloe excited for school?"

"Yes. I had to explain to her that the school wasn't going to be like her pre-school. It's going to be smaller."

My mother lifted her brows and asked, "Well how big was her pre-school?"

I laughed. "Mom, I lived in Portland, Oregon. Hundreds of thousands of people live there. How many people live in Oak Springs? Six hundred?"

"We're getting closer to twelve hundred. If you count the out-skirts of town," my father said as he took a drink.

Lifting her glass to her lips, my mother gave me a smirk that hinted she was up to something. "I have a feeling Chloe is going to *love* Oak Springs elementary much better than she would love some overcrowded school in Oregon."

I sighed. "I hope so. Hopefully Mrs. Bagnet isn't still the kin-dergarten teacher. That woman was mean as hell."

My father and mother exchanged glances. Dad acted like he was about to say something when my mother cut him off. "Oh, no, she retired four years ago. We have a new kindergarten teacher who's been there a few years."

"Thank, God," I mumbled as I finished off my drink.

CHAPTER 2

Steed

Chloe walked between my mother and Amelia as we made our way down the long hall. I couldn't help the small smile that tugged at my mouth. I hadn't been in these halls in a long time. A small part of me panicked, thinking I'd see Paxton. It had been her dream to become a teacher, but I made it a habit to never talk about her. My mother had tried to get me to tell her what happened, but if I told her the truth, she'd hate me. I made her vow to never talk about Paxton after my mother told me Joe Miller's mother said he and Paxton were close to becoming engaged. I guess they had started dating their senior year at Texas A & M.

That little bit of information is what sent me into Kim's bed and threw me into a depression that lasted for months. It was part of the reason I asked Kim to marry me. I was running from the past desperately. After that one conversation about Paxton and Joe, I never asked about her again, and if my mother brought her up, I'd threaten to end the call. She quickly learned it was a subject I didn't want to breach.

"I can't wait to meet my teacher!" Chloe said. "I hope she's pretty!"

Amelia laughed, and my mother replied, "Oh, she's *very* pretty. You're going to love her, Chloe."

"Mom, do you know who the teacher is?" I asked as they rounded the corner and slipped into the classroom before answering. I stopped to let another family go first. The guy seemed familiar, but I couldn't place him. We stared at each other for a moment before we both let it go. When I walked in, I quickly scanned the room. It was cuter than any of the pre-school classrooms Chloe had been in. I grinned when I saw the reading nook. When my eyes landed on the beanbag chair, a memory of Paxton hit me so hard it took my breath away.

"One day when I'm a teacher, I'm going to have a special reading area for my students. One where they can curl up in a beanbag chair and get lost in the words of a book."

"What grade do you want to teach, Pax?" I asked, holding her in my arms as we looked at the stars.

"Kindergarten. I think that's where my calling will be."

I took a few steps back. My head spun and my heart slammed against my chest.

Oh, holy fuck.

When I turned around to search out my mother, Paxton's blue eyes met mine. We stood there for a few moments, staring. Her brown hair was pulled up in a ponytail with a few loose curls hanging down. My eyes swept over her body. The young girl I fell in love with had turned into a beautiful woman. The most beautiful woman I'd ever laid eyes on.

Paxton seemed totally stunned to see me, just as I was stunned to see her. I thought I saw a smile start to form at the corners of her mouth, but then it pulled into a frown. She headed my way, and I had the urge to cover my balls when I saw a dark look in her eyes. Her last words to me—that she would cut off my dick and shove it down my throat—flashed through my mind.

I grinned and that seemed to make her even angrier.

"What are you doing here?" she asked in a low voice.

"I'm here because—"

She grabbed my arm, digging her nails into my skin, and pulled me into a large supply closet. With a look of pure anger, she shoved her finger into my chest. "How dare you show up here. You have got some nerve, Steed Parker. You're lucky I'm not holding scissors or I'd make good on my threat."

I swallowed hard and tried to take a step away, but bumped into something.

"Get out of my classroom."

"Hey, wait one second, Paxton. I didn't even know—"

She shook her head. "Don't make a scene. There are people we went to high school with out there, Steed. I'm begging you to please leave."

Yes. That's who that was.

"Manny Patterson. That's who that was." I said snapping my fingers when the realization hit me.

Opening the door, Paxton stepped out and softly said, "Please leave." Her voice broke, causing my chest to tighten. My eyes searched the room. A few people were staring so I quickly stepped out of the supply closet with Paxton following me out. "I don't know why you're here, but *please* leave. I can't do this. This is my job, Steed. Please."

Before I had a chance to explain, Chloe ran up to me. "Daddy! Daddy! Come look at my desk. It's so pretty!"

I bent down and smiled. "I'll be right there, pumpkin. I'm talking to an old friend."

Chloe glanced up and gasped. "You're beautiful. Are you a princess?"

I watched Paxton's anger melt. She gazed lovingly at Chloe even though I could see the hurt all over her face. "No, sweetheart. I'm Ms. Monroe, the teacher."

My heart dropped as Paxton confirmed what I had already known.

My eyes swung over to my mother. She was smiling at us. She knew. She fucking knew.

Fuck. My. Life.

"Daddy! Did you hear that? Your friend is my kindergarten teacher!" Her arms wrapped around my neck as I stood. My entire world came to a stop as I watched Paxton's eyes fill with tears.

Damn it. Fucking hell this is not how I wanted to tell Paxton about Chloe.

"Daddy?" she asked as her voice shook. Chloe turned to face her.

"We moved here from Oregon. It rains there all the time. Daddy said I can have my very own goat and ride a cow!"

Paxton stared at Chloe for the longest time. My heart was pounding so hard in my chest I was sure everyone in the room could hear it. The memory of Paxton's cries filled my head so loudly I wanted to cover my ears and run until I couldn't hear anything. Couldn't feel anything.

Like I did ten years ago.

Finally, Paxton let out a small chuckle. "It does rain a lot in Oregon. And a goat? How exciting is that? Chloe, why don't you head on over to your desk. There's a surprise in it for you."

I set Chloe on the ground and watched as Paxton bent down to my daughter. She studied her face and blinked back tears. "I'm so happy you're here, Chloe. I can't wait to get to know you. Welcome to Oak Springs."

With a huge grin, Chloe wrapped her arms around Paxton's neck. "Oh, thank you Ms. Monroe! I'm going to go find my surprise."

Jetting toward her desk, I glanced down to Paxton who was still bent down. Her hand covered her mouth as she tried to keep her emotions in. She stood slowly and faced me.

"I'm so sorry, Paxton. I had no idea you were the teacher. I'd have come and talked to you first had I known. I'd never just spring this on you. I hope you know that."

Her chin trembled before she lifted it higher and cleared her throat. "If you'll excuse me, I need to talk with the other parents. Please … um … take a look around the classroom. Up at my um … the um … my desk there are a few examples of what we'll be working on the first week of school. There's also a supply list so please pick that up before you leave."

She paused for a moment before she regained her composure. "Feel free to sign up for volunteering or have your wife. It's much appreciated."

I took a step closer to her. "Paxton. There is no—"

She shook her head and a devastated expression moved across her face. It felt like someone had punched me in the gut. "Stop. Please don't. I can't do this right now. I can't."

Spinning on her heels, she walked toward another family. I watched as she smiled big and bright and introduced herself as if I hadn't just shattered her world…again.

My mother's happy expression was now replaced with one of confusion. Anger swept over my body. I walked to where she stood with Amelia.

"Why didn't you tell me Paxton was the kindergarten teacher?"

She shrugged. "You forbid me to speak about her."

"I need to speak with you in private, Mom. Now."

Leaning over, I kissed Chloe on the cheek. "Daddy and Grammy have to go talk grown up talk. Aunt Meli is right here okay?"

She was searching through her desk, looking for her surprise. "Okay, Daddy."

I followed my mother out of the room and down the hall. The town of Oak Springs was small enough still that kinder through twelfth grade was on the same campus. The high school was separated by a small breezeway. When we finally came to a deserted area, I lost my self-control.

"What were you thinking? Why in the hell didn't you warn me Paxton was the teacher? Mom! I wasn't even sure she lived here in town!"

Pinching her brows, she placed her hands on her hips. "Do not talk to me in that tone young man. You're the one who said no one was to talk about her. That you didn't want to know what she was doing or where she lived. I was only going by *your* wishes. Now I don't know what happened between the two of you, but you were meant to be together."

I raked my hand through my hair. "Goddamn it, Mom. Why did you do this?"

She slapped me on the back of the head. "Do *not* use the Lord's name in vain."

I dropped my hands to my knees and dragged a few deep breaths. My emotions were all over the place. The moment I saw those eyes, my stomach dropped and I wanted nothing more than to kiss her and beg for her forgiveness. She looked at me with such hate that all I could feel was fear and regret. Guilt. Add that shit in there too. Lots of it.

Then the sadness in her eyes about dropped me to the floor. All I seemed to do was hurt her.

"Steed, I don't know if you had a fight or what it was that caused you to run away to Oregon, but think of this as a second chance."

I held up my hand to stop her from talking. "Mom, don't. You have no idea what you're trying to do."

"You both loved each other so much. Don't you remember the plans you two made together? You were both going to go to Texas A & M. Then move back home and build a life together. You talked about marriage and kids."

"Please stop," I begged.

She kept talking and my stomach cramped. I could no longer understand her words. The only thing I heard was Paxton crying.

Louder. And louder, until it became so deafening I yelled out. "Stop!"

Mom jumped. "My goodness, Steed, what has gotten into you? I think you're tired from that drive."

I couldn't stop the words before they slipped from my mouth. "Did you ever think the reason I left was pretty damn big, Mom? I was gone for ten years!"

"You were being stubborn. It's a Parker trait," she said.

I shook my head. "No, Mom. Paxton was pregnant and lost the baby the day before graduation."

Her eyes widened in shock and her hand clapped over her mouth.

I covered my face and let out a loud grunt before looking at her. "When she told me she was pregnant, I told her I didn't want to be a father. That we were too young, and that it was going to ruin our lives."

Her hand dropped to her side as she whispered, "Oh, Steed. Please tell me you didn't ask her to—"

"No. But I told her I couldn't be a father, which was just as bad. I avoided her for a week after she told me. Then she lost the baby, and I … I was so relieved. She screamed and yelled and told me she hated me and never wanted to see me again. I didn't know what to do. Cord said she needed time."

Anger moved across my mother's face. "Cord knew?"

"He was the only one who knew."

The anger on her face quickly fell to horror. "You left her alone to deal with losing your child?"

Old guilt ripped through me newly. My mother was staring at me for the first time in my life with disappointment in her eyes.

"Yes," I whispered.

She turned away. I closed my eyes and wished like hell I could travel back in time. I'd have done things so differently. I would have held Paxton in my arms and told her everything would be okay. That we would get through it together.

Instead, I ran like a coward. I walked onto the football team at Oregon State and played for them for four years. Never once coming back to the only woman I ever loved.

"That's why you never came home?" She turned and looked me in the eyes. I stood there in silence. "Answer me, Steed Parker."

"I knew what I had done to her was beyond wrong. I did the one thing I promised myself I would never do...I hurt her. I couldn't stand the thought of her glaring at me with so much hate. It was easier to stay away."

Her head slowly moved from side to side as she took a few steps closer. "Easier for who, Steed?"

Turning away again, my mother paced the hallway for a good three minutes. She shook her head and wrapped her arms around her waist. "If I had known, I would have never thrown you together like that. Paxton deserved a warning ... especially with Chloe." She covered her mouth as horror filled her eyes. It was then she realized how it probably had affected Paxton to find out like that.

I nodded. "I'm sorry I never told you and Dad. I knew you would have been angry with me."

Her hands dropped to her sides. When she looked me in the eyes, I held my breath. "Not angry, Steed. A child is *never* something to be angry about. But your actions and the way you handled it, I'm deeply disappointed in you. We didn't raise you to be a coward."

Wincing, I took a step back. The words hurt more than I imagined they would.

She headed back down the hall. I couldn't move. My legs felt like lead as I watched my mother walk away from me.

I deserved her disappointment and so much more.

I walked down the hall and out the door. I soon found myself sitting on the bleachers, staring out over the football field. All those years I had avoided coming home for fear of hurting Paxton again and facing what I had done to her. I hadn't even been here for a day and already I had hurt the two women I loved more than my own life.

When I glanced at my watch, I jumped down and headed back into the school. The halls were emptying as families headed out. I stepped into Paxton's classroom only to find her alone, staring out the window.

She didn't turn, but somehow she knew I was there. "They made a mistake on the spelling of her last name. It said Park."

I stood there motionless, the idea of Paxton being caught so off guard shattered me. "I'm so sorry, Paxton," I said barely above a whisper.

"Chloe's a sweet girl."

My chest ached. "Thank you."

Her voice cracked as she wrapped her arms around her body. "She has your eyes."

I nodded and tried like hell to keep my feet where they were. All I wanted to do was go to her. Pull her in my arms and tell her how much I loved her. How sorry I was for hurting her. But I didn't move. "I'm so sorry, Paxton."

Her shoulders lifted, but when she faced me, all I saw was the same angry eyes that had stared into mine ten years ago.

"Your family is waiting for you. You should go. They left a good fifteen minutes ago."

With a small nod, I took a few steps back. "Paxton, I—"

Holding up her hand, she shook her head. "Just go, Steed." Her voice sounded tired and defeated so I did what she asked.

I left.

Because I was so goddamn good at doing that.

CHAPTER 3

Paxton

After Steed walked out of the room, I counted to thirty before I covered my face and let myself cry.

He's back.

Steed is home.

He has a daughter.

The small knock on the door made me jump. I dropped my hands and saw my best friend from college, Corina, standing with a stunned expression on her face. We had been short on teachers this year and I had begged her to move from Austin to Oak Springs and teach first grade.

"What in the world? Why are you crying?" She rushed into the room, shutting the door as she walked in.

I practically threw myself at her. "He's back. Oh, God, Corina. He's back and he has a family!"

She pushed me away and stared into my eyes. "Steed?"

I nodded.

"Holy crackers. Okay. This is an emergency. I've got this. I'm in control of the situation."

My legs felt weak. I couldn't get the look in his eyes out of my head. The second I saw him, I was overcome with happiness. Then everything that had happened came rushing back. When he smiled, I lost control, and let the anger win.

Corina rushed around my desk, grabbed my purse, shut off all the lights, and pulled me by the arm out the door.

"Where are we going?" I asked numbly.

"We're going out for ice cream."

The cool night air felt good on my face as I walked aimlessly around town. Most everyone I passed said hello. Oak Springs was a small town and everyone pretty much knew everyone else. The more people moved outside of San Antonio and Austin, the more our little town grew, though. Especially with the new growth in our little town square. Business after business popped up, bringing our historical downtown back to life.

I stopped and turned. The pull to go inside the new bar was strong, but what if he was in there? The chances of that were pretty good. Then again, he was probably home with his wife and daughter.

A younger couple approached and said, "Excuse us."

"Oh, I'm so sorry about that!" I said as I stepped out of the way for them to enter. Country music blared from inside, and I strained to look in. The man held the door open for me.

"You coming in?"

"Oh. Um. No." I took a step back.

He shrugged and let the door close. Glancing up, I stared at the neon sign.

I took in a deep breath and walked in. I was risking a lot by going into the bar Cord owned. After all, he was Steed's younger
brother. Even though it was a small town, I had done everything in
my power to avoid the Parker family. Including Cord, who had been
a good friend after Steed left town. But even being around him
proved to be too painful.

I couldn't believe my eyes. Cord had really made this place into
something amazing. I hadn't been in here since he first opened it.
The bar was beautiful. Wood covered the walls and a giant sign hung
over the bar that read, *Hey Y'all*. Liquor bottles lined the wall behind
the long bar. My eyes swung around and I noticed that a second floor
had been added. People sat upstairs at tables that overlooked the
massive wood dance floor. A large number of couples were dancing
to a George Straight song.

"Paxton?"

Spinning around, I grinned when I saw him. "Hey, Cord."

He seemed happy to see me as he pulled me in for a hug then
pushed me back at arm's length. "Fancy seeing you here."

"He's back. I didn't know about her." I said while peering into
Cord's blue eyes.

He nodded and placed his hand on my lower back, leading me to
the hall that probably led to his office. The place had been remodeled and everything looked different. When we walked in, he shut
the door to his office and the music was muffled.

Cord leaned on the edge of his desk while I took a seat in a large
oversized leather chair. "You okay?" he softly asked.

My lips pressed together as I tried to keep my chin from trembling. Cord was the only other person who knew what had truly happened between Steed and me.

"No," I answered honestly.

His brows furrowed. "There were so many times I wanted to tell you, but it wasn't my place. I knew he had to be the one to tell you. Plus, any time I did see you, Paxton, you walked off in the other direction."

I let out a slight chuckle. "I avoided you *and* the family, too afraid to find out anything about him moving on with his life. It was pretty stupid to block y'all out of my life, looking back now."

Cord blew out a breath. "He didn't tell any of us he was coming back to Texas. Only my parents and that was only a week ago."

I shook my head in disbelief. *How could I have been so stupid to think I could live in this town and keep pretending the Parker family and Steed didn't exist?*

"He was a mess at dinner," Cord said.

My eyes swung over to him. "Dinner?"

"Yeah, our parents planned a welcome home dinner for him and Chloe. Steed was an emotional basket case, but was trying to keep things light for Chloe's sake. He told me what happened. He feels awful. No one told him either, Paxton. He had no idea you would be Chloe's teacher. I honestly figured my mother would have told you and Steed. But she didn't say a word."

"Yeah, he looked shocked to see me. Almost as shocked as I was to see him."

Cord sighed. "I guess he laid into Mom about springing this on the both of you. He, um, he also told her the truth."

I gasped and covered my mouth. What would Melanie think of me?

"She hasn't said anything to anyone else, don't worry. But Steed said she kept going on and on about the two you getting back together, and how you were meant to be. Steed kind of lost it and blurted out about the baby and what happened."

I fell back in the chair, my heart racing. "Your mother's going to think I'm a whore for getting pregnant in high school."

Cord chuckled. "Hardly. But she isn't talking to Steed."

I sat up. "W-why?"

"She's pissed. Disappointed. Angry. Sad. Guilty for not being there for you."

My arms wrapped around my queasy stomach. I hadn't thought about what it might be like for our parents to find out they had lost a grandchild. Swallowing hard, I closed my eyes. "When I saw him, I was so happy for about thirty seconds. Then every ounce of anger came rushing back. All I wanted to do was kick him in the balls. Then his little girl came running up and my heart broke all over again. I felt so angry that he had a child."

Peeking up at Cord, a small sob slipped from my mouth. "How could I be angry about an innocent child? But I was, and in that moment I wanted to tell him how unfair it was for him to have a baby with another woman when he didn't want ours."

Cord's eyes seemed sad. "Paxton, he was eighteen and scared shitless. It was a kneejerk reaction and he came to his senses."

"You didn't see the relief in his eyes. He was glad I lost the baby."

"And there wasn't a small part of you that didn't feel the same way?"

Tears made their way down both cheeks. "No. I had a part of Steed inside of me and even though I knew it was going to change everything, that baby was a part of us. A part of our love. I was scared, yes, but to say I was relieved, no. It was the opposite."

I glanced away and let out a soft chuckle. "Or at least I thought he loved me."

"He did. He *does,* Paxton."

"Ha!" I said. "He left town and never came back, Cord. He left me to deal with the loss of our child all alone. I almost failed out of my first semester of college because I was an emotional wreck. Not only did I lose a baby, I lost the love of my life."

Cord inspected the floor with a somber expression before glancing back up. "You did threaten to cut off his dick if he ever came back."

A small smile tugged at the corner of my mouth. "He could have called or written. Asked how I was. He did nothing."

"I'm sure he has a reason, Paxton. Maybe y'all should talk."

Cold swept across my body. All those feelings I had worked so hard to bury were rushing to the surface. "Why? He's moved on and has a family of his own now."

Cord looked like he wanted to say something, but he held back.

I fought internally over whether or not to ask the next question. My curiosity quickly won out. "What's his wife like?"

Cord roared with laughter. "Steed ain't married to that nutcase anymore."

Sucking in a breath of air, I tried not to let that bit of news show on my face too much. "What happened?"

Cord raked his hand through his hair. "You sure you want me to tell you? Maybe it ought to be Steed."

"Well, considering you never told me he was married or had a daughter, I think you owe it to me."

His face fell. "Damn it, Paxton. You've avoided me like the plague. Hell, you've avoided the whole family and you even admitted it. Besides, like I said before, it needs to be Steed telling you."

"I'm sorry. It was just so hard. You're all a reminder to me. Especially Mitchell. It hurt too much to see the family."

Cord nodded. "I know. I'm sorry I let you push me away. I'm no better than Steed to have let you deal with things alone."

I shrugged. "S'okay. And you were there after he left."

He nodded. I knew he felt terrible about what had happened. He was even younger than me and Steed, so for me to expect him to have been there would be crazy.

"What happened with Steed's wife?"

He took in a deep breath and pushed it out. "Steed hadn't dated anyone else until Kim. They met seven years ago and from what I could tell, it was only casual. Then her parents died, she threatened to do some serious shit, and Steed panicked. He didn't know what to do so he asked her to marry him. By the time he realized he had fucked up, about a month after they got married, he told Kim he wanted a divorce. She told him she was pregnant. Well, as much as he didn't want in the marriage, the guilt of what happened with you hit him and he stayed. After she had the baby she turned into a different person. She thought Steed was going to come into money. He tried a few times to file for divorce and she told him she would take Chloe and he would never find them. It got to the point where my parents had to meet Steed and Chloe in secret so Kim didn't find out."

"Why did they have to keep the visits a secret?" I asked.

Cord pushed his hand through his hair. "It was a mess, Paxton. Kim was money-hungry and had it in her head Steed was going to inherit the ranch. Even though he had kept her away from Texas, he still helped Dad with some of the financial stuff with the ranch. Investments and shit like that. Kim had stumbled upon information and all she could see was dollar signs. They eventually came up with a plan to pretend to disown Steed to get Kim out of his life. When Kim realized she wasn't getting anything out of her life with Steed except a loveless marriage and a daughter she didn't want, she filed for divorce and signed over her rights to Chloe. The first thing Steed did was move here."

By the time Cord finished, I felt numb. A small part of me was glad to see that Steed had been through hell and back with this woman, but the other part of me felt pain for him and especially for Chloe.

"So the mom signed over her daughter without a second thought?" I asked stunned.

Cord nodded.

Worry moved across his face. "What? What is it?" I asked.

"Steed talked to me tonight about the emotional abuse his ex put Chloe through. She was hateful towards Steed and basically ignored Chloe. He tried to shield Chloe from it as much as he could, but some of Kim's screaming about how much she hated her life reached the poor little thing's ears."

My heart broke. "That poor child. There is a special place in hell for a woman like that."

Cord agreed. "Yeah, I hope she never tries to set foot in Texas. I'm actually afraid of what Steed might do to her."

Chewing on my lip, I stood. "I'd better leave. It's getting late."

Cord walked over to me. "I'm glad you came in, Paxton. It was nice seeing you. Please don't stay away. The family misses you."

His warm smile got one out of me in return. "Will you tell everyone I said hello and I miss them? I spoke with Amelia for a bit earlier at Back to School night. I can't believe how beautiful and grown up she is. I remember her as a little girl in pigtails running around."

Rolling his eyes, Cord groaned. "Yeah, I've gotten into a few fights because of that sister of mine."

I hid a chuckle. Amelia must be taking after her older sister Waylynn in the rebel department. "Thank you for everything, Cord."

He wrapped me in his arms. "You're still a part of our family, Paxton. You're always welcome here."

The door to Cord's office opened, and I knew he was there before I even had to see him.

Cord dropped his arms as I turned around. Steed's eyes bounced between the two of us, confusion quickly turning to anger. Trevor clapped his hands and walked into the room.

"Paxton! My girl! Where in the hell have you been?"

He hugged me and spun me around. I laughed as he put me down. I guess with me being in Cord's office and his arms wrapped around me, that was a sign for Trevor to do the same. "I'd say you sure have grown up, Trev."

His grin widened. "What are you doing here with Cord?"

I glanced over at Steed. He was staring at Cord like he wanted to rip his head off. I knew how it looked when they walked in and saw us in an embrace. What he didn't know was I hadn't talked Cord in a few years. "I was walking by and thought I'd stop in. I hadn't been in since Cord opened the bar."

"We were catching up," Cord added with a wink.

My body trembled as I felt the intensity of Steed's eyes on me.

Trevor laughed. "Well hell, you still want to rip Steed's balls off, Paxton?"

Our eyes met. The way he stared into my soul had me feeling unsteady. My heart was telling me to run to him, but my head was guarding my heart. I'd promised to never let another man destroy me like Steed did.

A small smirk formed. "It was his dick. And I was going to cut it off and shove it down his throat."

Trevor lost it laughing and Cord chuckled. Steed's eyes turned darker as he smiled. A warmth spread through my lower stomach, and I tried like hell to ignore it. When I finally couldn't take the intensity of his gaze or the way his sexy smile made me feel, I turned back to Cord.

"Thank you for listening. I'll see you around."

He nodded. "Anytime, Paxton."

Trevor hugged me again. "Dance with me before you leave."

I laughed and pushed back at his broad chest. I'd forgotten how built these boys were. Trevor seemed to be following in his older brother's footsteps. The Parker boys were not only drop dead gorgeous, but they had hot as hell bodies.

"Rain check?" I asked with a smile. Trevor nodded and took off his cowboy hat to give me a kiss on the check.

Taking a deep breath, I headed through the door where Steed still stood. He was in a cowboy hat and it took everything out of me not to lick my lips. I stopped in front of him. He opened his mouth to say something, then quickly snapped it shut.

He stepped to the side to let me pass, but when I walked by, he took my hand. My heart jumped and I sucked in a breath as the familiar energy ripped across my skin. "Pax, can we please talk?"

Everything inside was screaming to run. Everything but my heart. Steed was the only person who called me Pax and he usually said it in a whispered voice while making love to me.

My eyes darted back to Cord. He grinned.

Focusing on Steed, I sunk my teeth into my lip and forced a breath. "I can't tonight, Steed."

His eyes looked hopeful, and he squeezed my hand lightly. My heart was pounding so hard in my chest I could hardly think. "When?"

I rubbed my lips together. My head was spinning and I was so confused. I wanted to be angry. I wanted to hate him. Everything in me wanted to walk away and tell him I never wanted to talk to him again. But I couldn't. Not with the way he was staring. Not with the way my heart was aching for him. "I'm not sure when I'll be ready."

"Can I call you in a few days?"

I swallowed hard. "You don't have my number."

And then it happened. He smiled and his dimples went on full display. My fingers itched to brush his day-old stubble. I longed to feel it against my lips.

"Your cell phone is in the information packet that Chloe brought home earlier."

"Oh," I managed, dreaming of what his touch would feel like as he gave my whole body attention. I couldn't pull my eyes off his mouth while my naughty thoughts continued to plague me.

Jesus. Get it together Paxton. Remember what he did to you.

Pulling my hand from his grip, I took a step back. I narrowed my eyes and lifted my chin higher. I was not going to let my desire for Steed control my emotions. He'd hurt me more than he could ever realize and a sexy smile wasn't going to fix it.

My voice cracked as I said, "I have to go."

Steed's smile faded. The throbbing ache in my chest was hard to ignore as a familiar pain settled into it. I found the strength to turn and walk away. If I had stayed longer I was either going to kiss him or kick him in the balls.

Keeping my breathing even, I headed out the door. My head was wrestling with my heart and I had no idea who was going to win.

CHAPTER 4

Paxton

Stepping inside my house, I turned on the lights and let my eyes travel from the living room to the kitchen. Calmness washed over my body. I loved my house. It was built in 1898 and the most recent owners had moved out ten years ago and left it to fall apart. When I stumbled upon it for sale, it felt like we had something in common.

We'd been left alone and broken.

With the help of my father and a few friends, I had gutted and remodeled, bringing it back to life. In the process, it had brought me back as well. The entire first floor was open with the exception of the formal dining room and downstairs half bath.

Kicking off my shoes, I slowly made my way up the stairs. The second floor consisted of two guest bedrooms I'd yet to decorate, a guest bath, and the master suite. I walked into my bedroom and smiled.

It had been the first room in the house I'd painted and decorated. The calming tones of gray were evident all over the room, from the dark gray curtains to the lighter shade of gray on the walls. The custom chairs were the same color as the walls but finished out in a blue trim. The bedding was a mixture of blues and silver. At the time I picked the colors, I hadn't even realized what I was doing. Now... now it all came back in one giant memory, seizing my heart and causing me to drop to the floor and bury my face in my hands.

"Some day when we get our own house, how do you want to decorate our bedroom?"

Steed laced his fingers with mine. "Well, you like the color blue, and I like gray. I think we should mix the two together."

I nestled against his body and watched the Frio River meandering by as we sat in our favorite spot. "I like that. Maybe add in a touch of silver for some glam."

The rumble in Steed's chest made my body warm.

"It could be lime green and banana yellow for all I care. As long as I get to wake up in the morning holding you and kiss you every night."

The ringing from my back pocket pulled me from the memory. Wiping my tears, I took my phone out.

Corina.

Hitting the button on the side of my phone, I sent it to voicemail. I needed to be alone so I could figure out my game plan.

I walked over to the large silver dresser and pulled open the top drawer. Pushing my clothes out of the way, I pulled out the black velvet bag that held the memories of my past with Steed. I clutched it to my chest while a new round of sobs shook my body.

Taking in a deep breath, I blew it out and waited for the kids to ar-
rive. The first day of school was always stressful for both the kids
and parents. But today I was the one stressing out.

It had been four days since I saw Steed. He never called, which
didn't surprise me. I hated that I even let myself get worked up over
it.

I smiled when the first kids started walking in.

"Good morning! Moms and dads, give your goodbyes at the
door and then boys and girls please go to your seats. There is a fun
coloring activity waiting for you." I repeated the greeting about every three minutes or so.

This was one of the hardest parts. Each year, I fought to hold my
tears back as I watched parents hold onto their children. Their tears
were hard to ignore as I fought to hold my own back.

Smile. Just keep smiling.

Walking around the classroom, I helped each student get started
with their coloring project, waiting for the whole class to show up.
My body tingled as I glanced up and saw Steed standing in the
doorway with Chloe, but my heart broke when I saw she was crying.
Throwing herself at Steed, he wrapped her in his arms and whispered
something to her. She shook her head and squeezed him harder.

I normally never interrupted a parent and child on the first day,
but I could see both of them were not dealing well at all. With a deep
breath, I headed over. Chloe looked up at me. She dropped her hold
on Steed and gave me a weak grin. Bending down, I came face to
face with her. It wasn't lost on me how close I was to Steed as well.
My body could instantly feel his heat.

"Good morning, Chloe cat."

Her eyes lit up at the nickname. I wasn't sure why I called her
that. I *never* gave my students nicknames.

"Is everything okay?" I asked as I wiped her tears.

"I'm afraid." Chloe said between sobs.

Glancing at Steed, I could see this was killing him.

"It's okay to be scared, Chloe. You're not the only one who is nervous, but I promise you're going to have so much fun today."

Chloe tilted her head. "I'm just nervous? Not scared?"

I tittered. "Maybe a little of both."

She turned to Steed. "Will you be okay today without me, Daddy?"

My heart stopped. How precious was she? And the look on Steed's face left me breathless.

Steed took her hands in his. "I'm going to miss you, pumpkin, but I promise I'll be okay."

I stilled. That was the same pet name he had called me all those years ago.

He kissed the back of each of her hands. "Do the song, Daddy."

Steed's face turned white. "Um … we did it in the car, Chloe."

Her little lip came out in a full-on pout, and I was positive she was about to lose it again.

Turning to Steed, I said, "I think today is such a special day that doing your song twice will make it extra special."

Chloe nodded. We waited as Steed's eyes bounced from me to Chloe. It was obvious he was nervous about this song of theirs.

"I don't think it's a good idea," he mumbled.

"Daddy, please!" Chloe begged.

He swallowed hard then softly started singing. "*You and me.*"

I prayed he hadn't noticed the sharp intake of air I had sucked in.

Next, Chloe sang. "*Me and You.*"

"*No one has to tell me who,*" Steed sang.

"*For you will always be my truuuuue.*"

Steed's eyes caught mine as he sang the last line. "*Yes ... you will always be my true ... true ... love.*" He was singing so softly, I barely heard the words.

My eyes filled with tears as Steed stared at me.

"I love you, Daddy."

Not removing his gaze from mine, Steed whispered, "I love you." Turning to face Chloe, he cleared his throat and said, "I love you too. Have a good day, pumpkin."

When I stood, I nearly lost my balance, causing Steed to take my arm to steady me. I felt the sting of electricity zip through my body and I knew he had felt it too by the way he reacted.

He was singing *our* song to his daughter. My hand went to my stomach as my dream of Steed singing that to our child flashed before my eyes. I fought to hold back my tears.

"Paxton," he whispered with pleading eyes. "I'm sorry. I've sung it to her since the day she was born."

I wanted to tell him it was okay. But it wasn't okay. None of this was okay. Anger replaced whatever crazy emotion I was feeling right now. "You never called," I said sharply. "This past week. You said you would call."

Oh gosh. I sound like a silly wounded teenager.

He smiled. "I think you put the wrong number down on the packet."

Pinching my brows together, I pulled my head back. *What an excuse.* "What? I don't think so."

"When I called the number, it was an older man by the name of Frank. He talked to me for nearly an hour before I was able to get off the phone."

Oh no. Had I put the wrong number?

Steed took out his phone to show me.

Yep. I'd put the wrong number. I covered my mouth to hide my chuckle. "Crap," I whispered.

"Ms. Monroe, should I go and sit at my seat?"

Pulling my eyes off of Steed, I glanced down at Chloe. "Give your daddy a quick hug goodbye and let's get the fun started!"

She did just that before reaching up to take my hand in hers. She waved goodbye and Steed did the same. I walked Chloe to her desk.

"Well good morning my lovely kinders."

"Good morning!" fifteen little voices cried out.

I walked up to my desk and leaned against it. "Today is going to be what I like to call fun day."

"Will we never have fun after today?" a little boy named Timmy asked.

Laughing, I replied, "I hope we have fun every day, but today is an extra special fun day. We are going to learn all kinds of fun things. But first, we're going to take a tour of the school and go see the library!"

Cheers erupted as I glimpsed past the kids to see Steed still standing, staring at Chloe. He must have felt my stare because he looked at me. Lifting my brow, he nodded and left before Chloe turned to see him still there.

Clapping my hands, I pushed off my desk. I was in my element. I loved teaching. I loved being with these kids and I would certainly love the distraction of keeping my mind off of Steed Parker.

"The first thing we're going to learn is how to pay attention when the teacher is talking. I'm going to teach a song we'll use when I need to get your full attention."

I scanned all the adorable faces and stopped when I saw big blue eyes staring back into mine. She was the spitting image of her father.

So much for trying *not* to think of Steed. He'd conveniently left me a little reminder with blonde pigtails and bright eager eyes.

CHAPTER 5

Steed

The keys made a clattering sound as I dropped them in the small bowl Chloe had made last year. Walking into the large living room, I started talking to myself. "What the fuck am I supposed to do now?"

The doorbell rang and I spun to answer it. Opening the door, I smiled when I saw my baby sister standing there.

"Hey," Amelia said.

"Hey back at ya. What brings you here?"

She shrugged, then walked in. She was carrying a computer bag over her shoulder, a diet Pepsi in one hand, and giant shopping bag in the other. "Thought I would do some work here and keep you company. I figured today would be a rough day with dropping Chloe off at school and all."

I raked my hand through my hair. "Yeah, it was rough in a few ways."

Amelia placed her bag on the coffee table and turned to me.

"Paxton?"

With a nod, I dropped into an overstuffed chair. I still wasn't used to having all of this. Not that we didn't have a nice home in Portland, we did. But that was all it was. Nice. This was over the top. My parents were loaded; we knew that growing up. But they never spoiled us and we all had to work on the ranch learning every single aspect of the business. I always thought I'd come back from college and work alongside my father. Instead I got a degree in business management with a minor in math. I fucking hated math, but I was good at it.

"Since you left, Paxton has pretty much avoided the family. I mean if she ran into us, she was always pleasant. But when she came home from college she never stopped by no matter how many times Mom begged her to. Then when she moved back to town, if she saw us, she'd go out of her way to go in the opposite direction."

My stomach tightened.

"What in the hell did you to her, Steed? Whatever it was, I know you told Mom and that's why she isn't talking to you. She told Dad she's never been so angry with one of her kids in her life."

I opened my mouth to speak, but Amelia kept on. "She said she was ready to let Paxton make good on her threat. Now I remember that threat, even though I was twelve. You said something to her at y'all's graduation and she said she hated you. Was going to cut off your—"

"Oh. My. God. Meli, stop talking."

She leaned back in her chair. "Last week when you and Mom went out to talk, Paxton was a basket case. She tried to act like she was okay, but her hands were shaking, and she kept touching her stomach." Her eyes narrowed. "I'm not stupid and I've put two and two together. Please tell me you didn't make her do something you would both regret."

I froze. "What? What in the hell do you mean?"

She leaned forward. "Abortion?"

I jumped up. "Fuck no. I would never do that!"

Letting out a breath, she mumbled, "Thank God. So why is Mom so pissed at you?"

I shook my head. The memories hit me hard. Paxton's cries echoed through my thoughts. Maybe it was selfish to want to tell someone else, but I was tired of keeping it a secret. Tired of pretending it had never happened.

"The last day of school our senior year, Paxton told me she was pregnant."

Amelia covered her mouth. "She was pregnant?"

Swallowing hard, I was transported back to the day.

Paxton sat in the stands staring out over the football field. I'd gotten her text to meet her there not long before. The second I walked up, I knew something was wrong. My heart started beating harder. We were both set to go to Texas A & M that fall. We were moving in together much to our parent's disliking.

What if she changed her mind? Shit.

"Hey, pumpkin. Is everything okay?"

Paxton forced a smile. Then she started to cry.

Rushing to her, I pulled her into my arms. "Pax, baby tell me what's wrong."

She buried her face in my chest and pulled at my T-shirt. "Tell me it's going to be okay, Steed. Please."

The pleading in her voice scared me. "You have to tell me what's wrong, Paxton, before I can tell you it's okay."

I pulled back and found that her blue eyes were bloodshot, liked she'd been crying for hours. My heart was racing.

"It's okay, pumpkin. Tell me."

She chewed on her lip and stared at the ground before looking back into my eyes. "I'm pregnant."

The words felt like someone had thrown them at me with a brick attached to them. "W-what?"

She shook her head. "I know how scary it is, but we can make this work."

I dropped my hold on her and took a few steps back.

"I don't want to be a dad right now. Fuck. I can't be a dad right now. This is going to mess everything up."

Her face dropped. "I'm not giving up this baby, Steed."

Taking a few steps, I shook my head again. "I'm sorry. I can't do this right now. I need to think."

"So you left her standing there alone?"

I nodded. No use in trying to sugarcoat anything.

"What a total asshole move. No wonder Mom isn't talking to you. Prick."

With a frown, I replied, "That's not the worst part. I ignored her until the day before graduation."

Amelia gasped. "Steed Parker."

"I needed time to think. Shit, my whole life had just changed. Once the shock wore off and I realized that we could make anything work as long as we had each other, and how much I'd love the baby, I went to her. It was too late."

My sister's eyes grew wide. "Why? What did she do?"

Paxton walked slowly up the stairs of the high school, her head down. Rushing over to her, I called her name.

"Paxton!"

Her eyes filled with tears the second she saw me.

"Hey, I'm so sorry I've been avoiding you. I needed time to think about everything. I'm sorry."

She looked like she hadn't slept in a week, and I hated myself for putting her through all the stress.

"I know I said I didn't want to be a father, but…I've been thinking. We can make this work, Pax. I love you and I know I'll love the baby too."

A tear slipped down her cheek. "I lost the baby early this morning. I just got back from the doctor."

Relief washed over my body and I closed my eyes, whispering, "Thank, God."

When I opened my eyes, Paxton's horrified expression stunned me. "What?" she said.

"Nothing. I'm so sorry. Why didn't you call me, Paxton? Did you go through that alone?"

Her eyes seemed lost. "Why would I call you? You made it clear you didn't care about me or our baby. I need to sit down, I was supposed to go home and rest, not come here."

I stood there stunned as she turned and headed into the school for graduation practice. My stomach churned; what I had done was unforgivable. I'd left her alone to deal with the pregnancy. And the loss.

When I opened my eyes, tears were rolling down Amelia's cheeks. "Oh, Steed, how could you? Do you think the stress caused her to lose the baby?"

I shrugged. "I don't know. A few months after I left home, I started to do some research on miscarriages. It's likely there could have been something wrong with the pregnancy and it naturally aborted itself, but my heart tells me it was the stress Paxton was under. I caused her to lose our child. That's why I never came home. Not for holidays, not even after Chloe was born. The idea of seeing

Paxton … knowing what I did to her … the guilt has torn me up inside all of these years. A part of me thinks my marriage to Kim was my karma. My punishment for what I put Paxton through. But I got Chloe out of it."

Amelia walked over to me. "That is crazy, Steed. You don't know what caused her to lose the baby."

Letting out a gruff laugh, I nodded. "The day of graduation, I tried to get Paxton to talk to me, but she was so angry. She threw it in my face that I'd said I was glad the baby died. When I tried to tell her it was a strange mixture of emotions, she lost it. Told me she hated me, and threatened to seek revenge."

"Surely she's still not angry with you."

"You don't know Paxton. Me showing back up in town and having a daughter to top it off … it's like rubbing salt in a wound."

Amelia made a face. "Oh, I wasn't even thinking about Chloe. But Paxton would never do anything to Chloe."

My hand went to the back of my neck where I tried to rub the ache away. "I know. But the way she looks at *me*. It's like the hate is still as strong as that day ten years ago."

Taking my hands in hers, Amelia peered into my eyes. "Steed, I've done a lot of research on miscarriages, I wrote about one in a book of mine. For some women, it's a loss so great they feel it for years. Small things will trigger the memory of the loss. That has to be why Paxton avoided the family so much. We reminded her of you…you reminded her of the baby she lost."

"But she wasn't that far along."

She smacked the side of my head so hard I was positive it rattled my brain around in my skull.

"What the fuck, Meli!"

"You idiot! Steed, think about the moment you found out Kim was pregnant. How did you feel?"

"Honestly?"

She nodded.

"Sad. Angry. Because the only woman I've ever wanted to have a child with was Paxton."

Amelia's hands covered her mouth. "That's the saddest, sweetest thing you've said yet. You stupid asshole."

My shoulders slumped. "Stop calling me names!"

"Hey, if the shoe fits!"

I sighed. "After the shock of Paxton telling me she was pregnant, I *was* actually excited. Scared as fuck, but I knew we'd made something beautiful together. I wanted to tell her that. I just didn't know that when she dropped the bomb on me. When Kim told me she was pregnant, I had to deal with the guilt of having a child with another woman. The only thing I knew for sure was I was not walking away from that baby. When I saw the sonogram, I was instantly in love."

"If you'd seen the sonogram from your child with Paxton, would it have made you react differently?"

I shrugged. "Hell, I don't know. I was older when Kim got pregnant. Almost out of college. More sure of myself and my future."

"The baby was *inside* of Paxton, Steed. *Your* child growing in her. Think about what that loss was like for her, then remember she not only lost your child … she lost you too."

Fuck. Son-of-a-bitch. I ran to the half bath and dropped to the ground as my breakfast decided to make a second appearance.

CHAPTER 6

Paxton

Chloe and Timmy held my hands while parents walked up to pick up their kiddos. Kindergarteners got picked up on the south side of the school, away from the older kids. Parents had the option of walking up or driving up. The first few days of school almost every parent walked up.

"Today was fun, Ms. Monroe."

Glancing down to Timmy, I smiled. "I'm glad you had fun."

"I hope I get picked next week to take the class pet home," Timmy added.

I made a mental note to actually pick up a class pet. I had totally forgotten to get one with everything that had been going on this week. Another thing I could blame Steed for.

Ugh.

Steed.

"Where is the class pet, Ms. Monroe?" Chloe asked. I glanced down at her. Great. This one wasn't going to let anything get by. Apple didn't fall far from the tree.

I put my finger to my lips. Leaning down, I whispered, "I forgot to get one, Chloe Cat!"

Her eyes lit up and she tried to hide her giggle. I wasn't sure why I had started calling her that. I only did it when the other kids couldn't hear. My biggest fear was showing her more attention simply because she was Steed's daughter. But knowing her mother never gave her the love she deserved made my heart ache. I wanted to shower her with so much attention that I had to force myself not to. Again, Steed was to blame.

Ugh.

"There's my mom! Bye, Ms. Monroe!" Timmy called out.

A few parents asked how the first day went, but not all. Some simply wanted their kids and took off.

Chloe had dropped my hand when her new best friend Lilly walked up. I smiled as I watched the two of them giggle as they whispered about something.

"Oh, God. There he is."

I turned to see one of the moms talking to another mom.

"I saw him drop his daughter off this morning. I heard he's a widower."

The other mom gasped. "No!"

"Yes! Check out that body. You can tell he is a Parker brother. Give me one night with him, and I can make him forget his dead wife."

My eyes widened in shock. *What in the world?*

"Daddy!" Chloe cried out as she ran to Steed. He lifted her with one arm like she weighed nothing and both of the moms next to me sighed.

"Look how strong he is," one swooned.

I rolled my eyes.

Steed knelt, pulling out a small bouquet of flowers from behind his back and handing them to Chloe.

Now *I* was sighing right along with the two moms. I couldn't help but smile. That was such a Steed thing to do. He used to bring me flowers all the time for the simplest of things. It always made me feel so special.

Chloe wrapped her arms around her father's neck. She grabbed Steed's hand and pulled him over to where Lilly and her mother were standing.

One of the moms next to me grunted, causing me to peek over at them again. "Oh great. Gina Higgins is going to sink her teeth into him."

The other mom snarled, "Bitch."

Turning finally, I recognized both of them. "Wow, okay ladies, if *I* can hear you, the kids can hear you."

They turned to me, shades of pink covering their cheeks. "Sorry, it's just, he's so good looking."

The other mom wiggled her brows. "All the Parker men are gorgeous. I went to school with Waylynn, their oldest sister. I got to see them all. And damn they were hot as hell, even the younger ones."

Both moms covered their mouths and laughed.

"Wait." The one mom said as she faced me. "Oh. My. Gawd! Paxton, you dated Steed!"

The other mom's jaw dropped. "What?"

"Mom! I'm ready to go now!"

The tall mom turned to her son. "Hold on, Jerry. Mommy's saying goodbye to Paul's mommy."

I needed to change the subject and fast. "The first day of class was amazing. You should both be so proud of your sons. Jerry actually pulled Lilly's chair out for her when she went to sit down."

Jerry's mom beamed. "That's my boy!"

She turned to the other mom. "I've got to run. Tell me if Gina sinks her claws in." Turning back to me, she said, "We need the scoop on you two!"

After the tall mom left, the other mom frowned. "Paxton, I'm sorry we were gossiping like that and I'm sorry I didn't remember you dated him."

Clearly this woman knew me and I had no clue what her name was. Damn. I usually had all the kids' parents memorized by the first day of school. I gave her a polite grin. Turning, I glared at Steed.

His fault. Again.

Glancing over to Paul's mom, I replied, "It's okay. You were a couple of years ahead of me, I don't expect you to remember something that happened so long ago."

We gave each other small smiles before turning and watching the scene with Steed and Gina. I knew it was wrong, and I never gossiped, especially with parents. But I couldn't stop the words that flew from my mouth. "So, Lilly's dad?" I asked.

"Left her. For his boss. They moved to Dallas or something. She's not from here so she hates it. She's waiting to sell her house so she can move back to Denver I think?"

"Really?" I asked. "Chloe will be so sad if Lilly moves."

"Well, if Gina hooks up with Steed Parker, she won't have to go anywhere. Especially when she finds out he's the son of the wealthiest man in the county. Hell, probably in the state."

Jealousy raced through my veins.

"I've got to run, Paxton. I'm glad today was great!"

Forcing a smile, I waved.

The only two parents left were Steed and Gina. I watched them talk before I headed into the building. I tried not to, but I glanced over my shoulder. My eyes caught his and I quickly shut the door behind me.

I spent the next hour trying to get work done, but all I could think about was Gina and how she was laughing and placing her hand on Steed's upper arm. I imagined she was making arrangements for a play date for the girls … or maybe for her and Steed.

Throwing my pen down on my desk, I let out a frustrated groan.

"Steed," I hissed.

Someone knocked on the classroom door. "Bad day?" Corina asked with a frown.

"No. It was actually a great day. How about you? Your first official day as a first grade teacher. Well, a first grade teacher here."

She laughed. "It was nice having the smaller class. The kids are precious. The parents are a pain in my ass already. And the need for a glass or two of wine is pretty strong."

I lifted my brow. "That bad?"

"Let's just say one of the moms asked if I was free this weekend. She had the perfect guy to set me up with."

"What did you say?"

Her mouth dropped. "Well, I didn't say anything at first because I was utterly shocked she knew I was single."

I chuckled. "Welcome to small town USA. Everybody knows everyone's business."

"Hmm, I probably shouldn't have told her I had plans with BOB this weekend."

My eyes widened. "Please tell me you didn't say that to a parent."

She smiled. "I did."

"Did she know what you were meaning?"

Corina shrugged. "Heck if I know, but that will teach her to butt into my business again."

I dropped my head. "You're going to get fired and I recommended you!"

Laughing, Corina turned to leave. "I've got some work to do before I call this day over. Tacos tonight?"

My phone buzzed on my desk. It was a strange number. Not local.

"Yeah sure. Be at my place at seven."

Corina gave me a quick wave as she retreated. Sliding my finger over the phone, I answered it.

"Hello?"

"Paxton."

His voice cut straight through my body and I found myself unable to speak.

"Hello?"

Jesus. Get it together Paxton! Now!

"I'm sorry, who is this?"

Good. Good. Make him think you didn't immediately know it was him. I tried to keep my voice straight, unfeeling.

"Steed. Turns out you put your number in more than one place. I was hoping this was the right one."

Pulling the phone away, I dragged in a breath and slowly blew it out. "What do you want?"

Wow. That came out more bitch sounding than I intended.

"You told me to call you…so we could talk. Plus, I didn't get a chance to ask you how Chloe did on her first day."

"Right." *You're an idiot, Paxton.* "She did really well. She's very outgoing and made a number of friends today. There were a few times I could tell she was getting a little homesick, but all the kids went through that and will for the next few days."

"I'm glad to hear she did good."

I could hear the smile in his voice. It was obvious Steed was a good father.

"Are you free this evening? Chloe is having dinner with my parents tonight. They want to start a new family tradition where they get to take her out to eat once a week."

I beamed. That sounded like Melanie and John.

"I've actually made plans for dinner tonight."

"Oh." The disappointment in his voice both thrilled me and made me feel bad at the same time. He'd taken the time to track down my number. Maybe I shouldn't be so hard on him. Plus, I wanted to find out what he and Gina had talked about.

"But, it's with a friend from work. I'm sure she wouldn't mind if I cancelled."

"Yeah?" His voice sounded hopeful.

I didn't want to smile, but a small part of me was happy knowing Steed was free tonight and he wouldn't be spending it with Gina. "Yeah. I think it's best if we clear the air. I can't very well want to take a knife to your dick every time I see you."

"Um…"

Kicking my feet up onto my desk, I covered my mouth to hide my chuckle. *Paxton one. Steed zero.* "It's best we do this for Chloe. I'd hate to think I would be responsible for her not having any younger siblings. Especially with how friendly you and Gina were."

"Who?"

I huffed. "Puh-lease. Don't even pretend. I'm not in the mood for your games."

"My games?"

"Listen, do you want to meet for dinner or not?"

The silence on the other end of the phone had my chest squeezing. *Shit. I went too far in the bitch mode.*

"What time and where?"

I didn't trust myself to be alone with him. Not with the way he made my insides all hot and crazy. No matter how angry I was with him, I was still in love with the jerk and my fingers itched to touch him. "Somewhere public."

Steed laughed. "Fine. Cord's place, say around six?"

Glancing at my clock hanging on the wall, I smiled. It was only four. That gave me plenty of time to get ready. By the time I walked into that bar tonight, Steed Parker was going to wish he had never walked away from me ten years ago.

"Sounds good. See you then."

CHAPTER 7

Steed

The music filled the air as I drank my beer. I watched Cord flirt with a blonde at the end of the bar. She was putty in his hands, gawking at him. Of course my brother didn't really need to try that hard. All of us Parker brothers never lacked in the area of attracting women; we were blessed with handsome looks from our father. Cord was almost an exact replica of Dad. Dark hair, built body and the famous Parker blue eyes.

The next thing I knew, Cord was jumping over the bar and taking her by the hand and heading back to his office. I shook my head.

"Cord has a way with the ladies," I said to my older brother Tripp. He'd had his face in his phone since he walked into the place.

"Tripp. Are you even listening to me?"

He jerked his head up. "What? Yeah. Cord. You said something about Cord."

Laughing, I took another drink. Tripp was the politician in the family. Once he got out of law school, he came back to Oak Springs and started forming an interest in running for office. Maybe even mayor. He was only thirty and would be the youngest mayor elected if he won.

I placed the beer on the bar. "I said, Cord has a way with the ladies."

Tripp rolled his eyes. "Fuck, you have no idea. Mitchell's afraid he going to pull up one day and find Cord screwing some girl in a parked car on the highway."

Shaking my head, I said, "Damn. He hasn't dated anyone seriously?"

Tripp nearly lost it laughing. "Cord? Our brother Cord tie himself down to one pussy? Please."

My eyes widened. "You're not going to win any election if people hear you talk like that."

He winked. "Hey, I may enjoy politics and law, but I love women. I'm no different from Cord or Trevor. A nice pussy walks by and I'm going after it."

I laughed. "There's the Tripp I remember from high school. Whatever happened to Harley? Didn't the both of you get caught screwing in the library? By her dad, right?"

Tripp's beer paused at his lips before he smiled. "I haven't seen Harley in a few years. And yes, her dad caught us. Nothing like dating the principal's daughter then getting caught fucking her."

I slapped the bar. "I just remember you running down the hall, your ass on full display while Mr. Harvey chased you with a baseball bat."

Tripp laughed again. "That's right! Bastard would have caught me if Mitchell hadn't stepped out in front of him and made him trip."

"That's right! The future Texas Ranger aiding and abetting."

Tripp laughed as he tipped his beer back. "Damn, we've had some good times."

A tightness moved into my chest, followed by guilt. "I regret staying away so long."

He slapped me on the back. "Well, you're back now and you brought one hell of a good-looking girl home with you."

Smiling, I took another drink of beer. "Chloe loves being in Texas. The ranch alone had her flying high. Doesn't help that Dad has her on a damn horse every single second of day. I swear if I let her, she'd sleep in the barn. Plus, he got her a pet goat."

Tripp chuckled. "That's good. Get her to fall in love with horses. You remember how much Harley loved horses?"

Harley wasn't only the principal's daughter and the girl Tripp screwed in the library, she was also the girl he'd dated all through high school. I was pretty sure she broke his heart when she left him. He hadn't dated anyone since Harley.

"Yeah, I remember."

He smiled. "She loved those fucking horses. Loved them more than me. I honestly believed I would have gotten into her pants sooner had she not been so obsessed with them."

My heart dropped. A swift panic raced over my body. "Fuck. There's going to be boys trying to get into my daughter's pants."

Tripp peered at me with dread in his eyes. "No fucking way. Not with her dad and four uncles looking out for her."

A sick feeling settled into my stomach. "I'll kill the little bastard," I said.

Cord appeared in front of us with a huge grin on his face. "Who will you kill?"

"The little bastard that tries to get into my daughter's pants."

Taking a few steps back, Cord appeared to be sick. "What! This early? They're starting this early?"

"What?" I asked with a confused expression.

"Someone is trying to … with my niece!"

"No, asshole, I'm saying when she gets older."

Cord leaned against the bar and dragged in a few breaths. "Damn it, Steed. Way to ruin my post sex high."

My head jerked back as I stared at him. "What? No way." I turned to see the blonde sitting at the end of the bar giggling with her two friends while putting her hair back up. Swinging my eyes to Cord, I asked, "You fucked her that fast?"

Cord grinned from ear to ear. "Lick her, stick her, make her scream."

Tripp laughed. "Damn dude, I can't get a condom on that fast."

"She wanted fast. I gave her fast," Cord said as he brushed his knuckles across his shirt.

"Jesus, did you even let the poor girl get off?" I asked.

"Fuck yeah I did. I always take care of them first. I can't help it if I know how to fuck a girl and make her come fast."

"Well isn't this nice. Glad to see the Parker brothers haven't changed any. Still talking filthy and treating women like sex toys."

I froze.

Cord's smile widened, and he clutched his chest. "That wounds me, Paxton. I would never treat a woman that way. If she asks me for sex, who am I to turn her down?"

Paxton stepped between me and Tripp. My dick instantly came to life when I saw her sweet beautiful breasts peeking out from a red dress. Her dark hair was pulled up in a bun on the top of her head. A few loose strands falling out in the back had me itching to push them to the side and kiss her there. My eyes moved down her body to see black heels that made her legs look like they went on forever. I couldn't help but smile. My sweet Paxton had moved on from cowboy boots to fuck-me heels. I knew by the way she was dressed she was trying to show me what I had missed out on over the last ten years.

I moved on the stool to adjust the growing dick in my pants. Lifting my eyes back up her body, I had to suppress a damn moan.

She was fucking gorgeous.

"Goddamn woman, you look hot as hell! Still drink Buds?" Trevor asked as he leaned next to Cord and handed Paxton a Bud Light.

Trevor would sometimes come and help Cord at the bar to earn extra money; I was wishing tonight hadn't been one of those nights.

Paxton blushed and took a drink. "Thanks, Trev. You're looking pretty good yourself."

Trevor's smile grew. "Dance with me, pretty lady. You owe me a raincheck."

My head snapped to him as Cord and Tripp laughed. *What in the fuck? My own brother?*

Paxton took a drink, set down the beer, and nodded. I almost fell out of my chair.

"You can't dance in those shoes." It was out of my mouth before I could stop it.

"Oh damn boy. You fucked up," Cord said as Tripp shook his head and gave me a *what the hell* glare.

Paxton faced me. Her eyes were dark as she let them roam over my body before she captured my gaze with hers. "How would you know?"

The words felt like a knife in my heart.

Trevor jumped over the bar, hit me on the shoulder and laughed. "You fucked up, bro."

"So I've been told."

I watched Trevor wrap his arm around Paxton's waist and lead her to the dance floor. Anger boiled in my blood as he pulled her into his arms. "I'm going to kill that little motherfucker," I said, starting after them. Tripp jumped up stood in front of me.

"Whoa there. Steed, take a deep breath and think about what you're about to do."

Cord must have jumped over the bar because he was already in my face, pushing me back. "Sit your ass down. I don't do well with people starting shit in my place and I don't give a fuck if you're my brother or not. You can't expect Paxton to drop everything and fall at your damn feet because you're back in town, Steed. Trevor's screwing with you because he knows it'll piss you off. Let it go. You know damn well nothing will come from him dancing with her."

I watched as they hit the dance floor and took off. He was lucky it was a fast song.

"Steed. Are you listening to me? Steed!"

My head jerked toward Cord. "What?"

Shaking his head, Cord said, "Dude, you lost any say when you left her."

The pressure on my chest made it hard to breathe as I took a few steps back and sat on the stool.

Cord put his hand on my shoulder. "Look, I know this is hard for both of you. But you've got to see it from her viewpoint. You came walking into her life ten years later like nothing happened and you brought a kid with you. I'm sure no matter how much she pretends to hate your guts, y'all loved each other and she didn't just lose you, Steed. I can't imagine how that must make her feel knowing you have Chloe."

My body sagged. It seemed like the last few times I was with Paxton I couldn't put her feelings first.

I turned and grabbed my beer, quickly downing it.

A slap on my back had me nearly choking.

"Don't drink too much. I wouldn't want to pull you over."

I grunted as my twin brother Mitchell sat down next to me. The only way you could tell us apart was a small scar above my right eye I got from being hit by Tripp with a baseball bat when I was fourteen. And we wore our hair differently.

"S'up, Mitchell?" I asked with a half-smile.

He grinned and motioned for Cord's new bartender to give him what I was drinking.

I hadn't realized how much I had missed my brothers. We had caused some serious hell growing up. I glanced around to each of them and wondered how in the hell they were all still single. It wasn't like we didn't come from a good gene pool. Not one of them was even dating a girl, let alone thinking about settling down.

"You off tonight?" Cord asked, putting another beer in front of me. He'd walked around the bar this time instead of hopping over it.

"Just got off. Rough day. Found the body of a woman on the banks of the Frio."

"Damn, any idea who it is?" Tripp asked.

Mitchell shook his head. "No. We're checking missing persons reports. Fucking sucks knowing someone's daughter is missing and she might be dead." He took a drink of his beer and glanced around the place.

"Fuck me. Who is Trevor dancing with? I'd like to tap that ass… Oh hell … is that…?"

My body shook as Tripp placed his hand on my shoulder. "Paxton," I grunted.

Mitchell jerked his head back. "That's Paxton? Sweet innocent kindergarten teacher, Paxton? Fucking hell. Look at that body."

He laughed, then turned to me. His smile dropped. "Shit. Sorry, Steed. I kind of forgot you were here."

My eyes widened in shock. "I'm sitting right next to you, asshole. How could you forget I'm here?"

With a shrug, he took a drink of his beer. "I think I'll take a walk around the place. See if there's a girl here I haven't hooked up with yet."

Shaking my head, I asked, "Are all of y'all man whores?"

Mitchell shot me a smirk as he took off toward a table of young women. Each of them had their jaws on the floor, hopeful looks in their eyes.

"I'm out of here," Tripp said standing. "I've got a meeting tomorrow morning I can't miss."

"Later," Cord said as they shook hands. Tripp reached for my hand, and I shook it. Then he leaned down and whispered, "Go cut in, you idiot."

I gave him a weak grin before focusing in on Trevor and Paxton. She threw her head back and laughed at something Trevor said.

Tripp started to leave before he stopped and turned back. "If you don't, Mitchell will. He's making his way over there in case you haven't noticed."

Jumping up, I made my way toward the dance floor. Trevor saw me coming and spun Paxton around so that she came to a stop in front of me.

I smiled and her grin evaporated.

"It's about damn time," Trevor said with a slap on my back.

Paxton chewed on her lip as I stared at her. "Dance with me?" I asked. Her eyes fell to the floor. "Please, Pax?"

Her gaze snapped back up, and she stepped closer. I took her into my arms. My entire body felt as if it had come alive after years of feeling dead. Damn, it felt amazing to hold her again. I closed my eyes and took in a deep breath as I pulled her a little closer. When she didn't say anything, I led us farther onto the dance floor.

Her head was against my chest, and I couldn't help but remember how good we fit together. In everything we did, not just dancing. "I've missed you, Paxton."

She didn't say anything, but I felt her body tremble.

"Please don't hate me. I can't stand the thought of you hating me."

Pulling her head back, she stared at me with those big blue eyes. "And why shouldn't I hate you, Steed? You left me to deal with everything. All alone with absolutely no one to talk to. You never even called to ask if I was okay."

A stab of pain hit my chest, and my voice caught in my throat. Her eyes swam with tears, but I knew she was fighting to hold them back. "If I could go back to that first day when you told me, Paxton, I would do everything different. But I can't, and all I know to do is tell you why I left and stayed away."

Our eyes were locked as we moved slowly on the dance floor even though there was a fast song playing.

"The way you looked at me that day…when you told me you hated me. I knew you meant it. I hated me too because I knew I was the reason you lost the baby."

Her eyes widened and her mouth parted, but she didn't say anything. She didn't have to deny it. I knew she blamed me, like I blamed myself.

"I was gutted when you started crying. I'd never seen you so upset, and I knew I was the reason for it. I caused your pain and it about destroyed me. I made a promise to you the first time I told you I loved you that I would never hurt you. I broke that promise and I honestly couldn't bear to look you in the face. I have no idea why I picked Oregon. It was far away. No reminders of us. I was going to come back after summer and go to A and M, but the thought of staring into your beautiful eyes and seeing your pain was too much. When I walked on and tried out for the football team and they took me, I was honestly stunned. I took it as a sign that maybe you were better off without me."

She let a small sob slip from her lips as she shook her head. "How could you think that?" she asked in a whisper. "I loved you, Steed."

"I was stupid. So fucking stupid and damn it all to hell, Pax." My forehead dropped to hers. "I never wanted to hurt you. I never wanted to leave you. I swear to God. *Please* believe me."

Paxton grabbed at my T-shirt and dropped her head to my chest to hide her tears.

The song changed, and I couldn't believe what started playing. Chris Bandi's 'Man Enough Now' came across the speakers and my body trembled.

Paxton tugged on my shirt harder as she cried. I pulled her closer. I'd give anything to take her away from this bar and be alone with her. There were so many things I wanted to tell her. So many things I wanted to do to her beautiful body.

The song ended and the DJ announced a quick break. Paxton and I stood in the middle of the dance floor as everyone walked around us, heading back to their tables.

I didn't want to let her go. The smell of her perfume, the same one she wore all those years ago, was holding me captive. Not to mention how on fire my body was against hers.

Finally, she pulled her head back and looked at me. I wanted to fall to the floor. I hated seeing her cry. Always had and forever will.

"You left me," she barely said.

My eyes closed as the pain in my heart became almost unbearable.

She dropped her hold on me and stepped back.

"I was stupid."

She nodded. "But you moved on."

I shook my head. "No, Paxton. I didn't move on."

A small huff of air left her mouth as she gave me a befuddled expression. "You got married. You had a child."

Her arms wrapped around her waist. "You had a child," she repeated as a tear slid down her cheek.

Reaching up, I wiped it away. "I didn't love my wife, Paxton. She knew I didn't love her because I told her about you."

With wide eyes, she jerked away as if she had been burned. She shook her head as she took a few steps back. Paxton spun on her heels and went back to the bar. I watched her walk away like she couldn't stand to be near me. *What in the hell just happened?*

Making my way through the crowd, I came up behind her. She was drinking her beer when I put my hands on her waist. Jumping at my touch, she set the beer down and turned to me. The idea that she didn't want me touching her made me feel ill. We were inches from each other. Paxton's breath came faster, heavier as her eyes landed on my mouth.

Fuck I wanted to kiss her. My fingers dug into her body, and she sucked in a breath. Even though the bar was getting crowded, it felt as if we were the only two people. The heat between our bodies was growing by the second. The passion we shared for one another was still present. There was no denying it.

I licked my lips and bent closer. Her eyes never left mine. "Paxton," I whispered.

"Tell me something, Steed," she said, our lips inches apart.

"Anything."

Her eyes turned dark. "How is that you didn't want our baby, yet you wanted the baby you had with a woman you didn't even love?"

It felt like every ounce of air in the bar had been yanked out as I fought to breathe. "W-what?"

Placing her hands on my chest, she pushed me back. "I think our conversation is done."

She left.

My feet were frozen. I stared at the spot she'd stood moments ago as her words hit me like a fucking Mack Truck. No matter how hard I tried to say something…do something…I couldn't.

CHAPTER 8

Steed

"Daddy!"

I sprung up in bed and groaned. I had the worst fucking head-ache ever. "Oh Mother of God," I said as I dropped back onto the pillow.

Chloe crawled on the bed and started jumping. "Daddy! Get up! I'm going to be late for school!"

"Chloe, baby, please stop jumping on the bed. Daddy has ..."

"A hangover?"

Snapping my head to the door, I shot Amelia a dirty look.

"Have fun last night?" she asked with a smirk.

Chloe kept jumping.

"Chloe, please stop."

"Cord said you drank until you damn near passed out," Amelia said. "Mitchell had to bring you home. I was already fast asleep by then."

I swung my legs off the bed and attempted to stand. "It was a rough night."

Amelia let out a gruff laugh. "You don't say. I take it things didn't go well with Paxton."

"Who's Paxton?" Chloe asked.

Before I had a chance to answer, Amelia did. "Paxton is Ms. Monroe, Daddy's old girlfriend."

Chloe gasped. I turned to Amelia. "What in the hell, Meli?"

With a shrug, she shot me the finger behind Chloe's back.

"What? Do you have a problem with me drinking, Meli?"

Chloe pulled on my T-shirt. I was wearing the same damn thing I went out in, minus my boots. "Daddy, did you and my teacher really go out on dates?"

Fuck. I don't want to have this conversation with Chloe. Especially right now.

"You couldn't keep your mouth shut, could you?" I spit at Amelia.

"Chloe, princess, will you run to your room and give me and your daddy a few minutes of grown up talk?"

"Sure!"

The second she was out my bedroom, Amelia shut the door and turned to face me.

"I'm not in the mood for your shit today, Amelia."

Her brows rose as she gave me a defiant look. "Well tough shit. You're an asshole, do you know that?"

I headed into the bathroom and turned on the water. I needed to splash my face and wake the hell up. "Yep. Figured that out years ago when I walked away from the only woman I loved."

"So what in the hell are you doing getting drunk out of your damn mind and then calling Paxton?"

My hands froze under the cold water as I peered up at Amelia's reflection in the mirror. "What?"

She nodded. "Yeah, you kept calling her. She didn't have Mitchell or Cord's number but I gave her mine at back to school night. She was worried sick because you were so drunk. I had to assure her that Cord and Mitchell were with you and would get you home okay."

Looking back at the water, I shrugged. "Why does she care?"

"So that's how this is going to be?"

"Yep. I tried to tell her I was sorry. Tried to explain and all I seem to do is make things worse, so fuck it."

"Fuck it?"

I turned off the water and grabbed a towel. Wiping my face, I dropped my hands in front of me. "Yeah, Amelia. Fuck. It."

She nodded. "Okay. Fuck it. So I guess you won't care that Joe Miller walked her home last night after finding her crying and alone."

My heart jumped to my throat. "How do you know that?"

"He was there at her house when she called."

My eyes widened in horror. "He was at her house? What time was it?"

Amelia shrugged. "I don't know. Ten thirty maybe."

"She had to work this morning!" I shouted.

My sister laughed. "Oh, so because she works she's not supposed to have a life?"

I swallowed hard. "Is she dating him still?"

Amelia pursed her lips. "I have no clue, and I didn't feel it was my place to ask her why he was there."

Scrubbing my hands down my face, I moaned. "Fuuuck." I dropped my arms to my sides. "What do I do, Meli?"

Her expression turned soft, and she shook her head. "Do you have any idea how much I long to have a man look at me the way you do Paxton? A love like that is worth fighting for and, unfortunately, I've never experienced it. So I don't know what to tell you, Steed. The only thing I can say is don't give up because I'm positive she doesn't want you to."

The sadness in my sister's eyes made my heart ache. I walked over to her and kissed the top of her head.

"You know there will never be a guy out there good enough for you, Amelia."

She chuckled and hugged me. "Fight for her, Steed. Show her you made a mistake and that you'll do whatever it takes to make it up to her."

"Feel any better?" Tripp asked as he walked on the other side of Chloe. Each of us held her hand, swinging her every now and then. He'd been at the house this morning and I'd snagged him to help me drop Chloe off at school, afraid to face Paxton alone.

"No," I grumbled.

"Mitchell said you did a number on yourself last night."

I laughed. "Yeah well, nothing like drowning your sorrows in alcohol, right?"

"Did it help?"

Glancing at him, I half smiled. "For a little while."

"And there lies the problem. It's a temporary numb."

I nodded. "Sometimes it feels good to feel nothing."

"That doesn't make any sense, Daddy," Chloe said as she tugged our hands.

"One. Two. Three," I said. Tripp and I swung her again. We rounded the corner of the school and my breath caught when I saw her.

"Uncle Tripp, this is my school! That's my teacher!"

Chloe dropped my hand and pulled Tripp toward Paxton. About half the parents were already dropping their kids off in the morning drop off line rather than walking them up. Fuck that. I knew if I walked Chloe up I'd get to see Paxton. Plus, I wanted to spend as much time with Chloe as I could.

"Long time no see, Paxton!" Tripp said while Paxton flashed him a smile.

"You saw Uncle Tripp last night, Ms. Monroe?"

I breathed a sigh of relief. Thank God Chloe didn't call her Paxton.

With a sweet laugh that settled nicely in my chest, Paxton answered, "Yes. I saw your daddy and other uncles too."

Chloe grinned from ear to ear. "Are you and daddy going to date again?"

Everyone turned to look at me. Including one of the moms.

Oh shit.

"Chloe, why don't you go line up with the other students."

"But—"

Paxton regarded Chloe and raised an eyebrow. The argument was over and Chloe walked to the other kids. Turning her focus on me, Paxton's hands went to her hips.

Lifting my palms in defense, I said, "Amelia said something in front of Chloe. I didn't say a thing."

Tripp frowned. "Why would she say something?"

"I don't know. She's stupid?"

"Steed!" Paxton said. "We don't use those words! Honestly, I'm going to have to ban the parents from walking up!"

The first bell rang and Paxton turned quickly, making her way to her students. Chloe turned and stared at me. Her eyes started to build with tears.

"Oh no. She's going to cry again," I whispered.

"What?" Tripp said with horror in his voice.

Paxton walked up to the students and called out, "Shave and a haircut."

They all stopped talking and replied, "Two bits." With their complete attention, she gave them instructions on walking into the building.

I couldn't help but smile. I glanced over to Tripp, who wore a happy expression too.

"Remember Mom used to sing that to get all of our attention?" I said with a laugh.

"Yeah. Looks like Paxton uses it for the same thing."

Nodding, I glanced at the door, hoping Paxton would turn back. She didn't and that wounded me more than I wanted to admit. At the same time, my heart soared as I watched her walk into the building holding Chloe's hand.

Tripp hit my arm. "Let's go. Dad needs me to pick up some paperwork for him."

We headed back to my truck. "So how much do you know what happens in this town of ours?"

Tripp laughed. "I know a lot."

"Do you know if Joe Miller is dating Paxton?"

Tripp stopped walking and looked at me. "I can find out, if you really want to know."

I felt like a creeper, but I needed to know and if I asked Paxton, she might lie and tell me yes just to piss me off.

"Do it," I said as I opened the truck door and climbed in.

CHAPTER 9

Paxton

September flew in like a storm. Literally. The cold front toppled the tents set up for the fall festival, one of our main fundraisers, and if we couldn't get everything set back up it would mean a lot of lost money for the school.

"Paxton! We need more help! I can't hammer this stupid tent stake in," Corina called out.

I let out a frustrated groan.

First and fourth grade were in charge of parent volunteers for this year's fall festival. It rotated with each year for the different grades. Corina was having a hell of a time trying to round up this year's first grade parents to help with anything. We were almost a month into the school year, and she still didn't have a classroom parent.

Who in the hell could I call to help?

Joe crossed my mind, but if I called him, he'd get the wrong idea like he did three weeks ago when he walked me home from

Cord's bar. It was stupid of me to use him as a shoulder to cry on. When he leaned in to kiss me, I put the brakes on fast.

"Um, let me call my dad," I said.

The wind blew hard, and the temperature was dropping. If it kept falling, it would be too cold for the kids to enjoy themselves. My father's phone rang, and I prayed he would answer.

"Hey there, sweetheart."

"Dad. I need help. We're trying to set up for the fall festival and none of the dads showed up to help us. This wind is kicking our butts."

"Who's all there?"

I glanced around. "Me, Corina, about three other teachers who got subs and four moms."

My father covered the phone, talking to someone. "I think I found you some help."

"Really? Oh, Dad! That would be amazing! Are they strong?"

He simply laughed.

"I'll take that as a yes. Are you at a delivery?"

"Yes, darlin'. We'll be there in a bit to help."

Smiling, I gave Corina a thumbs-up. "Okay, Daddy. Be careful."

Hitting End, I ran over to Corina. "My dad was at a delivery and rounded up some help."

"Thank goodness. I'm sorry my volunteers bugged out."

"It's okay. We may need to pull out last year's list and see if we can recruit some parents. If they didn't show for set up, it's unlikely they will want to work the booths tomorrow. Especially if it's on the cold side."

Corina placed her hands on her hips. "If I see them walking around with cotton candy I'm going to shove it up their a-holes."

Smiling, I shook my head. I loved my best friend. I'd have been kicked out of A and M if it hadn't been for her. When a position opened for a first grade teacher, I pretty much told her I'd do any-thing to have her here.

We got to work taking turns hitting the stake with the hammer.

"Damn rock!" I said as I hit it and nothing happened.

Corina dropped to the ground and sighed. "I'm exhausted. How are you not tired?"

Laughing, I answered, "My father delivers feed remember? I used to help with fifty-plus pound bags of the stuff."

She stared. "That explains your upper arm strength. To be hon-est, when you said your father grew and sold feed, I had no idea what in the hell you were talking about. At first I thought you said weed."

I stopped mid swing and stared at her before we both started laughing. "Let's hope he was delivering at a ranch with lots of young guys to help."

Corina's eyes lit up. "Cowboys. Yes, please, and thank you."

Growing up outside of Chicago, Corina still wasn't used to all the cowboys, especially in our small town. At College Station she got a taste of it, but there was nothing that screamed real cowboy as much as living in small town Texas. They were everywhere.

Thirty minutes later, a truck honked. I smiled and waved as my father pulled up and parked. Then two other trucks pulled in next to him. I swallowed hard.

Please God no.

Then the fourth truck pulled up and my heart dropped to my stomach. "Oh. No."

"What's wrong?" Corina asked.

"He was at the Parker ranch."

"Parker as in the ex? As in the richest family in this county?"

With a fake chuckle, I replied, "Yes, as in the ex. And expand that to at least ten counties."

Truck doors starting opening, and they all piled out.

"Holy mother of all creations. Sweet Jesus. I've died and gone to cowboy heaven," Corina purred.

Slowly turning to her, I had to smile. She truly did look like she had died and gone to heaven. "Corina, you've got a bit of drool on the side of your mouth there."

She mindlessly reached up and wiped her mouth with the back of her hand. "Cowboys. Look at them all. They're all…are they all…oh lord."

Squeezing her on the arm, I said, "Oh stop it. Yes. It's the Parker boys. Now snap out of it, Corina. They're just guys."

Her head snapped over to me. "Are you *not* seeing what I'm seeing? Because what I see is five guys … five guys in jeans and cowboy hats. No wait! Five drop dead gorgeous guys, in cowboy hats, and cowboy boots." She glanced back at them then focused on me. "And they're dirty."

I laughed. "That they are. Every single one of them."

Corina swallowed hard. "I meant their clothes are dirty."

Peeking back over at them, I replied, "Yeah. That too."

"Oh lord. My heart."

My father walked up, wearing a shit-eating grin. I knew exactly what he was doing. He'd always loved Steed. Hell, he loved all the Parker boys. I could only imagine the smile on his face when I asked for help, and he was standing in the middle of them all.

"Look who I stumbled upon this morning."

I lifted my brow. "I see."

My parents had stopped pressing me long ago about why Steed left town and why we had broken up. I didn't think I would ever have the courage to tell them. Once my mother found out Steed was back, I could tell her and Daddy had been itching to start up with the questions again. I'd talked about Chloe a few times, but not in great detail. I had thought it would be harder having her in my class, but I found myself drawn more and more to her, and it wasn't only because she was Steed's daughter. She had a heart of gold and was one of the sweetest students I'd ever had.

"You asked for help," my father said with an evil smirk as Mitchell, Tripp, Cord, Trevor, and last but certainly not least, Steed, walked up.

I tried like hell not to let my eyes linger on Steed, but it was hard. His tight black T-shirt showed off how he'd gotten in even better shape than he was at eighteen, and those jeans... I had to fight to make myself breathe. The matching black cowboy hat made his steel blue eyes pop and when my gaze caught his. I quickly glanced away. My heart was beating so fast, and I had a hard time focusing.

Get it together, Paxton.

"So you brought all five of the Parker boys?"

"Boys?" Trevor said with a laugh. "Hell woman, you've got yourself a bunch of strong men."

Corina mumbled something I couldn't understand. Grabbing her, I pulled her toward the four set of hungry eyes. The only one who wasn't looking at Corina was Steed. He hadn't taken his eyes off of me yet.

"This is my best friend, Corina. We went to A and M together. She teaches first grade here in Oak Springs."

Mitchell and Tripp pushed each other to get to Corina first. Tripp won.

Taking her hand, he lifted it to his lips. "It's a pleasure to meet you, Corina. The name is Tripp Parker."

Something slipped from her mouth. A giggle moan? I rolled my eyes, but deep down I was happy to see the guys giving her attention. Corina was beautiful. She had a sweet innocence to her. She almost always wore her blonde hair in a pony, unaware of how beautiful she was. Men tripped over themselves, and she was clueless to all of it. She had dated a couple guys while we were in College Station, and one of them had broken her heart when she caught him cheating.

Corina finally found her voice. "Nice to meet you, Tripp."

Mitchell pushed Tripp out of the way. Imitating his brother, he took Corina's hand and kissed the back of it. "Mitchell Parker. It's a pleasure to meet you, ma'am."

"Lord have mercy," Corina whispered.

Mitchell flashed that smile, and I was pretty sure Corina was melting on the spot. When he winked, she leaned into me.

"Oh, for the love of all that's good." I pushed Mitchell away. "We have work to do! Corina, stay away from Tripp. He's in politics."

"Hey!" Tripp cried out.

"Mitchell here, he's a Texas Ranger."

Corina perked up. "A baseball player!"

Mitchell laughed. "You're not from Texas are you, sweetheart?"

Looking at me with huge eyes, Corina smiled and then turned back to Mitchell. "Chicago."

He nodded. "Well, Corina from Chicago. Texas Rangers are a baseball team, but they are also an elite group of police officers."

Tripp huffed behind Mitchell.

"You're a police officer?" Corina asked with dreamy eyes.

Mitchell's grin grew wider. "Yes, ma'am."

When her teeth sunk into her lip, I pulled her away.

"Corina, this is Cord Parker. He owns Cord's Place."

Corina reached out her hand, and Cord followed suit. "Pleasure is all mine."

"Nice to meet you, Cord."

Stopping in front of Trevor, I took a deep breath. He was the one I was most worried about. "Corina, this is Trevor. He may be the youngest brother, but I think he is the most dangerous."

Trevor tossed his head back to laugh before staring straight at Corina. "Hell yeah, I am."

"Nice to meet you, Trevor," Corina said as she held her hand out. Trevor looked down at it and then grinned like he had just made the catch of the day. "Hell girl, any friend of Paxton's is a friend of mine. Come here."

Before I knew it Corina was wrapped up in Trevor's arms. He lifted her off the ground. She let out a small yelp and laughed. When he put her down, her cheeks were flushed.

"Nice, Trevor," I said with a roll of my eyes.

I wanted to turn and walk away without even introducing her to Steed, but I couldn't do that in front of my Daddy. He'd raised me better than that.

Steed was still staring at me, but turned to Corina and smiled politely. He reached his hand out and shook hers. "Steed Parker, it's a pleasure meeting you."

Corina snapped her head over and gave me an inquisitive stare. "Steed? This is him."

I chewed on my lip. *Please don't make a scene, Corina.*

With pleading eyes, I replied, "Yes, Corina, this is Steed. He just moved back from Oregon with his daughter, Chloe."

Corina plastered on a fake smile. "Well, I've heard a lot about you."

Steed's grin faded as he cleared his throat. "I'm sure you have."

Leaning in so only he could hear, Corina whispered, "I'd like to grab you by the balls and push them up into your throat for what you did to her."

His eyes grew wide, and he took a step back.

I clapped my hands. "Great. Okay. Since we have man power here, we need to get all these tents up, and they have to be staked into the ground good with this front blowing in."

Trevor was the first to get after it. "Let's do this shit!"

Steed paused in front of me, but then followed Cord to another tent without saying a word. I tried not to let the hurt show. After all, I was the one pushing him away. Why should I expect him to stop and talk?

CHAPTER 10

Paxton

"He can't keep his eyes off of you," Corina whispered.

"So what," I said as I peeked over at Steed. I wouldn't admit to Corina and could barely admit it to myself, but my chest fluttered and my stomach dropped each time I caught Steed watching me.

She sighed and I stopped setting up the booth and turned to her. "What?"

She shrugged. "I don't know. He looks so…sad."

"So? I really don't care if he's sad or not."

"Paxton, you don't really mean that. I know you still care for him."

She was wrong. I still loved him.

My father walked up with a smile, as usual. "Darling, we've got all the tents up, but I think the boys need to be getting back to their place. I pulled them away and they've got work to do."

I hugged him. "Thank you, Daddy, for bringing help."

He pushed me back and gave me a wink. "Well, as soon as they heard y'all were in trouble, they were eager to help."

A rush of guilt washed over me knowing I had avoided the Parker family for so long, and the moment I put out the call for help, they didn't think twice. With a chuckle, I said, "Sounds like the Parker boys."

Corina stood next to me. "Paxton those are not boys. They are one hundred percent men."

My father laughed while I rolled my eyes.

Mitchell approached, wiping his hands, and I couldn't help but notice how Corina seemed to stand a little taller and her eyes got a little brighter. "It was a pleasure meeting you, Corina." Mitchell reached out for her hand and shook it. I could tell she was a bit disappointed. Maybe she wanted another swoon moment with him kissing the back of her hand.

Tripp was next and practically pushed Mitchell out of the way. He was happy to kiss the back of Corina's hand. "Corina, it's been an honor working alongside you. Maybe we'll meet up again soon."

With a wide grin, Corina replied, "I'd like that."

My eyes swung over to Mitchell. He didn't look pleased as he headed to Trevor's truck.

I thanked each of the guys with a hug then glanced around for Steed. He wasn't standing with his brothers. I glanced over my shoulder and saw him talking to Gina Higgins.

"When did Gina get here?" I asked Corina.

She shrugged. "No clue. Seems like she has her eyes on your man."

I huffed. "He isn't my man, Corina." Turning away, I walked my father to his truck.

Cord stood there, smiling. "Paxton, you really should stop by my folks' place sometime. I know Mom would love to see you."

The ache in my heart grew. I loved Melanie and missed her more than I could say. "I'd love that," I replied softly.

He nodded, then stared past me. "He's not interested in her."

I glanced over my shoulder. Gina was trying her best to keep Steed's interest. When our eyes met, I looked back at Cord.

"I wouldn't care if he was."

His brows lifted. "Really? Because the way you glared over there a minute ago screamed like you cared."

Before I had a chance to respond, Trevor honked, causing me to jump and yell. Cord shot him the finger. Tripp and Mitchell laughed as the Ford backed up and headed out of the parking lot.

My father waved goodbye from where he stood beside his truck. "Bye, sweet girl. I need to run."

"Thank you again for coming to my rescue, Daddy."

He laughed. "Don't thank me. Thank the boys."

I smiled. "Be careful, and give Mom a kiss and hug for me."

Climbing into his truck, he shut the door and called out, "Will do!"

Cord still stood there, staring like he knew something I didn't. I opened my mouth to talk but instantly shut it when a rush of energy zipped through my body...starting at my lower back where Steed had placed his hand.

"Paxton, do you have a minute to talk?"

My eyes were fixed on Cord as if my life depended on it. The bastard turned and headed to the passenger side of Steed's truck.

"Please, Pax?" Steed said.

My eyes closed. The sound of his pleading settled around my aching heart.

When I turned to him, I had to hold my breath. My god, he was so handsome. An older version of the boy I fell so madly in love with.

"Fine, but not here. I don't want parents gossiping."

"Okay. Where?"

The words were out of my mouth before I could stop them.

"We can meet at my house later this evening."

He smiled and my legs wobbled. Pointing at him, I said, "Don't get any ideas."

The way his gaze searched my face had me fighting for air. He looked like he wanted to kiss me and honest to God if we hadn't been where we were, I probably would have let him. Before I kneed him in the balls of course.

"What time? I'll need to make arrangements for Chloe."

There went that ache in my chest again.

"Five. Is that early enough so you won't miss her bedtime or anything?"

His eyes turned sad. "Yeah. Yeah that works great."

I nodded. "Fine. I'll text you the address."

Spinning on my boot heels, I walked toward the booth where Corina was standing. I had to concentrate on breathing, especially since I could feel Steed's eyes on me. One glance over my shoulder proved I was right. I gave him a weak smile as my heart raced. I didn't want to forgive him. I wanted to be angry, but my heart was beginning to win the war against my head.

When I got to the booth I felt more eyes on me. This time they were Gina's...and they were filled with anger.

I stood in front of the mirror and groaned. "Why did I tell him to come here?"

Corina sat on the edge of my bed. "Because deep down you want something to happen."

My mouth dropped open as I stared at her in the mirror. "I do not."

She laughed. "Please. You two gaze at each other like you're starving for one another." Falling onto the bed, she covered her heart. "Oh, to have a love like that."

I huffed. "You're insane. I don't look at him like that, and he certainly doesn't look at me like that. Besides, you saw him talking to Gina."

Corina sat up. "Puh-lease. Gina is a money grubbing S. L. U. T. Steed's not interested in her. She keeps throwing herself at him. Trust me. I was watching."

"Since when did you become a Steed fan?" I asked, pulling my hair up and braiding it.

"Oh, I'm not. Believe me, when he introduced himself I wanted to junk punch him. His pretty face was a bit of a distraction though."

Corina winked, and I couldn't help but chuckle. "He is handsome, I won't argue with you on that."

"Hell, they are all handsome. And bodies like gods. What in the heck did their mother drink while pregnant?"

Laughing, I dropped in one of the chairs in my bedroom. "When we were younger, oh man, the girls would go crazy for the Parker brothers. Tripp's the oldest brother and lord did the girls throw themselves at him. It was almost kind of sad."

"Did he ever date anyone?"

"Yeah, he had a serious girlfriend, Harley. They broke up, and he kind of started the path for the whole Parker man whore legend. I think she broke his heart and the only way he could get over it was to sleep with every girl he could."

Corina rolled her eyes. "What about Mitchell?"

I smiled. "He's always been the serious one. Anytime the boys wanted to do something that was borderline wrong, Mitchell tried to talk them out of it."

"Explains the cop thing then."

"Yeah. I think he's probably the shyest out of all the guys."

"Huh. Interesting." Corina stood. "I guess I better head out before Steed gets here."

My chest tightened as panic set in. "Maybe I should call and tell him another night."

Corina placed her hands on my arms and pierced my eyes with hers. "Paxton, you need to talk to him. You've been needing to talk to him since the day he walked away. You won't be able to move on if you guys don't sort this out. I know you say you don't have feelings for him, but I'm your best friend and I know that's a lie. I see the way you look at him. Talk to him, honey. You can't keep this inside much longer."

A single tear slipped from my eye and made a slow trail down my face. "I know," I whispered.

Squeezing my arms, Corina gave me a reassuring smile. "Tell him how he hurt you, Paxton. Get it out there in the open and close this chapter of your life. Then you can decide if Steed Parker is part of the next chapter or not."

My chin trembled and all I could do was nod.

Corina kissed me on the forehead and turned to leave. A quick peek at the clock told me I had fifteen minutes until Steed would get here.

Corina stopped at the door. "Maybe you should take a shot of something."

Jerking my head back, I asked, "Why?"

"Because you're shaking like a leaf." She winked.

After Corina left, I stood there for a few moments staring at the door. Taking a deep breath, I let my mind go back to the day that changed everything.

Everyone was celebrating the fact that we had graduated high school. Everyone but me. The cramps in my stomach were a constant reminder that I had lost the baby in the early morning hours. I was so tired. I'd driven myself to the hospital and sat there alone while the doctor told me what had happened.

Steed sat down next to me and reached for my hand. Pulling it from him, I turned to him. "Don't touch me."

His eyes were sad, but I didn't care.

"Pax, please. I'm so sorry I wasn't there."

"You did this."

The horror on his face should have made me regret my words, but I didn't. I meant every single word I said.

"Please can we go somewhere and talk?"

"Talk about what, Steed? There's nothing your words can say to make it better."

He reached for my hand again, and this time I didn't fight it. "Maybe I should leave for a few weeks."

My head whipped as I stared at him. "What? Why?"

He looked at the ground. "You're upset, and we both need time to wrap our heads around this."

Standing, I glared at him. "You're running. That's what you're doing. You piece of shit! You're leaving me! Again! How could you do this?"

Steed stood. "Wait, Paxton, that's not what I meant."

I pushed him as hard as I could. "I hate you! I hate you so much right now. Leave! Go run and hide! I never want to see you again. And I swear to God the next time I see you if you even think of speaking to me I'll cut your dick off and shove it down your damn throat!"

"Paxton, wait."

He reached for me, and I screamed. I'd never seen Steed look so scared in my life. The way he jerked his hands away with a look of horror had me wanting to tell him I was sorry. But I didn't. "I'd never hurt you, Paxton. Ever."

"You've already hurt me more than you could ever know. Please...just leave me alone, Steed. Just leave."

My eyes snapped open and I inhaled a quick breath. The memory of that day swirled in my head. Turning, I walked into the kitchen, grabbed a bottle of rum and a Diet Coke, and made myself a drink.

The drink hit my empty stomach, making me groan. My eyes closed.

I pushed him away. I was the one who told him to leave and never come back. I never in my wildest dreams thought he would take it to heart.

CHAPTER 11

Steed

When I pulled up to Paxton's house I couldn't help but smile. It looked like a place she would fall in love with. Paxton had always talked about owning one of the older homes in the center of town. I'd bet anything she bought it and remodeled it, bringing it back to life from an old dull farmhouse.

Turning off the truck, I ran my hand through my hair and took in a deep breath. I'd waited ten years to have this conversation, and I couldn't get my damn hands to stop shaking.

As I stepped onto the porch, I took a quick peek around. I chuckled when I saw the two black rocking chairs. All the times we had sat on my parents' porch and talked about our future…I couldn't look at a black rocking chair without thinking of Paxton.

My arms felt like lead as I stared at her door. I finally pressed the doorbell. Less than ten seconds later, the door opened.

The air from my lungs was gone in an instant. The most beautiful woman in the world stood in front of me. Paxton was wearing a light blue dress that hung from her body in all the right ways. My eyes lingered on her bare feet before I dragged them back up and smiled when I saw the braid coming around the side of her head.

"Hey," I said barely above a whisper.

I couldn't read her eyes, but it was like she could read mine. She didn't say a word as she turned and walked into the house. Lifting my eyebrows, I followed her in and shut the door.

"Want a drink?" she called out as she made her way to the large open kitchen. I scanned the living room as I made my way through it.

"No thanks."

She laughed. "Well, I'm having another."

We stopped at a large island, and Paxton poured rum into a glass followed by Diet Coke. When she downed it, my mouth nearly dropped to the floor. "You okay?" I asked.

Her eyes snapped on mine, and she slowly shook her head. "No, Steed. I'm far from okay. I haven't been okay since you walked away from me the night of graduation."

I swallowed hard. "I was confused, Paxton. You were telling me you hated me. You told me to leave."

"I did hate you, and I did want you to leave."

A tear made its way down her cheek. "Some nights when I'm alone in bed, I hate you all over again."

"Pumpkin, I'm so sorry."

She laughed. "So sorry for what? That you left me to deal with the loss of our child? That you didn't care enough to come back? Or maybe that you ended up knocking up another woman, but decided she was worth sticking around for?"

Anger raced through me. "You told me it was my fault, Paxton! That you never wanted to see me again. What in the hell was I supposed to do?"

She slammed her glass on the granite counter. "Stay! You were supposed to stay goddamn it! Not leave me!"

I shook my head. "You *told* me to leave."

Her lips pressed together. "I didn't want you to leave, Steed. I was hurting and scared, and I'd just had to deal with taking myself to the hospital where I lost *our* baby. I had no one to talk to."

A loud sob slipped from between her lips, and it hit me right in the gut.

She dropped her head and started crying. I moved around the island, but she held up her hand to stop me. Taking a few steps away, she looked up and I nearly fell to the ground.

Her face was soaked in tears.

"I lost her. T-then I-I lost you."

"Paxton," I whispered.

"Then I lost *me*, Steed. A part of me never came back until you walked into my classroom that night. That small…small…" She attempted to keep her sobs at bay but struggled speaking. "Th-that small part of m-me that died when you left. It came back to life and I think…that made me…hate you all over again."

This was the reason I never came back. I was a fucking coward.

Paxton looked me in the eyes and asked, "Why didn't you come back?"

I didn't even bothering trying to keep my tears back. The only woman I ever loved was hurting and it was my fault. Again.

"Because of this. Seeing how much I keep hurting you. It kills…" I had to clear my throat to keep speaking. "It kills me knowing what I did to you and our child. When I left, I was…consumed with researching miscarriages. When you said I caused it to happen, I…knew it was the truth."

Paxton stood there staring at me. Her arms wrapped around her body.

"I started drinking to try and drown out your cries." My jaw ached from trying so hard to keep my emotions in check. "It never worked. They only got louder. Your voice repeated in my head that you hated me, and I knew if I came back, this would happen and you'd hate me all over again. I was a coward and I couldn't handle seeing you...seeing you..."

My head dropped and I had to take in a few deep breaths.

"I almost quit school," she said.

Jerking my head up, I asked, "What?"

Paxton leaned against the counter as she wiped her cheeks. Streaks of black smeared her beautiful face.

"When you never came back that summer, I knew you never were coming back. It hurt so much without you there. Everywhere I turned there was a memory of you. Of us. My life was nothing but heartache. I was in the middle of a storm, and I had no idea how to run from it. So I pretended everything was okay. I did what my parents expected me to do, and I went to A and M. But all I felt was pain. When I met Corina I put on a good front for the first couple of months until I saw an Oregon football game and your name was announced. You were the star player from Texas who walked on and made it at Oregon State. I found myself outside in the rain just standing there. The storm cloud had followed me, and I knew I would never be able to stop hurting. I stopped going to class. I partied, drank, and more than once I almost did something I knew I would regret the rest of my life."

My breath stalled in my chest.

She smiled. "But they weren't you, Steed. So I always walked away before anything happened. But the hurt kept growing, and I didn't know how to deal with it. Corina made me tell her everything. She's the only person I've ever told about the baby and what happened. Well, besides the counselor I started going to. I finally learned..."

Covering her mouth, she closed her eyes. I walked up and put my hands on her arms. Paxton dropped her hands. "I learned to grieve the loss of the baby and the only man I've ever loved."

I closed my eyes and struggled to take in air. My lungs burned as each breath moved in and out painfully.

"I'm so sorry I wasn't there." Opening my eyes, I gazed into hers. The sadness told me Paxton was not done grieving. "Paxton, if I could go back." I dragged in a shaky breath. "If I could change how stupid and selfish and…I don't even know the words I'm looking for to describe what an asshole I was. But if I could go back to that day you told me you were pregnant, I would have never walked away. I fucked up twice, and there isn't anything I can do to take it back."

She wiped her tears away. "I know that."

Lifting my hand, I pushed a piece of loose hair behind her ear. "Paxton, I never stopped loving you."

Her chin trembled. "Why…why did you move on then?"

I shook my head. "I never moved on."

With a frown, she glared. "I'm sorry, what? Steed, you got married! You had a baby! You moved on."

"No. This is what I wanted to talk about. The other night at Cord's place you didn't let me explain. Mom used to keep me up to date with what was going on with you. She'd ask your mom how you were. It killed her that you stopped coming around."

Paxton sniffled. "It killed me too."

I placed my hand on the side of her face, and I thought for sure she would move away, but she didn't.

"One day she told me you were dating Joe Miller. I didn't even know the fucker went to A and M. His mom told my mom she thought y'all were going to be getting engaged and that a wedding would follow soon after."

Paxton's eyes widened in shock. "What?"

Dropping my hand, I took a few steps back and leaned on the other counter across from Paxton. "I went fucking insane with the thought of you marrying him. Hell, you simply dating him drove me crazy. All the guilt and anger I had tried to bury came rushing back. The thought that I walked away from the love of my life left me sick to my stomach. I told my mother I didn't want to hear anything else about you. I forbid her to talk about you and if she brought you up, I'd threaten to hang up."

Confusion laced her face.

"I met Kim at a party a few weeks after my mother told me you were getting engaged. She was supposed to make me forget, as fucked up as that sounds. I never felt a connection with her, but she was the total opposite of you. We dated for a bit, and I realized I needed to be honest with her. The night I was planning to break up with her was the same night her parents died. She was a mess for weeks. Her best friend talked me into asking her to marry me because she was afraid she would kill herself if she didn't have anything to look forward to. I felt so guilty and if only I had known at the time all that guilt was for what happened with you and had nothing to do with Kim…"

I paused and took in another long deep breath. "At the same time, I was still angry about Joe and the idea of you dating him. I thought you had moved on, Paxton."

Her brows pinched together.

My heart was pounding so fucking hard in my chest as I tried to get everything out as fast as I could. I'd waited so long to tell Paxton everything. Now that I was standing in front of her, I was more scared than ever that she'd hate me even more.

Taking in a deep breath, I continued. "So I asked Kim and we got married. It didn't take me long to realize what a huge fucking mistake it was. I told Kim I wanted a divorce. Then I called Mom, told her I was coming back to Texas as soon as I graduated and get divorced. I was going to try and work things out with you."

"What?" Paxton covered her stomach and her mouth like she was about to get sick.

"Pax? Are you okay?"

She shook her head. "No. I need to sit down."

CHAPTER 12

Paxton

I was going to be sick. Steed was going to come home? He was coming back for me?

Sinking into the chair, I reached for the bottle of rum and went to take a drink when Steed took it. "Let me get you water instead, pumpkin."

Pumpkin. Each time he called me the pet name my lower stomach pulled with want.

Steed opened the refrigerator and looked around for the waters. He handed me one, and I quickly took a drink. "Keep going," I managed to say.

When his hand pushed through that dark brown hair, I had to hold back a moan.

"Um, well, I told Kim I wanted a divorce. She had told me she was on birth control, but even after we got married I kept using condoms."

92

The idea of Steed sleeping with another woman nearly killed me. I knew he had of course, but hearing him say it hurt more than I ever dreamed.

"Was she…was she not?"

"I don't know. I'm pretty sure she stopped taking them before we got married. From what I could piece together from her crazy ass friends, Kim saw an article in Texas Monthly that had my parents listed as one of the wealthiest families in Texas. She started talking about us moving to Texas. I knew that was never going to happen. It was then I realized I was lying to myself. I was in love with you still and I needed to get out of the marriage."

I swallowed even though my throat felt like it was coated in cotton. "But she was pregnant?"

Steed's eyes fell. "Yes. When she told me I felt sick. The only thing I could think was how it was supposed to be you."

He slowly lifted his eyes to meet mine. "You were the woman I dreamed of marrying and having kids with. Even after I left Texas. Kim was nothing but a mistake."

Pressing my lips together, I tried not to start crying again.

"Then the guilt hit. Hard. As much as I wanted to tell her it didn't matter, I was too afraid to make the same mistake. I'd already told her about you. That I could never love her because I'd given my heart to another woman. She insisted the baby would change things. I knew it wouldn't. I was too afraid to upset her though…if she lost the baby it would be my fault. Again."

A tear slipped down his cheek and my heart ached at the sight. "Steed, it wasn't your fault. Our child wasn't meant to be."

His head dropped and I sat there stunned as I watched his shoulders rock while he cried. "Every damn day I wake up and I think about it, Paxton. There's not…there's not a single day where I don't think about it. I *need* you to know that."

I couldn't move. I was frozen in place as I watched Steed grieve for our child. Covering my mouth, I cried along with him.

"There was no fucking way I was doing it again. I couldn't live with myself."

My heart ached.

He wiped his tears and looked back at me. "So I stayed. And she had the baby and then I felt the guilt all over again because I fell madly in love with this...b-beautiful child. But she wasn't...she wasn't *your* child. I didn't know how to deal with that. I had planned on telling Kim I wanted a divorce after she had the baby, but I wasn't sure how the custody would work. When I did finally tell her, she threatened to take Chloe from me and said I'd never be able to find them."

Steed took a few minutes to get his emotions in check as I sat there, silently crying, as I tried to let everything soak in.

"Kim never loved Chloe. The moment she was born, she pretty much had nothing to do with her. I learned pretty quick she was only after money. I tried like hell to get Chloe away. I begged Kim for a divorce. Each time I would bring it up she would make the threats about taking the baby, and say I'd never see them again. If I left the house without Chloe I would wonder if my daughter would be there when I got home."

I shook my head as I tried to keep the bile down. How could a mother be so cruel? "Poor Chloe."

"For years I tried to figure out how in the fuck to get away. One day Dad came up with the whole idea of cutting me out of his will. It took a while to do it. I didn't want Kim knowing I was on to her. Dad made a fuss about me not coming back to Texas to help him full time with the ranch, we pretended to fight about it and he had fake documents sent to the house. I knew if Kim saw legal documents from Texas delivered to the house she would open them. Dad had it arranged to have them sent while I was at a meeting at the office. The next day she walked into my office at home with a lawyer, took out the legal documents and signed her parental rights away. Her exact words were, "I wasted seven years of my life on you. No more.""

I gasped.

"She didn't even say goodbye to Chloe. She just left."

Steed's hands ran down his face while he let out a gruff laugh. "It's so fucking confusing. I wish like hell I never walked away from you, but then I wouldn't have Chloe." Closing his eyes, he sucked in a breath as he attempted to hold his emotions in.

He failed.

When he looked at me, his eyes spilled over with tears. "I have Chloe, but I don't have you. I have this amazing little girl who I love, but I don't have the dream we both wanted. And the fucking vicious cycle of guilt keeps spinning around, and now here I am, and all I want to do is hold you in my arms and tell you how much I love you, Paxton. I've never stopped loving you. But I destroyed our dream and I don't blame you if you hated me for that."

My entire body started to shake. Everything spun. I slowly stood and walked over to him. I couldn't help but notice how Steed held his breath as I stopped in front of him.

I wanted more than anything for him to take me in his arms and hold me. Tell me everything was okay because he was back.

But he didn't. He didn't move as his gaze locked on mine.

I took in a shaky breath, barely getting the words out. "I did date Joe for a while, but we were far from being engaged."

Knowing what I was about to say was going to cause Steed further hurt, I should have stopped. But I didn't, because everything needed to be out in the open for both of us to move on. I just wasn't sure if we would be moving on together…or apart.

"I never even slept with him."

There was no doubt I could see the sick feeling move across Steed's face. "W-what?"

"We dated off and on, it was never anything serious. I have no idea why his mother would say that to Melanie. I never even visited his parents while we dated."

It was in that moment that everything came full circle. Every stupid thing we said to each other in anger. Every mistake we each made. Every single regret, out in the open.

Steed covered his face with his hands and cried out as he slid down to the floor. He repeated the same three words while his body shook violently. "I'm so sorry."

My heart dropped to my stomach as I fell to the floor next to him. I'd never seen Steed cry like this. He pulled me into his arms and buried his face into me, his body shaking as he let all his emotions out.

"Paxton, I'm so sorry. Please forgive me. Oh God. I'm so sorry."

Closing my eyes, I held onto Steed as he wrapped me tighter in his embrace.

I had been wrong all those years. The storm cloud hadn't only been over me. It had been over Steed as well.

Steed and I had been sitting on my kitchen floor for the last thirty minutes, neither of us saying a word. I cried until I no longer had tears left, and I was pretty sure the same was true for him.

Leaning against the cabinets, I turned to look at him. His head was resting against the cabinet as he stared straight ahead. My chest tightened at the sight of this man sitting next to me. I still loved him.

Probably more after what happened here than ever, but I was still hurting and I had no idea when I would be able to open my heart again.

Steed finally spoke. "There was this quote I read one time that always stuck with me."

"What was it?" I asked.

"Fear is temporary, regret is forever."

He turned and caught my gaze. "I'm never going to let fear lead me down the road to regret ever again, Paxton."

His eyes dropped to my mouth where I instinctively licked my lips. "I love you, Pax. I've never stopped loving you and I'll love you until the day I take my last breath."

Dragging in a shaky breath, I whispered, "Steed, I—"

He held up his hand. "Wait. Let me finish, please." Reaching for my hands, he guided me up along with him. Standing face to face, he searched my face with such an intense look it caused me to shudder.

"I don't know where life is going to lead us, but I know I won't stop fighting for us, Paxton. If it takes me the rest of my life, I'll earn your forgiveness and love back."

My heart had never beat so fast or so hard in my entire life. I'd been fighting the urge to kiss him since he first walked into my classroom. I was tired of fighting.

One kiss.

That's all I wanted. All I needed.

Who am I kidding? I needed this man.

Taking a step closer, I captured his beautiful blue eyes with mine. "You never lost my love, Steed."

His hands reached up and cupped my face.

Just *one* kiss.

Slowly moving closer, his eyes drifted to my mouth once more. I silently begged him to kiss me as he grew closer and closer. When his lips finally brushed against mine, I let out a soft moan.

It was a slow and tender kiss and my body came to life. Reaching up on my toes, I deepened the kiss a little more. Steed groaned into my mouth before pulling back just enough to break the kiss. He rested his forehead on mine and sighed.

"I'm sorry," he whispered.

Closing my eyes, I replied, "Don't say that. Not when I know we both wanted it."

The doorbell rang, and we both jumped. I felt lightheaded and needed to grab onto the kitchen island to steady myself.

Steed's eyes looked hungry with desire, but his expression was sad.

When the person rang the bell again, then knocked, I cleared my throat. "I better get that."

He simply nodded while his fingers pushed through his hair. *Shit, he is so damn hot when he does that.*

Focusing on trying to get my breathing under control, I opened the door without looking to see who it was. My eyes widened in shock.

"Joe?"

A wide grin moved across his face as he purred, "Hey beautiful. Miss me?"

CHAPTER 13

Steed

The pounding in my chest was echoing in my ears. I hadn't needed the kiss to remind me of how much I loved Paxton, but when our lips met and our bodies rushed with energy, I knew deep in my heart that this was the woman I would love for the rest of my life. She was the reason my heart beat.

When the doorbell rang I silently thanked God. It was taking every ounce of strength not to pick up Paxton and lay her over the island and bury my dick inside of her. The constant battle between my head and my heart was getting exhausting.

I reached down and adjusted my rock-hard dick.

"Jesus, get a grip, Parker," I whispered to myself as I walked to the bottle of rum. I poured a shot into the glass and went to drink it when I stilled at a familiar voice.

"Joe?"

"Hey beautiful. Miss me?"

What in the fuck is he doing here?

I tossed the shot back and set the glass on the counter.

Paxton stood there in silence for a little longer than I would have liked.

"Um, Joe now isn't really a good time."

His eyes lifted and met mine. When his smile faded, mine grew bigger. *That's right motherfucker. I'm back.*

He let out a gruff laugh and said, "Steed Parker. I heard you were back in town. Planning on sticking around this time?"

Asshole.

"I sure do."

Paxton cleared her throat and stepped in front of Joe as he attempted to walk in.

"Now's not a good time, Joe."

"Nonsense, looks like you're having a bit of a reunion here."

Walking around the island, I made my way into the living room. "And I don't believe you were invited."

Paxton glanced over her shoulder. "Steed. I can handle this."

Joe laughed again. "So you think you can ride on back into town and pick up where you left off?"

"Excuse me?" Paxton said as she placed her hand on Joe's chest. "I think you need to leave now, Joe."

He looked down at her and then back at me. "You've got a lot of nerve showing up here, Parker."

It was my turn to laugh. "You don't even know why I'm here, asshole."

"That's enough, both of you stop. Joe, I'm asking you nicely, please leave."

A frustrated expression moved across his face as he glared and then finally focused in on Paxton while pushing himself into her house. He grabbed her by her upper arms and shook his head as he spoke.

"Why, Paxton? Why would you let this lowlife back into your life? He left you, remember? He doesn't love you and never did. All you were was a sex thing for him to play with until he found something better."

I walked up to him and grabbed him by the shirt, pulling him away from Paxton.

"Fuck off, you son-of-a-bitch!" I hit him in the face, causing him to stumble back.

Paxton screamed and rushed to Joe. "Steed! Are you crazy?"

"He had his hands on you, Paxton. I'm not going to let him touch you and say bullshit things like that."

Joe wiped the blood from his mouth as he glared at me from the floor. Paxton was kneeling down next to him. Why she gave a shit how he was, I couldn't imagine.

I pointed at him. "You ever say something like that again and I'll—"

"Enough!" Paxton cried out. "Steed, I think you need to leave."

My eyes widened in shock. "What? Why in the fuck do *I* need to leave? He's the one who came bursting in here and manhandled you!"

"I could have handled it, but it looks like some things never change. Your hot-headed temper likes to take control."

There was no way she was taking that asshole's side right now. "Pax, are you serious right now? We were talking …we were… I thought… Why are you doing this?"

"I need you to leave, Steed. Now."

Joe stared up at me with a shit-eating grin on his face.

Nodding, I glanced between the two of them and settled my gaze on her. "Fine. If that's what you want."

She stared up at me, anger still visible.

"I guess maybe you were wrong," I said.

The anger on her face immediately melted away. "What?"

"Maybe you did stop loving me."

One more survey of Joe, and I simply nodded. "You got what you wanted, fucker."

Paxton stood. "Steed. Wait."

Without looking back, I walked out the front door and to my truck.

"Steed!"

I opened the door to my truck and glimpsed back at the house. "You asked me to leave, Paxton. I'm doing what you asked, unless you want me to stay. Do you want me to stay?"

She wrapped her arms around her body and said nothing.

I slowly nodded. "Okay, I guess I'll see you around."

My heart felt like it had been ripped from my chest all over again. This time, before I walked away, I asked her twice if she wanted me to leave. I started up the truck and drove away.

Chloe was practically pulling my arm out of socket as she dragged me behind her.

"Hurry, Daddy! The carnival is about to start!"

Glancing around, I couldn't help but notice all of the people. Where in the hell were some of them yesterday when Paxton needed help setting up? They must have gotten more help after we left.

"A petting zoo!" Chloe shouted.

Laughing, I shook my head. "Pumpkin, you live at a zoo practically."

She rolled her eyes. "It's not the same, Daddy!"

As we walked over to the zoo on wheels, I searched the crowd for Paxton. I knew she was here and a part of me dreaded seeing her. Especially since she let me walk away from her last night, leaving her alone with that fucker, Joe.

Before I knew it, I was in the damn pen chasing a duck down for Chloe to pet.

The battle was won, and it was worth it when I saw the smile on Chloe's face. Her little blue eyes stared up and pleaded. "May I get a duck?"

My heart dropped. "Huh?"

A light chuckle came from my left. Turning, I wanted to groan when I saw Gina standing there. "They are so adorable at this age. Lilly wants a duck too."

Chloe jumped up and down. "We can get sister ducks, Daddy. And then they can have play dates."

Lilly jumped around in agreement. When I looked at Gina I had to turn away. Holy shit if she wasn't giving serious fuck-me eyes.

"Chloe, we're not getting a duck. Sorry pumpkin." I took her hand and glanced back at Gina. "Good seeing you. We've got to run, meeting someone."

Her lower lip jutted out in a pout. "Bummer. Let's plan a play date! Soon!"

Lifting my hand, I called back to her. "Sure. I'll get with you on it."

The second we got out of the mini-zoo I took off. "Daddy, why are we walking so fast?" Chloe asked.

I slowed down my pace. "Sorry, pumpkin. How about we go find some games to play?"

Her smile grew bigger. "Games! Yes!"

We headed over to the area that had all of the games set up. Each one they got to play for something. A homework pass for the older kids, tea with your teacher, a trip to Build-A-Bear, a floating raft trip down the Frio.

"Daddy! It's a fishing game."

Something in the air changed, and I quickly looked around. Paxton was nowhere to be found so I shook it off. Chloe was yanking on my shirt, trying to get me over to the small circular pond where the kids were fishing.

When I walked up, I glanced down. Real fish. Yep, we're back in Texas all right.

"Please may I fish?"

My Chloe loved fishing. She and Dad had already been to the lake on the ranch about a dozen times. Smiling, I motioned for the kid manning the booth to give us a pole.

"Just one, sir?" he asked confused.

Laughing, I stated, "She fishes better than me."

When the kid handed her the fake worms, Chloe stared at him with a confused expression. "Those ain't real."

"Those are not real," I corrected.

She quickly glanced around and dashed over to the open field.

"What's she doing?" the kid asked.

A smile spread across my face. "Looking for a worm."

"But we have worms. She has to use these."

My eyes swung back over to the kid then I glanced around at their setup. "I don't see where it's posted they have to use your bait."

He glanced over to the older man who laughed and winked. "Hey, if she's got the guts to dig her own worm, she deserves to use it."

I gave him a nod as my way of saying thank you.

Chloe came back with a huge fat earthworm.

"I got me my worm, sir."

"Would you like me to hook for you?"

By the look on Chloe's face, he knew her answer and handed her the pole again. Promptly getting her worm on the hook, Chloe tossed it into the water. Peeking up at me, she grinned and my heart fluttered in my chest.

I was in so much trouble with this little girl.

So much trouble.

CHAPTER 14

Paxton

Standing to the side of the giant sign, I watched as Chloe dug up her own worm and proceeded to fish with it. Steed stood there with a proud expression.

My heart ached as I watched them. The moment I saw him earlier I wanted to run up to him and tell him I made Joe leave immediately after he left. Well, after I told him there was no way he had a chance with me. Telling Joe I was still in love with Steed had visibly hurt him, but it was the truth. Besides, we had nothing in common and it was one of the reasons we had never worked out as a couple. That and I wouldn't give it up for him.

I hated I had asked Steed to leave and not Joe. When Steed hit him though, I was so angry. I hate violence, and Steed knows that. Plus, it was my way of avoiding what had happened between us in the kitchen. His admission to loving me still, my admission, and that kiss. So much more was said with that one kiss. I wasn't sure I was ready to deal with it all.

"Whatcha doing?"

I nearly jumped out of my skin as I spun around and clutched at my chest.

"Jesus, Amelia! Why would you sneak up on me like that?"

She tried to hide her smile and failed. Lifting her brows, she glanced past my shoulder. "Were you watching Steed and Chloe?"

My cheeks heated. "What? No! Are they here? I haven't seen them. Why would you say that?"

When her eyes moved back to mine, I knew she saw right through my blunder of lies. "Uh-huh. I know I was little when you and Steed dated, so we really don't know each other all that well." She smiled. "But I can already tell you're a terrible liar, Paxton."

I dropped my head then peeked up at her. "I wasn't spying."

Amelia held up her hands. "I didn't say you were."

Chewing on my lip, I sighed. "Okay. I was spying. I'm lost, Amelia."

With a soft sympathetic grin, she glanced at her brother. "So is he, Paxton. His eyes are so sad. Earlier this morning we all had breakfast together as a family and both Mom and I noticed it."

"The family was all together?" I asked.

She nodded with a grin. "The boys have been working the ranch the last two days so they're all staying at the house. It's been nice having Steed home again. Dad's thrilled he's back and digging deeper into the business side of the ranch. The idea of having another son run day-to-day operations has him all kinds of happy."

Guilt hit me square in the chest. It was my fault he left. I told him to leave.

He left his family and stayed away because of me.

"I'm so sorry he left town," I said.

"Paxton, you didn't keep him away all those years. That was his decision. A poor one, but his nonetheless."

I shrugged. Turning, I glanced back at Steed and Chloe. "He's such a good father."

The sadness in my voice caused Amelia to put her hand on my shoulder and gave it a squeeze. "Steed told Mom y'all talked last night."

Worrying my lip, I pulled in a breath. "Yeah. I think we understand a few things better, but the pain is still there and I don't know how to move past that."

"Do you want to move past it? I mean, do you still love him?"

My chin trembled and I opened my mouth, but nothing came out. I wanted more than anything to admit the truth. But admitting the truth opened me up to being hurt again. I didn't think I could live through another heartbreak at the hands of Steed Parker.

"Aunt Meli! I won! I won!"

My breath caught as Chloe came running up. Only because I knew her father wouldn't be far behind.

"That's amazing! You take after your granddaddy when it comes to fishing," Amelia said with a proud expression covering her face. She grinned when her brother walked up. "Look who I found. Paxton."

Chloe threw her arms around my legs. "Ms. Monroe! I won at fishing."

Squatting down, I pushed a piece of her blonde hair behind her ear. "That's wonderful, Chloe Cat. What did you win?" Her smile quickly dropped.

"Well, I can't really use the prize."

I frowned. "Why not?"

She shrugged. "It's a mommy daughter date package for a spa."

My eyes swung up to Steed. He wore a devastated expression on his face.

"Daddy said maybe Grammy can go."

Amelia shook her head. "Well, when is it? We can go together!"

Steed cleared his throat. "You'll be out of town. There's only a two-week window."

I wasn't sure where in the hell my head was when I opened my mouth. "I can go with you."

Amelia dropped down next to me. "That's a great idea!"

Chloe lit up like the Christmas tree they put up every year in the town square.

Shit. Shit. Shit. I should have asked Steed first. Standing, I studied him. "I mean, if you approve."

He showed no emotion whatsoever, but it almost seemed like there was a hint of appreciation. "You don't have to do that, I'm sure my mom—"

Chloe interjected. "Daddy! I want Ms. Monroe to go! Please? Oh, Daddy please. This would be the bestest day ever if my favorite teacher got to take me."

Her words wrapped around my heart like a warm blanket. Of course, I was her only teacher, but still. I was her favorite. I looked at Steed with an apologetic expression. "I'm sorry. I didn't mean to put you in such a position."

He shrugged. "Nah, it's fine. If Chloe wants to take her *teacher*, that's fine with me."

Amelia sucked in a breath. I tried to hide the fact that his words felt like a slap on the face. I swallowed hard then dropped back down to Chloe.

"I think Chloe Cat and I are more than teacher and student. We're friends. And when we're outside of the classroom, you can call me Paxton."

"Cause your Daddy's old girlfriend, but you're just friends now, right? Is that why I can call you Paxton?"

Oh dear. I think I've made this situation worse. "Um, yes."

Wait. What was I saying yes to?

Clearing his throat, Steed asked, "Amelia, would you mind taking Chloe over and getting her a drink?"

Steed's sister looked between the two of us. She took Chloe's hand. "Come on, pumpkin. Let's see what goodies we can find to eat."

As they walked off, she glanced over her shoulder. "Don't be a d.i.c.k. Steed."

He rolled his eyes.

"What's that spell, Aunt Meli?"

Steed watched them walk away. Once they were out of hearing range, he turned to me. "I don't need you feeling sorry for Chloe. I would have figured it out."

I was stunned and taken back by his tone. He'd never talked to me like that before.

"I'm sorry I didn't ask you first. It sort of slipped out."

"Well, if you didn't mean to say it I can explain to her you can't go after all. Mom can take her. It's some sort of spa day. Nails and toes and all that shit."

My hands began to sweat. "If you'll allow me, I'd really like to take her."

He narrowed his eyes at me. "Why?"

"Why not? She's an adorable little girl. *Your* little girl. I'd love to get to know her better."

"She's not a replacement."

The sharp intake of air from my mouth had Steed closing his eyes and cursing under his breath. "Shit. I didn't mean that, Paxton."

My entire body started to shake and bile moved to the base of my throat. "Is that what you think? You think I'm using your daughter as some sort of sick pretend game?"

He shook his head. "No. Of course not. I'm angry, and I shouldn't have said it."

"I'm sorry you left last night. I tried to get you to stop."

Steed laughed. "What? I asked you if you wanted me to stay, and you stood there on the goddamn porch staring at me. If you had wanted me to stay, I'd have been the one watching Joe drive away. Not the other way around."

"I was confused and emotional. Everything we talked about…and then that kiss. Joe showing up threw me, and then you had to go all caveman and hit him."

"He grabbed you, Paxton!"

I shook my head. "I needed to tell him there was no future with him, Steed. He was getting the wrong idea, and I needed to nip it in the bud and make it clear to him."

"I'll say the fuck he was. How often does he come over?"

With pleading eyes, I softly said, "Not here. Please don't do this here, Steed."

His shoulders dropped. "There never seems to be a good time or place, Paxton."

"Steed! There you are." Gina hooked her arm around Steed's, smiling. "Lilly has been searching all over for Chloe. Do you want to take the girls on the train together?"

Steed went stiff, and I was almost positive I was giving Gina the stink eye. I turned away, getting ready to excuse myself.

"Sorry, Gina. Paxton's already promised me and Chloe she'd ride the train with us."

My head snapped back to look at him. "Um, yes. Yes I did."

"Paxton! I got a pretzel!" Chloe cried out as she ran up to me. Gina's eyes about popped out of her head when Chloe called me by my first name.

"Lilly!" Chloe cried out as both girls hugged. "Guess what? Paxton is taking me on a mother daughter date, but she's not my mommy, but she *is* Daddy's old girlfriend and best friend now. But they like each other. *A lot*."

My mouth fell to the ground, and I was pretty damn sure so did everyone else's. Steed and I looked at each other, and I could feel Gina's glare.

Where in the hell did Chloe get all that from?

"Well, oh my, I hadn't realized you two were an item again," Gina said as Steed and I still stood there speechless.

Amelia laughed. "You know what they say about true love." She winked at me, and I opened my mouth to speak, but I had nothing.

Oh lord. Rumors were fixin' to fly.

CHAPTER 15

Paxton

After Gina walked off with her daughter, Steed pointed to Amelia. "What in the heck was that?" Then he looked down at Chloe. "And why did you say Paxton and I liked each other?"

With a huge grin, Chloe giggled. "Cause Aunt Meli said you two liked each other. A lot."

My cheeks heated as my gaze met Steed's. We both looked at Amelia.

"What? She asked me if y'all liked each other still. Do you deny it?"

Pushing his fingers through his hair, Steed groaned. "Amelia. You've got to learn to keep some things to yourself around Chloe."

"Really? Is that how things are going to be? How long are the two of you going to lie to each other. To yourselves?"

Chloe gasped. "Daddy! It's not nice to lie!"

Steed looked exasperated. "I didn't lie, pumpkin. I'm not lying."

Amelia's hands went to her hips as she flashed Steed a doubting smirk. My head was spinning. I wasn't ready to admit anything to anyone, let alone myself. We'd barely just scratched the surface last night. There were so many things we needed to work out.

"Paxton, do you like my daddy?"

The air caught in my throat and burned, unsure of what to say or do.

Steed gazed at me with pleading eyes, just like last night. "Um, excuse me. I really need to go check on a few things."

I spun on the heel of my cowboy boots and walked away. Covering my mouth with my hand, I attempted to keep myself in check. It appeared I was not only good at pushing people away, but I was great at running away as well.

"Do you know what we need?" Corina asked.

Looking up from my book, I asked, "What do we need, Corina?"

"A night out. Like a night out dancing and having fun. Let's go to Cord's Place."

I chewed my lip. I doubted Steed would be there.

"Come on, Paxton. I need to rub up against a dick or two."

My mouth dropped in shock. "Oh my gosh! Corina!"

She giggled. "I just want to do some silly flirting. Feel a guy's hands on me. Please. It's been forever."

Her puppy dog eyes made me laugh. "Fine. I could use going out."

We were soon ready. Our hair and make-up was done to perfection. I chose a mid-thigh, black, curve hugging dress, my favorite pair of black cowboy boots finishing out the look. Corina was wearing a light purple dress she had found in my closet. It was slightly low cut and showed the perfect amount of cleavage. Luckily, we wore the same size both in clothes and shoes. She rounded out the sexy look with a pair of teal cowboy boots. As we walked into Cord's Place I felt eyes on us. I scanned the room and couldn't believe how packed it was.

"Ohmygawd!" Corina said as she elbowed me ten times in excitement.

"What?" I asked.

"They're here. Well, a few of them are. The Parker brothers."

My breath stilled. "Who? Where?"

She laughed. "Don't worry. I don't see Steed. I only see Cord, Trevor, and Mitchell."

I panicked. "How do you know it's Mitchell and not Steed?"

She laughed. "Please. Yes they're twins, but they wear their hair different and Mitchell is hot as hell."

I huffed. "They're all hot as hell."

"Touché."

We walked over to the bar, and it didn't take long for the three of them to notice us. I got a polite smile from each, and Corina got heated stares. The kind that said they wanted to see her naked and bent over. Damn men.

"Hey, Paxton, Corina. How you ladies doing this evening?" Trevor asked while sliding two Bud Lights in front of us.

"Could be better," I stated as Corina grinned.

"We are doing great! Totally in the mood for dancing," she said as she drank her liquid courage.

Mitchell took that as his cue. "Then let's go cut a rug."

Corina's eyes narrowed in confusion. It was cute how she was thrown off by some of the things folks said and did down here. Being from Chicago she was used to a fast and crazy lifestyle. Here in small town Texas things moved slower.

"Cut a rug?" she asked, her nose crinkled up. I couldn't help but notice the way Mitchell smiled at her. *Dear lord, don't tell me he is attracted to her.* I may not have been around the family much the last ten years, but there was one thing I knew for a fact. Every Parker brother was a player. None of them were the least bit interested in settling down with one woman. I'd heard the rumors and even found myself listening to a few conversations in the coffee shop of some of the Parker men's one night stands. They usually hooked up with tourists, but a few of the local women had been the flavor of the week a time or two.

But the way Mitchell was laughing with Corina had me second-guessing that stereotype. Maybe Mitchell was ready to set down his wild ways.

Mitchell took Corina's hand. "It means let's go dance, Corina from Chicago."

Tipping my beer back, I watched them make their way to the dance floor, almost choking on my beer when I noticed how close Corina let Mitchell get. His knee was damn near in her vagina!

"Wow. Mitchell's not wasting any time is he?" I said with a chuckle.

Trevor laughed. "She's hot as hell, and I'm afraid she's got Mitchell's eye as well as Tripp's."

I glanced over to Cord. "Really?"

Trevor sighed. "Yeah, the two of them were arguing over her all the way back to the ranch. I was fucking sick of hearing about your friend by the time we got back."

Resting my chin on my hand, I asked, "What were they arguing about?"

"Who got to go after her."

"Seriously? Go after her? What does that even mean?"

"It means they both like her. So if they both like her, they have to figure out who is going to go after her and who isn't. Brother code and all."

I laughed. "Brother code? Seriously? Y'all have that?"

Trevor made a martini and gave me a serious face. "Fuck yes, we have that. Dicks before chicks, especially when the dicks are re-lated."

There was no way I could hide my smile even if I wanted to. "They do know I'll kill them if either one of them hurts her. Corina's not a stick and leave kind of girl. She doesn't do random hook ups."

Trevor smirked. "Yeah, I got that impression, and that's the reason I backed out right away. Not worth it for me."

"You're still young."

He winked. "Fuck yeah, I am and I like pussy way too much to settle with just one."

I should have winced, but this was Trevor Parker. All the Parker boys talked that way. Even Steed. The countless times he'd whispered dirty things into my ear nearly drove me over the edge. Yet, at the same time they treated woman like princesses. Whether it was a girlfriend or a random hookup. At least, that's what I had heard. They also spoiled their sisters and would die to protect them.

Oh yes, the Parker brothers were a rare breed. Smart, strong, sexy, and not afraid of anyone.

The guy next to me laughed, pulling me from my thoughts. Trevor set a drink in front of him and moved down the bar to help someone else.

The guy lifted his drink and drank it almost in one go. Narrowing my eyes, I tried to place him. I'd seen him before, but I couldn't think where. He must have felt my stare because he turned to me. My cheeks heated, and I gave him a polite grin.

When he smiled back, I couldn't help but notice how nice it was. Then his eyes roamed my body, and I focused back on watching Trevor behind the bar.

"You're not tired, Trev? I mean working on the ranch all day and then coming here?"

He laughed. "Nope. Cord does it too."

"Yeah, but you work on the ranch full-time right?"

Nodding, he replied, "Yep. It's been nice having Steed back. I can tell he's trying to get back into the swing of things, but the extra hands are nice."

Cue the guilt. Steed's plans were to go to college for business management and then come back and start learning the business end of the ranch. I wondered if that was still his plan.

"Does it bother your dad that not all the boys are involved with the ranch like you are?" I asked while taking another drink.

Trevor handed one of the waitresses a few drinks and looked at me. "I don't think so. I mean, they all still come and work. He gets that they all had their own dreams they wanted to follow. But for me, the ranch is what I breathe. Nothing will take me away from it."

"Why do you work here?"

Trevor stopped and studied me. "Seriously, Paxton?"

"Yeah."

He leaned against the counter and tossed a white rag over his shoulder. A cocky grin moving across his handsome face. "Free beer and endless pussy. Need I say more?"

Little Trevor who used to run around and chase the chickens was now all grown up and talking about pussy and beer.

I snarled. "No, you don't need to say anymore."

When I glanced over my shoulder, Corina and Mitchell were spinning around the dance floor, and she was laughing.

"At least one of us is having fun," I mumbled under my breath.

Finishing my beer, I held it up for Trevor to give me another. The guy who was sitting a few seats down stared so hard I shot him a look. He smiled, and I returned the gesture.

Corina's voice filled my thoughts. "Harmless flirting will do us good."

"You're not from here," I stated.

His eyes lit up. "No. Here on business."

Okay, he was cute. Really cute. Maybe some harmless flirting was what I needed to forget about Steed for a bit.

"You?" he asked.

I laughed. "Born, raised, and will most likely die here."

He got up and moved to the seat next to me. Sticking his hand out, he flashed me that nice smile of his, but this time it was wider and showed a dimple on his right cheek. "Mike Ryan."

Taking his hand, I replied, "Paxton Monroe. It's nice to meet you, Mike."

He kissed the back of my hand. "The pleasure is mine."

"What brings you to Oak Springs, Texas?" I asked, taking another drink.

"I work for an accounting firm in San Antonio. Hoping to pick up a rather big client."

Laughing, I asked, "Here?"

"Ranching. Makes for good money."

I grinned. "That it does if you know what you're doing."

"And this ranch knows what it's doing. The Parker ranch. Cord here was kind enough to show me this place after I spent the afternoon with the owner."

"John Parker," I said.

His eyes lit up. "Yes. Do you know him?"

Laughing, I replied, "Well everyone knows John. But yes, dated one of his sons a long time ago."

Mike pointed to Cord then Trevor with a questioning look. I chuckled. "No. His name is Steed."

His smile faded. Oh gesh. That must mean he had met Steed.

"Ah, yes, Steed. The prodigal son who has returned home," he said. I lifted my brow. "I met him this afternoon and introduced myself. I have to say, he's making things a bit difficult for me."

Rolling my eyes, I took a long drink of my beer. "Sounds like him."

Mike stood and held his hand out. "Dance with me, Paxton?"

A part of me needed to say no. But another part needed to have a bit of fun and that was exactly what I was going to do.

"I'd love to dance with you, Mike."

CHAPTER 16

Steed

I walked into the crowded bar and saw her. Paxton was dancing with that fucker Mike Ryan. The bad feeling I got about him earlier only intensified.

"Hey, Steed Parker! Are you fucking kidding me? Dude. When did you get back into town?"

I had to force myself to pull my eyes off Paxton and Mike. Todd Schneider stood in front of me wearing a huge grin. I shook his hand and returned his smile. "A month or so ago."

"Fucking hell, man. It's been a long time. I bet Paxton was happy to see you again."

My eyes lifted to the dance floor where she was getting a little too comfortable with Mike. Todd followed my gaze.

"Or maybe not. I figured y'all would hook right back up. Especially since Paxton hasn't dated anyone since you left."

I shot him a look. "What about Joe?"

He lost it, laughing. "Joe Miller? You're kidding, right? Shit, they dated off and on but even I could tell there was nothing there, much to Joe's disappointment. I'm sure he was happy as hell you took off. Remember how he liked Paxton in high school?"

"Yeah. I remember."

"Who's the guy she's dancing with?"

"Accountant from San Antonio."

"Oh fuck. That spells boring."

I laughed, and Todd hit me on the back. "Let me buy you a drink."

"Sure, why not." I followed Todd to the bar. Trevor glanced up and almost had a look of relief on his face. He'd called me almost an hour ago and said Mike had been feeding shots to Paxton, and she was willingly taking them. One quick call to mom to ask her to come sit at the house while I went out, and I was out the fucking door and speeding to get here. I'd imagined the different ways I was going to pound my fist into Mike's face. Then I remembered how things went with Joe, and I simmered my ass down.

I glanced over my shoulder and searched the dance floor until I saw them. The ache in my chest grew. Clearly Paxton was enjoying herself with Mike. Maybe she was over me. Maybe I read too much into that kiss and what she said in her kitchen. She said she never stopped loving me…but was she *in love* with me?

"Hey, Todd. What can I do ya?" Cord asked, pulling my attention back to the bar.

Todd reached his hand out for Cord's. "Sup, Cord. I'll take a Bud.

Trevor set a shot of whiskey in front of me as his eyes met mine. I reached for it, lifted it, and smiled. Damn, I'd missed my brothers. I didn't even have to say a word, and Trevor knew what I was thinking. He also knew I needed something to take the edge off.

It was good to be home.

"Thanks for calling," I said after the shot burned down my throat.

He nodded and went off to help someone else. Cord was talking to Todd, but he looked over and gave me a warning.

I grinned. I wasn't about to start any trouble in his bar. Yes, I was only here because Trevor told me some asshole was all up in what was mine, but I wasn't going to make a repeat of what I did the other night at Paxton's house.

Todd hit me on the side of the arm. "Hey, let's get together sometime. Catch up. I'd love for you to meet my wife. She's expecting our first baby in a few months."

I stood and shook Todd's hand. "I'd like that."

We exchanged numbers and Todd headed back over to the guys he was here with. I knew a few of them from high school, but we never hung out. Todd had worked during the summers at the ranch and that's how we had become friends.

"Don't start any shit, Steed."

Dragging my eyes back across the dance floor, I caught sight of Paxton and Mike before focusing in on Cord.

"I'm not here to make problems. Trevor was worried and gave me a call. I'm only here to keep my eye on her."

He lifted a brow. "And if he goes home with her?"

The thought made me sick to my stomach. I didn't answer. If Paxton did indeed leave with the fucker, I'd let it go. It would kill me, but I couldn't and wouldn't force myself on her.

"Then it will be her choice, right?"

Cord's eyes grew sad. "She might, Steed. They've been pretty flirty with each other. Her friend Corina's been dancing all night with Mitchell, pretty much."

I didn't want to look back out in the crowd. The last time I did, Mike had his hand on Paxton's ass.

Pointing to the shot glass, Cord smiled. "I'm not letting you get drunk."

Laughing, I replied, "I don't want to get drunk. Only want one more shot then I'm going to leave."

His eyes widened in surprise. "What?"

I shrugged. "She survived before I was here, right?"

A small line appeared between his eyes. "Yeah, well, she was never in here when you were gone. I've seen her in the bar more now that you're back than I have in the five years it's been open."

"I'm not her babysitter, Cord."

He pulled his head back and studied me. "So this is how you're going to handle it, huh?"

"What do you mean?"

"You're going to give up?"

Sliding my shot glass over to him, I said, "I'll take one more, then I'm leaving."

He lifted his hands in surrender. Everyone thought they had all the answers. Well, they fucking didn't. Paxton still hated me. She wanted nothing to do with me and that was pretty damn clear.

I glanced over my shoulder just in time to see her laughing as Mike spun her around. She didn't look too torn up to me. I was the one sitting at home reliving our entire conversation over and over. Seeing her cry about gutted me. Hearing the pain and hurt in her voice killed me. And where was she? Out fucking dancing with some douche motherfucker who probably didn't even know how to jack himself off let alone take care of her needs.

Cord put the shot in front of me. I downed it. He set one more in front of me, and as I picked it up, the hair on the back of my neck lifted.

"Steed?"

Her voice sounded like an angel's. Putting the shot glass to my lips, I tossed it back, set it on the bar and turned to face her.

Mike stood there with his hand on her back. Paxton took a few steps away from him, breaking the contact.

"Hey, how's it going?" I glanced over to Mike and gave him a head nod before turning back and facing Cord. I stood, pulled out my wallet and threw some money on the bar.

"I'll see y'all later!" I called out to a confused Trevor.

When I walked around the barstool, Paxton stepped in front of me, blocking my escape.

"Where…where are you going?"

"Home. Not really in the mood to be out."

She worried her bottom lip. "Did you just get here?" she asked.

My gaze swung over to Mike. *Fucking dick. What in the hell did she possibly see in this guy? City slicker asshole.*

"Yeah, enjoy your evening. Mike, good seeing you again."

Mike nodded, then gave me a fucking smirk that had me balling my fists. I had to take in a deep breath to calm myself down. I really wanted to punch the motherfucker.

Stepping around Paxton, I made my way to the door. Each breath I took felt as if it burned my lungs. My feet were heavy as I made my way out into the cool fall night. How stupid was I to think I could walk back into her life like nothing happened?

I was an idiot for leaving her in the first place.

The lights on my truck flashed off and on as I unlocked it.

"Steed! Wait!"

Turning, my eyes widened as Paxton make her way over to me. She stopped in front of me and flashed that smile I fell in love with so long ago.

"Would you be able to give me a ride home? Corina's, um, she's having fun with Mitchell and doesn't want to leave."

I glanced back over to the bar entrance and frowned before staring back into those beautiful blue eyes of hers. "You want me to give you a ride home?"

She chewed on the corner of her mouth. "If that's a problem I'm sure I can talk Corina into leaving."

Paxton wasn't leaving with Mike. A sense of relief washed over my entire body, and I let out the breath I was holding.

"No. No, I don't mind taking you home. Not at all."

There went that smile again. When she put her hand on my arm, my heart stopped. "Thank you."

Nodding, I placed my hand on her lower back and guided her to the passenger side of the truck. Opening her door, I waited for her to climb in, but she didn't. She stared into my eyes.

"I'm sorry about the other day with Chloe, if I stepped over the line."

I was lost in a swirl of blue. Even in the dark of night with just a few parking lights her eyes lit up.

"You didn't. She was so excited to win and then they told her what the prize was and her little face fell, it about killed me. She's been talking about going with you non-stop."

She beamed. "It'll be fun."

I nodded. The urge to reach out and touch her was overwhelming. "I'm sorry about Amelia. For what she told Chloe. And I'm sorry for what I said to you. It was heartless and I didn't mean it."

Her eyes searched my face. Bouncing from my lips back up to my eyes then back down again. It was like she was struggling with some deep eternal thought. Finally, she giggled then gave me a wink. "I do like you, so it's not a lie."

I laughed. "Well, that's better than you hating me."

Her smile faded while her gaze dropped to the ground.

"Let's get you home, pumpkin."

Slipping into the truck, she didn't say a word.

The drive back to her house was silent. It took less than ten minutes, but it felt like a fucking eternity.

My heart was pounding as I pulled up and put the truck in park. Paxton sat with her hands folded in her lap. The weight of whatever she wanted to say was heavy in the truck. The only thing I knew to do was be patient. When it was clear she wasn't about to, I opened my mouth to speak, but she beat me to it.

"Will you come in?"

Okay. That wasn't what I thought she was going to say.

"Um."

She closed her eyes and shook her head. "No. What I mean is, will you let me show you something."

I wiggled my brows. Paxton let out a soft chuckle before reaching over and hitting me on the leg.

"That's not what I meant."

"Sure, I'd love to come in."

I jumped out of the truck and jogged around to the passenger side where I reached my hand out and helped Paxton down. She smiled, and I led the way to her front door.

When we walked in, she tossed her keys into a small square bowl. My eyes about popped out of my head; it was the bowl I'd made her in eighth grade pottery class. I didn't say anything as I continued to follow her. When she made her way over to the steps, I paused.

Paxton glared. "I don't want to sleep with you, Steed. I only want to show you something."

My ego took a serious hit, and I couldn't help the look of disappointment on my face. Not because I realized I wasn't going to have sex with Paxton, because trust me, I was fucking disappointed in that. But because she didn't seem to want me. At all.

"Is it something naughty?" I teased while following her up the stairs.

"No," she replied with a lighthearted laugh. I could tell she was a little tipsy with the way she was walking. I had to admit it was nice to have a bit of lighter banter between us.

"You feel okay, pumpkin?" I asked, watching her ass as she climbed the stairs.

"Yeah. I think I drank more than I thought I did. I feel a bit lightheaded."

My breathing increased with the idea of being in Paxton's bedroom. My dick was already thinking of what it wanted to do, and I adjusted myself. But the moment we walked into her room and she turned on the lights, I knew it was going to be a battle keeping my hard on at bay.

I scanned the master bedroom. It was done in different shades of gray. The touches of blue in the room made me smile. It was almost exactly how we'd talked about all those years ago.

Paxton sat down on the bench at the end of her bed and pulled her boots off. I stood there with my hands in my pocket still looking around the room.

"Um, Pax, is there a reason you brought me up to your bedroom or are you trying to make me fucking crazy?"

Her brows lifted and a small grin tugged at the corner of her mouth. "You're going crazy being in here? Why?"

I stared at her like she was insane. "Do you want me to answer that honestly?"

She slowly nodded. "Always."

My tongue ran over my lips, and I was suddenly parched. I needed water. My head was spinning.

Did I tell her the truth? What I was really thinking? Hoping?

Fuck it. What could it hurt?

"I'm going crazy because all I want to do is bury my cock inside you and stay there all night."

CHAPTER 17

Paxton

My mouth dropped open, and I had to fight to hold back the moan slipping from my lips. My panties instantly dampened.

Steed shrugged. "You told me to be honest, Pax. I'm being honest."

I had to shake my head to get rid of the mental image of Steed making love to me. No. The image was of Steed fucking me. Hard and fast. I would be kidding myself if I said I didn't want that more than ever. *But could I open my heart up to him again?* Not until it was healed, and I needed to do one more thing for that to happen.

Swallowing hard, I ran my tongue along my lips. Steed's eyes turned dark with desire.

"I... I... Um, I need a moment I think."

He stepped closer, and the air crackled between us. Gently lifting his hand, he placed it on the side of my face. "I'm sorry, pumpkin. I didn't mean to make you uncomfortable."

I shook my head then placed my hand over his. With a soft smile, I pulled my lip between my teeth. Steed's eyes dropped and focused on my mouth. The need to have him kiss me was over-whelming. My stomach twisted and turned, my clit ached with want, and my heart was pounding.

Closing my eyes, I knew what I had to do. My gaze lifted up to meet his. "I need to show you something."

He nodded and dropped his hand.

Walking to the dresser, I opened the top drawer and searched for the velvet pouch. I picked it up and held it to my chest. Closing my eyes, I shut the drawer and held it out to Steed.

My heart was beating so loudly in my chest I was sure he could hear it. He glanced at the bag and smiled. "Is that the same bag I gave you the promise ring in?"

Tears pricked my eyes as the memory of Steed giving me the promise ring on my eighteenth birthday. He'd taken me to our favorite spot on the ranch where we had sat and watched countless sunsets. We'd talked about our dreams and our future. He had promised me no one would ever love me like he did. He had promised to love me forever.

"Y-yes."

The smile on his face faded. I could hardly breathe. He stared at the bag. "I promised to love you forever that night."

A tear slipped down my cheek.

When his eyes lifted and caught mine, he let out a pained sigh. His thumbs came up and wiped my tears away. "I've never stopped loving you, Paxton. I know that's hard to believe, but I never once stopped loving you."

A part of me knew it was true. He called his daughter the same pet name he called me. He sang her our song. I could see it in his eyes, the way he was looking at me this very moment.

My chin trembled as I dropped my gaze to the velvet bag. The ache I always felt when I looked at this bag hit me like a brick wall, but something about having Steed here made it hurt a little less.

"I…I need to show you this." Lifting my head, our eyes locked. "I've tried moving on. I mean, I have moved on, but a part of me remains held back. Still lost in that storm."

My words fell out between sobs. "I hated you for leaving me alone. I hated you for leaving me. You were my entire life, Steed, the reason I breathed, and you left me."

His eyes filled with tears as he waited for me to keep talking.

Swallowing hard, I opened the bag. It still held a beautiful card and the velvet blue ring box, but now there were two other items.

I pulled out the box and card. Steed never took his eyes off of them as I set them on the end table next to my bed. Facing him, I dragged in a shaky breath. His eyes searched mine, desperate to figure out what I was going to take out.

Reaching in, I took out a piece of paper along with the little plastic bag that held the pregnancy test I took the day I found out I was pregnant.

Steed sucked in a breath and took a step back.

"My therapist kept telling me I needed to find to way to say good-bye. But I couldn't say good-bye." Tears streamed down my face.

"I needed you to be here with me. I needed…you…to be h-here."

Steed's eyes bounced from mine to what I held in my hand. "Is that…?"

His voice shook and I watched a tear slip from his eye and trail down his face.

Lifting my hand, I handed him the sonogram picture of our child. "When I took the test and found out I was pregnant, I went to the doctor to confirm it."

Steed's shaking hand took the picture. "Our baby," he whispered while running his finger over the picture. My breath caught in my throat, and my heart slammed against my chest. There were countless times I wished I had showed him that picture when I told him that day. Maybe it would have changed things. But it didn't matter. I needed to let go of the what-ifs.

"Oh God, what did I do?" His eyes snapped to mine. "I'm so sorry."

I shook my head. "You didn't do anything. It wasn't…meant to be." The words were hard to get out of my mouth, yet at the same time, to hear myself say it was almost healing.

Closing his eyes, Steed broke down. He dropped to the floor. "Our baby. Paxton, our baby."

My hands came up to my mouth as I tried to keep my own sobs back. Steed was on his knees, leaning over with his head dropped down. Sobs rocking his body.

"Our baby. Paxton, our baby. I'm so sorry I wasn't there. I wasn't there."

My heart seized. Steed was mourning the loss of our child. My eyes locked on his trembling body. I wasn't sure how he would react when I showed him the picture. I simply wanted him to see our child. Feel that love like I had so many times. The only way I could move on was if I shared this with him. I never in my life imagined he would fall apart…exactly like I had done so many times. I dropped down in front of him. He lifted his head, and I gasped when I saw all the guilt, pain, and hurt in his eyes.

Shaking my head, I forced myself to speak. "I'm so sorry. I didn't mean to hurt you."

He pinched his eyes together. "You don't have anything to say sorry to. I left you. I left you alone, and I'll never forgive myself. Never."

We kneeled in front of each other, so vulnerable and open. Bleeding hearts exposed for each of us to see. He saw my pain; I saw his hurt. Guilt engulfed me. *Was it selfish of me to show him this? Was it wrong of me to want him to know the child we lost?*

"I'm not trying to hurt you. I wanted you to know."

He cupped my face in his hands. The fire from his touch shot through my veins like a bolt of lightning. Even in our darkest hour, his touch thrilled me.

"I'm sorry I wasn't there. I'm sorry you went through it all alone." He closed his eyes and took in a shaky breath before focusing back on me. "Please...please tell me you forgive me. Paxton, I'd rather die than know you won't forgive me."

His pleading words felt like they wrapped around my broken heart, healing the tear that his leaving had left. So many days I spent alone, crying like my entire world had ended because I had lost the baby. But now, staring into the eyes of the only man I'd ever loved, I realized I mourned the loss of Steed more, and I was just as much to blame as he was.

"When you left and didn't come back—" My voice shook and I needed a moment to steady myself before I continued. "I didn't see it then, but it was my fault. I pushed you away because I was devastated we lost the baby. But when I realized you weren't coming back, I died inside knowing I lost *you*."

His eyes widened in horror. Realizing that most of my pain was from losing him. "I swear to God I will never leave you again. Please tell me you forgive me and I will make it up to you for the rest of my life."

A lightness in my chest settled in. Something I hadn't felt in over ten years was taking root again.

Peace.

I knew I wanted Steed in my life. I also knew we had to take things slowly.

"I forgive you, but I'm scared, Steed. I don't think I could survive it if you broke my heart again."

The way his eyes searched mine, I could see his pain, but something else was in there. Something dark that was eating at his soul.

His hands were still holding my face. "I love you, Paxton. Tell me what to do to earn back your love."

My chest tightened. "Oh, Steed. You never lost my love. Never."

His expression brightened, and I couldn't help the small grin that moved across my face. With a slow nod, he leaned in closer. His lips inches from mine. "Then tell me how I win your trust back. I'll do anything."

I was aching for him to kiss me. Truth be told, I was aching to feel him inside me. But we needed to go slow. Sure, we could jump into my bed and fuck like rabbits all night, but would that really be the right thing to do? Besides, we had Chloe to think about. I couldn't just suddenly show up in her world.

My hands came up and grabbed onto his arms. "I know how you could start."

The hope in his eyes was hard to miss. I knew if I told him to make love to me, he would do it in a heartbeat.

He smiled. The tears had stopped flowing for both of us. My emotions felt like they were all over the place. I was happy, relived, horny, scared. *Gah!* I was all over the place. But I knew we *needed* to go slow.

I flashed him a flirty grin. "You could take me out on a date."

Steed stared at me like I was insane. "A date?"

Nodding, I replied, "Yeah. A date."

He pinched his brows together, and I almost wanted to laugh.

"Um, pumpkin, I was kind of thinking of something else."

I lifted my brow. "Such as?"

"Well, not to sound like a total dick, because honestly all of that was emotional as fuck, but when I said I wanted to sink my cock into you, I wasn't lying."

Lord. Help. Me.

"Um," I whispered as I chewed on my lip. "I just... I'm not... What if..."

He pulled me closer. The heat from our bodies made me dizzy. *We can't do this. It would be better to go slow.*

I inhaled deeply. His musky scent filled my senses and shot right between my legs. Who was I kidding? I wanted him too. More than anything. The way he was looking at me and the slight alcohol buzz I still had going on was starting to lean me towards his idea.

"Please let me hold you, Pax. I want to feel your body against mine. That's it, I swear."

That one sweet gesture was the only thing I needed to push me over the edge. I started to stand, and Steed followed my lead. With shaking hands, I reached for his shirt and slowly pulled it over his head. When I had a hard time getting it off, we both laughed. Steed reached for it and gave it a pull before tossing it to the ground.

My eyes lingered on his perfect body. His broad chest had gotten bigger. The boy I fell in love with was now a man. His six pack abs made my fingers itch to touch them…so I did.

When my fingers moved lazily over his skin, Steed drew in a sharp breath. Chewing on my lip, I couldn't help smiling knowing that I'd made him shudder like that. Lifting my eyes, I noticed his were shut. As if he was trying to take in this moment and remember it forever. His breathing had sped and a slight moan slipped from his soft plump lips.

When I'd had enough of abs and chest, I moved my hands to his pants. It felt like the first time all over again as I held my breath and unbuckled his belt, then his jeans. I smiled when I noticed he had no underwear. Peeking up, I found him watching me, his eyes full of lust and desire.

"No underwear, huh?" I asked with a giggle. He shook his head and kicked off his boots.

My nerves were starting to build as Steed reached behind my back and unzipped my dress. It fell to the floor into a puddle at my feet. His eyes roamed my body with greed. Licking his lips, a low growl came from the back of his throat.

"Fucking hell," he said. "You are perfection."

I stood before him in nothing but pale yellow lace boy shorts and a matching push up bra. I started to question if we should remove all of our clothes. Maybe we were moving too fast. Could we both resist the urge to be together?

Steed must have seen my internal struggle. He cupped my face and gently brushed his lips over mine. I longed for his kiss. More than I ever imagined.

"As much as I want you right now, we can wait, Paxton. We can take things slow."

My stomach twisted with a flurry of flutters. He had no idea how much it meant for him to say that to me. How much it showed he was putting my feelings above all.

"Will you stay the night with me? Hold me in your arms like you said?"

He smiled, and my knees grew weak. "Yes. Nothing would make me happier than to fall asleep in your arms. But, I want to feel you against me."

Reaching around, he unclasped my bra. I fought a momentary urge to keep myself covered before I let it fall away. Steed licked his lips, and I felt my already hard nipples grow harder. His hands touched my hips, and I jumped at the spark I felt against my skin. Slowly, he pulled my panties down. A soft groan came from his mouth that instantly had my lower stomach pooling with desire.

He kissed my belly button, and my head dropped back. I could probably come with only his lips touching my body. Not only had I not had sex in forever, I hadn't had a decent orgasm in months. Years!

Steed moved back up my body, placing soft kisses on my stomach, between my breasts, up my neck and right under my ear. His hand cupped one of my breasts, and I was instantly dizzy with lust.

"So fucking sexy," he whispered against my ear. "I can't wait to taste you again, Pax. To feel you come against my mouth. My name moaning off your lips."

Jesus.

I grabbed onto his arms, needing something to hold me up.

Opening my mouth, I panted a few breaths before finding my voice. "Maybe slow is overrated."

CHAPTER 18

Steed

Holy fucking shit. Paxton was standing before me naked. Beautifully naked. She was breathtaking. I could smell the desire coming from that sweet bare pussy that was begging me to bury my face into it. The urge to slip my fingers inside her was so fucking strong it made my body physically ache. I had no clue how I was holding it together. The last time I had sex was the night Chloe was conceived. I was about to fucking come in my own jeans, and I honestly wouldn't have cared if it meant I got to keep touching Paxton.

Her head dropped back when I cupped her breast. A soft hiss slipped from her lips.

Fuck.

"So fucking sexy," I said against the soft skin below her ear. She was driving me crazy. I wanted more. So much more. I decided I needed to tell her how much.

"I can't wait to taste you again, Pax. To feel you come against my mouth. My name moaning off your lips."

Her body shook with need. I loved what my touch was doing to her. Driving her so far over the goddamn ledge she had to grab onto me to stay up.

"Maybe slow is overrated."

I pressed my lips to hers. Our kiss started slow. Biting on her lower lip, she gave me access to that delicious mouth. The lingering taste of alcohol reminded me she'd had a lot to drink tonight. As much as I didn't want to stop, I would.

Soon.

For now, I want to taste her, touch her, feel her body against mine. Drawing back from her lips, she groaned in protest. I quickly pushed my pants down and kicked them off. Paxton's eyes widened as she looked at my rock-hard dick. Her tongue slowly moved over her lips, as if she was thinking about wrapping those plump pink lips around my cock.

Hell yes.

But not now.

My hand moved behind her neck, causing her to drag her beautiful baby blues back up to me. Pressing my lips to hers, our kiss deepened. I reached down and picked her up, carrying her over to her bed. Her warm soft body felt like fucking heaven against me.

"Steed," she softly spoke while I laid her down. Crawling on top of her, I nestled between her legs, my cock pressed against her warm pussy. I could probably come by simply rubbing against her like a damn dog in heat.

"Shhh," I whispered against her lips. "I only want to feel you."

Her eyes had a mixture of need and fear in them. As I pushed against her, Paxton arched her back.

"Oh God," she cried out.

My mouth was back onto hers and what started out as slow and sweet, now turned into fucking hot as hell passionate kissing. Our hands were all over one another. My hand cupped her perfect tits while I squeezed and pulled her nipple. Paxton's hand was on my ass as she pulled my hot hard length tighter against her. Her body rocked, and I knew she was close.

No. When she came for the first time, it would be by my mouth or my cock inside her. Not shit we did in high school.

I rolled off of her, and she grunted in protest.

"Steed, wait." Her chest rose and fell as she labored for each breath.

"Jesus Christ, Pax. It's killing me with my cock up against you. I only have so much strength, ya know."

Her cheeks had already flushed pink, now they were a beautiful red. "You're so crude, Steed Parker."

Pulling her to me, I adjusted her against my body. Her back to my front. "And you love it."

Paxton let out a contented sigh. "I do love it. And I love you."

Reaching for the covers, I pulled them over us. *Was I fucking dreaming? Or did I really have Paxton in my arms? Her naked body against mine?*

I placed a soft kiss on her back as she snuggled against me more. "I love you too, pumpkin. So much."

Cord and Trevor both stood there, their mouths dropped open with stunned looks on their faces.

Wrapping the wire around the post and fence, I asked, "What?"

"You can't just blurt out you stayed the night at Paxton's and then say nothing after that," Cord said.

"Did you fuck her?" Trevor asked with a wicked grin on his face.

"Don't talk about Paxton that way," I said, shooting him a dirty look. He laughed and picked up the fence pullers.

"Okay, let me reword it. Did you sleep with her? No, wait. Did you make love to her? Better?"

I frowned. "Yes, better. And no. She wants to take things slowly."

Trevor lost it laughing, and soon Cord was bent over laughing as well.

"Pricks," I mumbled as I went back to tying on the fence ties for the new fence.

Cord slapped me on the back. "Jesus, I bet that was the biggest case of blue balls if there ever was one."

I groaned. "You have no fucking idea. I had to wake up early to get back before Chloe got up. Talk about the walk of shame. Mom only smiled when I got home, but she knew I was with Paxton. I had texted to ask her if she wouldn't mind spending the night."

"Damn," Trevor said. "I don't know what's worse. Mom thinking you got laid, or the fact that you didn't get laid."

"Trust me, they're both bad," I said.

Cord lifted the roll of fencing and started to roll it out some. "How do you think Chloe is going to feel about you seeing someone?"

My chest squeezed a little. The memory of last night and seeing my first child's picture on the sonogram hit me again for about the tenth time. I had broken down big time in front of Paxton, but somehow I think my falling apart was a part of her healing.

"She already loves Paxton, and our noisy sister has already informed Chloe that Paxton and I like each other. I don't think it will be too hard on her. At least I hope it's not."

Trevor stopped working and wiped his brow. Even though it was October, it was still fucking hot as hell today. He sighed and walked over to the cooler. Lifting the lid, he grabbed three beers.

"This is why I will never settle down with one woman. Too much fucking drama to deal with."

I laughed. "Well, with Paxton and me, it's a little different. We have a history, and I have a daughter."

Trevor popped the tab on his beer. "Still. Women bring problems."

"A-fucking-men," Cord added.

I leaned against the tailgate of my truck and glanced between my two younger brothers. "Seriously, neither of you have ever met a woman who didn't make you want more than a hookup?"

They both shrugged, looked at each other, then focused back on me.

"Nope," they said together.

I actually felt sorry for my brothers. Damn. They were in for a ride when it did finally happen. And it would happen whether they liked it or not.

Trevor pointed to me, as if he could read my thoughts. "Trust me when I say there will *never* be a woman who will make me want to only settle down with one pussy. No, thank you."

"I've got to agree with Trevor," Cord added. "The thought of not being able to fuck someone any time I want or anywhere I want." He shuddered. "God, the thought alone hurts my dick."

Laughing, I finished off my beer and tossed the can into the back of ranch truck Trevor drove.

Walking up to each of them, I gave them each a hit on the arm. "I can't wait to see y'all eat crow."

CHAPTER 19

Paxton

Corina knocked on my classroom door Monday morning and strolled in whistling. Glancing up, I grinned.

"You're in a good mood for a Monday morning."

Her smile grew big. "I had sex this weekend."

Dropping back in my seat, I gasped. "What? With who?"

She covered her mouth like a schoolgirl about to tell the biggest secret ever. "Mitchell."

My pen dropped out of my hand while my eyes widened in surprise. "Mitchell Parker?"

She nodded then giggled. "Jesus, he was huge. I had to soak in a bath all day yesterday I was so sore."

I covered my mouth and gagged.

Corina lifted a brow. "Too much information?"

I leaned over my desk. "You slept with Mitchell? Like as in…" I glanced around as if someone was in the room. "As in sex? His junk in your…" I pointed.

She laughed. "Oh my gosh, I know! So unlike me to do something like that. But yes. I had sex with Mitchell. Actually, we fucked. Like rabbits. On my sofa, on the kitchen island, the kitchen floor, in the shower, in my bed." She lifted her eyes as if she was trying to remember if there were more spots she might have missed.

"Oh, and up against my front door when he was trying to leave, but something came over us again. He has a magical dick. I'm not kidding. His stamina. I've never had so many orgasms in my entire life. Six. I had S.I.X. orgasms, Paxton."

I sat there with my mouth open. Not only did my best friend just tell me she fucked a guy, but she proceeded to tell me all the places they did it and how many times she came. And it was with Steed's brother. His twin brother!

The silly dreamy look in her eyes should have caused me to freak out. After all, she'd slept with a Parker brother. Not exactly the type of guys who are rushing to get into relationships. And what about the brother code? I seemed to remember Tripp calling dibs on Corina.

Oh for Christ's sake. Listen to me!

"Okay, I need a moment, or a few days, to process this. Corina, you do know Mitchell probably assumed it was only a one-night stand kind of thing. Right?"

Her smile faded. "I didn't get that impression. Not with the sweet things he said. The way he made me feel. I've never had a guy worship me and love on me like Mitchell did. It was amazing."

"And how much had y'all had to drink?"

My question must have felt like a slap in the face. She turned away. What started out as excitement in her eyes now turned to shame.

I sighed. "Wait, let me try this again."

She stared back, her chin quivering. "Do you think it was a one-night stand? He was so sweet to me. The things he said…"

There was no way I was going to tell her how the Parker boys were known for being smooth talkers. They were romantics by nature, and if they wanted to show a girl a good time I had no doubt in my mind they couldn't swoon the pants off any woman they wanted to. But more than one night? No. I didn't think any of them had ever been in a serious relationship. Well, besides Steed and Tripp. His long-time girlfriend from high school, Harley, was the only woman he'd ever dated long term. Mitchell, he dated, but if I remembered right, as soon as things turned serious, he was gone.

Reaching for her hand, I smiled. "Don't listen to me. It really has been a long time since I've been around Mitchell. Maybe his player days are over."

Corina shrugged. "There was something there, Paxton. I felt it, and I've never felt that way about a guy. Our chemistry was crazy and it was like we couldn't get enough of each other." She frowned and focused on the floor. "Maybe I just thought all of that because I needed an excuse to justify sleeping with him."

I felt like an ass. Here she was so happy and I ruined it for her. "No! It sounds like y'all had an amazing night. Has he called you?"

By the look on her face, I knew I had asked the wrong thing.

Slowly, she shook her head then buried her face in her hands. "Oh God! What did I do? I slept with a guy who's a player! I'm so freaking stupid!"

I jumped up. "No! You don't know that! You had chemistry! You even said it."

I started to hear laughing and yelling down the hall. Students were starting to show up.

Corina stood. She straightened out her skirt, dabbed at the corner of her eyes, and stood taller. "No. You're right. I let myself think it was something more than what it was. He didn't even ask for my number and that should have been my first clue. I let my normal good sense down for a night and let my libido run the show. So I *fucked* a guy."

My eyes snapped over her shoulder to the door. Thank God there were no kids coming in. Corina rarely swore and the way she stressed the word fuck told me she was now feeling ashamed.

Shit. Shit. Shit.

"So what. I'm young and other women my age are out doing guys left and right. One hookup after another. I'm fine. It is what it is. It's all good." She forced a fake smile, but all I saw was humiliation and it was all my fault.

I didn't know what to say, and I hated that I had made her feel this way. But I knew that there was no way Mitchell Parker hadn't thought of last night as some random hook up. He wanted Corina and charmed her until he got what he wanted. Even after he had agreed to step aside for Tripp.

"Corina, I'm so sorry I even said anything. I feel like this is all my fault."

She shrugged. "You were being honest. Friends need to be honest with each other."

I reached for her hand as I walked around my desk. "Hey, maybe Mitchell will surprise me, and he'll call you for dinner or something."

Chewing on her lip, she forced a smile. "Well, considering he never asked me for my phone number, that might be hard to do right?" Corina turned on her heels and walked out of my classroom.

"Damn it!" I mumbled.

I made a mental note to talk to Steed about this. If anyone knew what would be going through his brother's mind it would be Steed.

With another quick glance in the mirror, I beamed. The black Capri jeans and light blue shirt should be casual enough for my date with Steed. My stomach fluttered as I thought back to Saturday night. I hadn't been that turned on since the last time Steed had touched me, over ten years ago. Sure, Joe used to turn me on, but it was never anything like what Steed could do. All Joe and I ever did was have make out sessions. He'd made me come a few times with his fingers, but nothing beyond that.

My fingers came up to my mouth as I let a soft chuckle slip from my lips. I swear they still tingled. I closed my eyes and let the memory of being wrapped up in Steed's strong arms engulf me. What a crazy night of emotions. I was so exhausted I immediately fell asleep. At one point he got up and told me he had to text his mother. All I could do was mumble under my breath before I was lulled right back to sleep when he climbed back into bed.

I jumped when my phone buzzed and vibrated on the end table next to my bed. Reaching for it, I smiled when I saw his name.

Steed: *Almost there. I hope you're in the mood for pizza. I let Chloe pick where to eat.*

Smiling, I typed back my reply.

Me: *Pizza sounds amazing!*

Small waves of nervousness rolled over my body.

Pushing down the nauseous feeling in my stomach, I headed downstairs. I opened a bottle of red wine and poured a small glass. The need to curb these nerves was real.

"What is the matter with me? It's Steed. Why am I so nervous?"

Then it hit me. I wasn't nervous about Steed, I was terrified about Chloe. It was my idea to invite Chloe along for our first official date, and I had to admit, I was scared to death of what she was going to think about us dating. Oh sure, she adored me as her kindergarten teacher and she knew we liked each other, but I was bid-

ding for a place in their world. Would she be willing to share her
Daddy with me?

My finger and thumb pinched the bridge of my nose while I
took in a few deep breaths. Not being able to take it anymore, I
texted the only person I thought would be able to help: Amelia.

Me: *Did Steed tell you what was going on?*

She responded almost instantly.

Amelia: *OMG Yes! I'm totally writing a book about y'alls
story.*

I rolled my eyes.

Me: *What if she hates me?*
Amelia: *Who?*
Me: *Chloe!*

Seconds ticked off while I waited for her reply. When my phone
rang in my hand I nearly threw it across the room it scared me so
bad.

"Hello?"

"Why would Chloe hate you, Paxton? She already adores you.
When Steed told her the three of you were going on a date, you
should have seen the way her eyes lit up. Mom of course started crying, which made Chloe ask why she was sad. She had to explain to
her that they were happy tears!"

Smiling, I inhaled a deep breath to shake away the jitters. My mother had almost the same reaction when I told her earlier the three of us were heading out for a date.

"I would never want her to think I was trying to take her father away from her."

Amelia sighed on the other end of the line. "Oh, Paxton. She won't feel that way. I think you inviting her on the first date was the absolute right thing to do. It's making her feel like she is a part of this. It's going to be a change, but if I know one thing for sure, it's Chloe is desperate for a mommy and you are all she talks about. Stop worrying."

I nodded, even though I knew she couldn't see me. "You're right. I'm just nervous."

"Don't be. Y'all will have fun."

A strange sense of confidence came rushing over me. "You're right! We will have fun! Thanks, Amelia!"

She chuckled. "Sure. Anytime!"

The doorbell rang.

"They're here!"

"Bye! Kiss my brother and niece for me!"

"I will. Bye!"

Hitting End, I rushed to the front door. After taking a few deep breaths, I opened it to find the most beautiful sight I'd ever seen.

I gasped and then smiled. Tears pricked the back of my eyes as I looked at Steed standing there, holding Chloe in his arm, while they both held bouquets of my favorite flower. Pink Peonies.

"Paxton! Daddy and I got you flowers. They're your favorites."

Reaching for both bouquets, I kissed Steed on the cheek and then Chloe. "They are beautiful! I love peonies!"

"See, Daddy? I told you the flowers were a good plan."

Steed laughed. "You sure did, pumpkin."

Chloe was for sure her father's daughter. Gesturing for them to come in, Steed put Chloe down, and she bounced into the house.

When he walked in, he stopped and pulled me in for a kiss on the lips. It was quick, but it left me dizzy all the same.

"Paxton, do you have any animals?" Chloe asked.

I laughed. "No. I've been thinking about getting a cat, though."

Chloe shrieked in excitement as Steed groaned. I reached for a vase and looked at him. "I take it Chloe wants a cat, and you don't."

"No cats."

"Aw, but Daddy!" Chloe said, a small pout forming on her face.

"Pout all you want, Chloe. No cat. Granddaddy and Grammy have five cats."

"But they all live outside. I want one to snuggle with."

"My mommy and daddy have a cat. I'll take you over there some time to meet him. His name is Milo."

Chloe's eyes lit up. "Milo! I love that name!"

After filling up the vase with water, I put the flowers in and set it in the middle of my kitchen island. "There. They look beautiful."

Chloe climbed up onto one of the stools and admired the flowers. Her dark blonde hair was pulled up into pigtails with a small yellow bow on each side. I couldn't help but wonder if Steed had done her hair or if Amelia or Melanie had.

"I like these flowers," Chloe stated.

My eyes met Steed's and I could feel the crackle of desire in the air. "I do too," I softly replied.

I was positive if we were to have a repeat of the other night, I would not be telling Steed to go slow. The ache in my lower stomach grew more and more, and my own hand wasn't going to make it stop.

It was like Steed knew where my thoughts were taking me. He walked around the island and stopped in front of me, his hand lacing into my hair. "You're so beautiful, Paxton."

The heat on my cheeks told me I was blushing. He didn't seem to mind saying that in front of Chloe so I didn't mind hearing it.

"May I kiss you?"

My eyes darted over to Chloe who was watching our every move, her smile wide. She nodded as if giving me permission, or at the very least, urging me to let her father kiss me.

Focusing my attention back on Steed, I replied, "Yes."

He leaned in and gently pressed his lips to mine. Then he pulled my body up against his. My hands landed on his chest, making sure we kept a safe distance from each other for the sake of Chloe.

Leaning his forehead against mine, he let out a contented breath. As if that simple kiss and me in his arms had just solved all his worries.

"I love you, Paxton," he whispered. I was stunned he would say that in front of his daughter. She was going to get confused.

Drawing back, he saw my confusion. With a wink and a crooked grin that nearly had my legs going out from under me, he said, "I talked to Chloe this afternoon. I told her how you and I used to date and how we both still love each other, but that something bad happened, and we were separated from each other."

My heart ached. I peeked back at Chloe, who was sitting with her chin resting on her hands, almost like it was story time, totally entranced by the prince and princess who found love again.

"I told her we were going to start dating again."

I nodded and looked at Chloe. "Chloe, are you okay with your Daddy and I dating each other?"

She grinned. "Oh yes! Daddy's been so sad and lonely. But he said he isn't sad anymore and his eyes aren't sad either. Your kisses make him happy. So kiss him again, Paxton!"

Steed and I both laughed. When we caught each other's gaze, Steed leaned in and pressed his lips against my ear and spoke so only I could hear him. "And me buried inside of you will make me even happier. So let's plan that…soon."

My stomach dropped at the delicious thought. All I could do was whisper back a needy, "Yes."

CHAPTER 20

Steed

I was going fucking insane. Sighing, I shut the books I was looking through and leaned back in my chair.

Fuck. I couldn't get her out of my mind. Last night I thought for sure I was going to rip her goddamn panties off and fuck her in my truck. The need to be inside her was growing by the minute. I wanted to respect her wish to take things slow. To date her, slowly bringing her into Chloe's and my world, but this was insane.

The last few weeks had been amazing though, if you didn't take into account my constantly hard dick and the never-ending times I had to jack off in the shower. Paxton and I spent an equal amount of time with each other as we did with Chloe. Paxton's fear was that Chloe would grow to resent her for taking my time away, but the opposite had happened. Grinning, I thought back to this morning with Chloe.

"Good morning, pumpkin," I whispered as I kissed her cheek.

Chloe opened her eyes and grinned. "Is today the day you're going to marry Paxton?"

Laughing, I gazed into her beautiful blue eyes. "Not today."

She frowned. "Well, will you make me pancakes then?"

"Yes! That I can do."

Jumping up, Chloe raced down the stairs and into the kitchen. Pulling the chair at the island out, she climbed up while I gathered everything needed for pancakes.

"Daddy, why is Paxton so different from my old mommy?"

My heart seized up. "Well, your mother doesn't have love in her heart. Paxton does."

"Why doesn't she have love in her heart?"

"I don't know, pumpkin. Some people only think of themselves and not others."

She stared out the window as I poured the batter onto the pan.

"Daddy, do I have to call her my mommy anymore?"

Lifting my hand to the side of her face, I tried not to let her see how I was dying inside. I hated that Kim was Chloe's mother. "No, Chloe. You don't have to call her mommy if you don't want to. She's never going to be in our lives again."

"She doesn't want to be my mommy, does she?"

Fuck. Did I tell her the truth? What would that do to her emotionally?

"Pumpkin, she doesn't deserve to be your mommy."

Her little eyes seemed lost in thought, before a huge smile covered her face. "Paxton's going to be my new mommy soon. You really need to hurry, Daddy."

Laughing, I kissed her on the tip of her nose. "You're bossy. Just like Paxton."

Her eyes lit up, and I didn't think I'd ever seen my daughter look so happy.

"I want to be like her! Just like her! I wonder if Paxton wants a pet goat too. Patches needs a friend."

Stopping what I was doing, I shook my head and winked. "You little stinker. Are you trying to figure out how to get yourself another goat?"

Her little hands covered her mouth as she giggled and nodded.

"Chloe Lynn Parker. You're a sneaky one."

My eyes drifted back to the ranch's financial books, and I felt my cheeks straining from the happiness of the memory. I shook my head and got back to work.

Something was off. Numbers weren't making sense, and I had a feeling the old CPA who took care of my father's books was up to no good. Dad wanted to hire that fucker Mike, but I put the halt on that when the asshole tried to hook up with Paxton. I sent his ass back to San Antonio almost two weeks ago. I didn't have a good feeling about him from the moment he set foot in my office and Dad introduced us.

Asshole. Of course if it hadn't been for him, I'd have never have gone to the bar that night, and Paxton wouldn't have asked me to take her home. When she started for her bedroom I couldn't help the dirty thoughts that flashed through my mind. My dick was growing hard remembering her in my arms. Naked. Her soft skin against mine.

Fuck. I wanted her.

I pushed all thoughts of my cock inside Paxton's pussy out of my mind and got back to reviewing last months' figures.

The knock on the door had me lifting my gaze.

"Steed?"

"Dad." I motioned for my father to sit down.

He walked into the room with all the confidence in the world. I remember being little and thinking I wanted to walk into a room like my father did. I constantly heard people say the most amazing things about my father, and as a little boy looking up to him, I knew I wanted to be just like him someday. The guilt of staying away from the family ranch business still weighed heavy on my heart.

"How's it going, son? Find what you were looking for?"

He leaned back in the large leather chair opposite my desk. Dad had insisted that I have an office in the main house. Right next door to his. Within a day of telling my father I was coming back home, he had the office ready. A large mahogany desk sat near the large floor-to-ceiling windows that overlooked the Texas Hill Country. In front of the desk were two large, oversized leather chairs that Mom had picked out. To the left was a sitting area with a sofa and table. The other side held a large table. Dad had used this space as a conference room before I moved back, and I had talked him into keeping it one as well.

Shit. How in the hell do I tell my father I suspected his former CPA was stealing from him?

"I think so."

"Trevor need to be here? I can give him a call."

My brother Trevor had an office as well, but it was down in the main barn, along with the two-bedroom studio where Trevor lived. Since he was the foreman, he wanted to be closer to the barn so Dad had the studio built onto the barn.

The barn. If you could call it that. Dad's prized horses were housed in the main barn. The damn thing had heat and air conditioning and I swore the stalls were nicer than my first loft apartment in Oregon.

"Nah, I don't think he cares too much about the logistics of numbers."

My father chuckled. "Then give it to me."

"I don't know how to tell you this, Dad, so I'm just going to say it. I think Fred was stealing from you."

I figured he'd laugh. Tell me I was insane and that I needed to look through the books again. Instead, he leaned forward, put his arms on his legs and cursed.

"Motherfucker. I knew it."

My eyes widened. "What? You *knew* Fred was stealing, and you didn't do anything?"

When his head dropped, I had to fight the urge to comfort him. If there was one thing I knew about my father, it was that he didn't show emotion. Weakness. Anything, when it came to his business.

His head was still down. Fuck. Was he upset? Or was he just that mad?

Finally, he looked up and I had my answer.

He was mad.

Hell, he was pissed.

"That pencil whipping, son-of-a-bitch, asshole, money hungry, dirt bag, asshole, fucker!"

Oh yeah, real pissed.

I chuckled. "You said asshole twice."

He glared at me. Apparently now was not the time for joking. "I want him dead."

"Well, I'm sure Cord knows a guy who knows a guy."

His eyes met mine, and I was almost sure he was trying to shoot daggers at me. "Okay, we're still not in the joking phase yet?" I asked.

"Find out how much the fucker took. I've been waiting for an excuse to beat his ass ever since he hit on your mother."

He stood and started for the door. I jumped up. "Wait, Fred hit on Mom? When?"

Dad glanced over his shoulder. "At our wedding reception."

My brows furrowed. "But y'all have been good friends. Why have you never done anything?"

"Because I'm a Parker, and we don't have to worry about our women looking elsewhere when they've got it all with us."

I snarled at the thought of my father and mother that way. My body shuddered.

"And I knew I didn't have to worry about your mother, I trust her. But Fred was another thing. Why do you think I kept the fucker so close to me all those years? I figured he'd have tried to go after your mother again, but steal from me? Oh, hell no. I've been waiting for another reason to kick his ass and now, thanks to my son getting off his stupid ass and coming home, I've finally got him."

He opened the door and closed it behind him. I smiled…until I realized my father hadn't just given me a compliment. He'd insulted me.

Another light knock on the door, and Amelia walked in. "Hey, I thought you were out of town."

She frowned. "The book event got cancelled. What's going on with Dad? He looked pissed."

I waved it off. "Apparently he's been in a pissing contest with Fred for forty years."

"Huh?" Amelia asked with a confused expression.

Laughing, I replied, "It's nothing." No need for me to tell Amelia about Fred's stealing. If Dad wanted the rest of the family to know, he would tell them.

She curled up in the leather chair and smiled at me.

"What?" I asked.

"Oh nothing. Just wondering how things are going with you and Paxton."

The simple mention of her name made my heart skip a beat. "They're going good. Slow, but good."

She lifted her brow. "Slow? How so? Y'all are with each other all the time."

I dropped my head and gave her a taste of her own medicine. I shot a *really* pained look.

Her mouth opened as her head kicked back. "Oh! Slow as in the sex area."

"Yes, and please don't say anything else to Chloe. I know it's you filling her head about marriage."

She appeared to be offended. "Excuse me, but I haven't mentioned anything about y'all getting married. Not one word."

"You haven't?" I asked.

"Nope. I'd take that shit up with our mother."

Damn. Mom. I hadn't even thought about it coming from her.

"Anyway, back to the sex. What's going on?"

I shrugged. "Paxton wants to go slow. So I'm going slow. Painfully fucking slow."

Amelia covered her mouth and giggled.

I sighed. "It's not funny. I go to sleep with blue balls and wake up with them."

"*Ew.* Seriously, I could have done without that bit of information, Steed." She made a gagging noise.

I laughed and pushed my hand through my hair. "Anyway, I don't know if I push a little harder or let her pick the pace."

"Want my advice?"

"No offense, squirt, but you're only twenty-two."

She gave me a dirty look. "Well, I'm a woman. I've dated. I've had sex. I think I can add my two cents."

Anger rushed through my body. "Who the fuck have you had sex with? I'll kick the asshole's ass."

"You didn't honestly think I was still a virgin, did you?"

I threw the pen out of my hand like it had burnt me. My hands covered my ears. "What the hell, Meli! Oh God." My hands dropped. "Do the rest of your brothers know this bit of information?"

An evil smile moved over her face. "My first was Bobby Bishop."

My eyes widened in shock. "Does Trevor know his best friend took your flower?"

Amelia lost it laughing. "My flower? What in the hell? Are you fucking kidding me right now, Steed?" She bent over laughing hysterically. "Oh. My. God. My flower! I'm dying! I can't wait to tell Waylynn! You know she's lost her flower too, right?"

I rolled my eyes and leaned back in the chair, waiting for her to get it out of her system. The thought of a guy touching either of my sisters pissed me off. Even with Waylynn being married, I still wanted to punch her husband every time I thought about it. "You done?" I asked.

She wiped her tears away. "Oh, man. Hells bells. I needed that laugh. And no, I certainly didn't tell Trevor."

"I take it my ideas of you being a sweet and innocent girl are shot out the door."

Standing, Amelia placed her hands on my desk. "I grew up with five brothers. Five brothers who I might add have made their own reputations. I learned from the best." She winked.

"Oh, shit. If Dad ever knew…"

The smirk that spread over my sister's face had me smiling too.

"What Dad doesn't know, doesn't hurt him."

"Daddy's little angel." I *tsked*.

She let out a curt laugh and spun on her heels. Before she made it to the door, she stopped, put her hands on her hips, and let a wicked smile spread over her face.

"And by the way. I'm giving you my two cents on Paxton. You need to spend the night with her tonight, seduce her, and make love to her, and then spend the rest of the night fucking her to make up for lost time. Trust me. It's what she *really* wants deep down. This going slow shit is a safety net she's using because she's scared."

I pulled my head back. "Scared of what?"

She winked. "I can't tell you all the secrets now, can I?"

And like that, she was out the door.

CHAPTER 21

Steed

"What crawled up your ass, dude?"

I rode next to Trevor on the horse my parents had bought me for graduation. I had never even ridden her before I left town. Now, I tried to ride her every day. She was a beautiful red and white paint that would do anything I asked her to do. Trevor broke her and trained her. I swear the boy missed his calling.

"Nothing's crawled up my ass. What's crawled up your ass, asshole?"

He laughed. "I ask a question, and you're either so deep in thought you don't hear me or you snap at me. Dude, if you don't get laid soon I swear you're gonna burst."

"Fuck off, Trevor."

"See!"

I groaned. "Shit. I don't know what to do. Amelia gave me her thoughts, but I'm not sure."

"Well, she's a woman, so she would probably know better than us."

We walked our horses side by side through the pasture. "Damn, I missed this place. Missed riding next to you, Mitchell, Tripp, and Cord."

"This place missed you."

I smiled. That was Trevor's way of saying he missed me. "You still friends with Bobby Bishop?"

Trevor brought his horse to a stop. "Why?"

Shrugging, I replied, "Just wondering."

"I haven't talked to him since I beat his ass one night. I caught him feeling Amelia up behind his truck at a party."

Laughing, I shook my head.

"I was positive Mitchell would find some reason to arrest him, and Cord probably threatened him with how he knew someone who knew someone who would break his leg and arm."

Damn, we all think the same.

I chuckled, and we rode the next few minutes in silence. "So listen, I went over the books. Fred's been stealing from Dad."

"No shit," Trevor said, kicking his horse, picking up her pace to keep up with mine.

"Yeah. Dad didn't seem surprised. In fact, I think he knew. He just didn't want to admit it."

"That's why he's been pushing you to look at the books since you scared Mike away."

"I didn't scare him away."

"Keep telling yourself that."

I didn't want to let Trevor know how much Fred had taken. It wasn't small change. It was thousands of dollars. When I told my father Fred had taken close to three hundred thousand, I thought he was going to have a heart attack. After he let out a string of curses, some I'd never heard of before, he got up, went to his gun safe and said he would be back later. I didn't even bother trying to stop him. I knew he wouldn't do something stupid, but he sure as shit would scare the piss out of good ole Fred.

"Was it a lot of money?"

Glancing over to him, I nodded. "Yeah. It was a lot of money."

"Fucker. I hope Dad puts his ass in jail."

"Let's hope."

We checked one of the fence lines and started back for the main barn when we found it still in good shape.

"You still roping?" I asked.

He looked at me like I was crazy. "I'm a rancher, asshat. I rope shit all the time."

My brow lifted. "So, what? You just ride around roping calves or something?"

"Why? You afraid you've lost your touch living as a city boy all those years?"

"Don't you wish. I can probably still rope circles around you."

"Prove it then."

I was the one who taught this little shit how to rope in the first place. If he thought he was better than me I was going to have to show his ass up.

"First one back to the barn," I said as I kicked my horse. She took off like a bolt of damn lightening.

Holy shit. This horse is fast.

There was no way I could help the smile on my face. Running through an open field on horseback was the best feeling in the world. Nothing was more beautiful. More calming.

As we approached the barn, I saw her. Sitting on top of the fence while Cord worked a horse in the corral. My heart stopped, and I brought Lady to a stop. Trevor raced by and headed to the barn, winning our bet. I didn't care, though. The only thing I cared about was the beautiful sight before me. I was wrong earlier; there was something more beautiful than running through a field on horseback.

Paxton Monroe.

Her hair was pulled up in a sloppy bun with half of it sticking out wild and untamed. She had on jeans, a T-shirt, and boots. A far cry from the sweet, innocent look she had on earlier today when she picked up Chloe for the mommy daughter spa day.

Slipping off Lady, I walked us over to the pen. Paxton looked at me over her shoulder. Her smile about knocked me off my feet.

"Hey," she said with a low sexy voice. "Cord said you and Trevor were out checking the fence lines."

"We finished up. I was about to show Trevor how one ropes."

She shot me a confused expression. "Doesn't he already know how to?"

"Fuck yes, he does," Trevor said from behind me. I grinned as he walked by, stopping long enough to hit me in the stomach with rope. "Let's do this shit. Paxton get in the middle of the pen. We're roping you."

Paxton looked frantically between Trevor and me. "Huh? You're not treating me like a damn animal!"

"I'm kidding, Paxton. Jesus, take it easy," Trevor said with a crooked grin on his face.

Cord laughed. "Let me get out of here before the two of you end up rolling around kicking each other's asses."

"Wait, what's going on?" Paxton asked worriedly. I walked to her and dropped the rope at my feet. Placing my hands on her hips, I pulled her body to mine and kissed her.

It didn't take her long to wrap her arms around my neck. A small moan slipped from her lips. It traveled straight to my dick.

Paxton broke our kiss, and I instantly missed her sweet honey taste. "What's going on?"

"Nothing. I need to prove Trevor wrong on something."

She shook her head. "Some things never change no matter how old you are."

I winked and slapped her ass. "Hey, when did you change your clothes from spa day?"

Trevor yelled, "Let's get this show on the road! I need to ride to the south pasture to check on a few pregnant mares."

We both ignored Trevor as Paxton answered me. "Figured maybe we could go for a ride later, so I brought a change of clothes."

My brow lifted. "You and me? Or *we* as in Chloe as well?"

She dug her teeth into her lip. "You and me. Your mom wanted to spend some time with Chloe."

Those words went straight to my dick as well. "One second, baby. Let me set Trevor straight."

I walked to the dummy calf. Trevor smirked and stood back. He started to spin the rope over his head and tossed it, ringing the dummy bull with ease.

Stepping up, I followed his lead and roped it just as easily.

"Beginner's luck," Trevor spit out.

"Beginner? I taught you how to do this!"

We stepped farther and farther away. Each time we both ringed it.

Before I knew it, we were roping real calves, and Cord was timing us. Of course it helped I had my own personal cheering team with Paxton, and then Chloe. Mom brought her down in the Mule after Paxton texted her about the contest.

"Go, Daddy! But don't hurt the baby cow!"

Smiling at my daughter, I winked and shouted, "I won't, pumpkin."

Trevor went next and had a small problem getting the calf turned over and on the ground. I knew I had it in the bag.

"If Steed beats your time that's five in a row!"

"Damn!" Trevor shouted as I nodded for Paxton to let the calf out. I took off, roped it, jumped off Lady and had the calf over and on the ground in the fastest time I'd ever run.

"Dude, that was six seconds!" Cord shouted. "You could be making millions!"

Paxton and Chloe jumped up and down, calling my name.

Mom walked over to Trevor. "Oh, honey. Remember he's been doing it longer."

"Mom! He was gone for ten years!"

Walking up to Trevor, I hit him on the back. "Dude, did you really think I wouldn't find a place up in Oregon to ride? How in the hell did you think my daughter learned how to ride?"

Trevor stared at me with a blank expression. "I hate you, Steed. You suck!"

Cord and I both started laughing as Mom tried to play peacekeeper. "Now, Trevor. I didn't raise you boys to be sore losers."

Chloe pointed to Trevor. "Oh, Uncle Trevor said hate!"

"Sorry, Chloe," Trevor said as he kissed her on the top of her head.

Turning to Cord, I said, "You should put a mechanical bull in the bar."

His eyes lit up. "You know, that's a damn good idea. Can you image the woman who would get on it drunk and—"

"Small ears, boys! We have small ears!" my mother called out as she pointed down to Chloe.

Cord winced. "Dang it. I forget sometimes."

Paxton sighed. "I swear, you boys will never grow up. You ready for our ride?"

There was something in her eyes that told me she had something other than riding on her mind.

I nodded and walked over to Chloe. "Hey, pumpkin. Daddy and Paxton are going to go for a ride. You going to be a good girl for Grammy?"

Chloe grinned. "Yes. We're going to make pumpkin bread! Your favorite, Daddy!" Her little arms wrapped around my neck, and she squeezed as hard as she could. When she leaned back, she did her best to whisper, "Are you going to ask Paxton to marry you?"

The sharp intake of air from Paxton had me cringing. I placed my hand on the side of Chloe's cheek. "No, baby. We're only dating. Remember? We talked about it."

Her little eyes turned sad. Mom and I had talked about how attached Chloe was becoming to Paxton, and she was concerned how it would affect her in school with Paxton being her kindergarten teacher. Chloe, however, didn't act any different at school according to Paxton, which was a relief...but she was becoming more and more obsessed with me asking Paxton to marry me. I knew Chloe longed for a mother. A real mother who showed her affection, and Paxton was stepping into that role nicely. Hell, I'd marry her tomorrow if I thought she would say yes, but I knew she was still dealing with her own issues, and I wasn't about to push her into anything.

Paxton leaned down so she was eye to eye with Chloe.

"Chloe Cat, I love your Daddy so very much."

Chloe smiled big and bright. My eyes lifted to see Mom staring at us. Her eyes threatening to spill over with tears.

"But, it's been a long time since we've been boyfriend and girlfriend. We have to...get to know each other again."

With her brows furrowed, Chloe asked, "But don't you already know each other?"

Paxton and I chuckled. "We do, sweetheart, but Daddy did something that hurt Paxton's feelings. I didn't do it on purpose, but I made her really sad."

Chloe's eyes filled with tears. "Would you ever do that to me, Daddy?"

My heart ached in my chest. "God no, Chloe. I didn't mean to do it to Paxton, but Daddy was not in a good place a long time ago. I promise you I'll never hurt you or Paxton. Ever."

Chloe leaned and asked, "Did you say you were sorry?"

I kissed the tip of her nose. "I did, pumpkin. And Paxton has accepted my apology. But we need to get back to how things were before I left. I know it's hard for you to understand."

Her next words nearly were nearly my undoing. My daughter would forever own my heart.

She nodded. "I trust you, Daddy."

CHAPTER 22

Paxton

I panicked the moment Chloe asked if Steed was going to ask me to marry him. It took me a few seconds to find my breath. She'd asked me to pretend I was her mommy during the mother daughter spa retreat we went to that morning, and my heart broke when I had to explain to her that would be lying.

Steed was talking to Chloe in that oh-so-sweet voice he used with her. My mind swirled as I tried to process what he said and the sad look on her face.

When he admitted that he'd hurt me, I had to reach out and hold onto the fence. He was so honest with her and with me. I knew it had been hard for him to take it slow. The kissing led to touching, which led to him waiting for me to give him permission to take things further. For some reason, I was hesitant. Oh, believe me I wanted to have Steed do all the dirty things he had been whispering in my ear over the last few weeks, but a part of me was still scared. If I opened that part of our relationship up again, I was opening my heart to the risk of being destroyed.

Steed's voice pulled me from my thoughts. "I promise you I'll never hurt you or Paxton. Ever."

Chloe leaned in close to her father. "Did you say you were sorry?"

My hand covered my mouth in an attempt not to laugh. I glanced at Melanie. She gazed lovingly at her son and granddaughter. The ache in my chest was hard to ignore. Knowing Steed had a child from another woman seemed to be my biggest hurdle. I loved Chloe, but I couldn't shake the idea that I wasn't the one to give Steed his first child. That some monster of a woman had made this precious, sweet, innocent little girl…the spitting image of her father.

Steed kissed Chloe on the nose, and her next words nearly knocked me off my feet.

"I trust you, Daddy."

Steed beamed, and I knew those words also affected him deeply. "That means so much to me, pumpkin. I love you."

Her little arms wrapped around his neck where she held on for dear life. He stood, taking her up with him. I watched as they stood there lost in one another. Steed held onto her until she was the one who was ready to break the contact. Chloe had trusted her father to never break her heart, and I honestly believed he never would. Not purposely. Just like he didn't purposely break mine.

A million things started running through my mind. We had handled everything wrong, yet we had been so young. Weren't we supposed to get stuff wrong? And I knew deep in my heart, just like Chloe did, that Steed would never hurt either one of us now.

Turning to me, Chloe grinned. "Paxton, do you like pumpkin bread too?"

The question threw me. I'd been so lost in thought that I had to force myself to push it all away and act normal.

"Yes! It's one of my favorites."

Steed set Chloe back on the ground, and she skipped over to Melanie. "Grammy, let's go make bread!"

With a lighthearted chuckle, Melanie took Chloe's hand, but not before glancing back at us. "You two kids have fun. Don't rush back."

She winked, and I felt my face flush. Cord lost it laughing. "And that's my cue to get the hell out of dodge. I've got to get to the bar. Y'all enjoy your ride."

Steed made his way over to me, took my hand, and led me to his horse. "Come on. Let's go saddle up a couple horses."

"What's wrong with riding Lady?" I asked.

"She's due for a break. I've been on her damn near all morning with Trevor."

I nodded and followed. Peeking over my shoulder, I watched Melanie and Chloe drive off on the mule, headed back up to the house. My chest squeezed as I thought about the amazing morning I'd spent with Chloe. I was falling head over heels in love with her. It wasn't hard; she was precious. Her heart so full of love and a need to be loved right back.

Steed set off to work, taking Lady's saddle off, brushing her, getting her some fresh water and a small snack of oats. Trevor walked into the barn, leading two horses behind him.

"Thought y'all might like to exercise a few of the horses for me. I don't get near enough time to give them all their fair share."

I walked over to the beautiful bay mare who was standing so patiently behind Trevor. My hand ran over her gorgeous reddish brown color. Her mane and tail were black and matched the lower half of her legs. She bobbed her head a few times as if to tell me to just get on her already. She was ready to go. I smiled as I pressed my face into her side and breathed in her heavenly scent.

Steed gave Trevor a light tap on the shoulder. "Thanks, Trevor! You didn't have to this."

He laughed. "Considering you kicked my ass at roping, I figured I'd do something nice for you."

Steed did the same thing I'd done with my horse. His hands moved over the Blue Roan. "Fucking hell, she's beautiful," he said.

Trevor nodded. "I just bought her not too long ago from a breeder in Mason. His wife trained her, and I've got to say, she did one hell of a good job. I've never had a mare behave like such a lady as this one."

"What's her name?" I asked while still running my hands along my horse.

Trevor pointed to my horse first. "This here is Allure."

My brows lifted. "Very fitting name for her."

He laughed. "Yeah, and this one is Marley."

I crinkled my nose. "That's an adorable name for her."

Steed took the reins from Trevor. "Anything you need us to do when we get back?"

"Hose them down, and make sure they have fresh water. They'll get oats tomorrow morning, so a bit of hay cubes is fine if you want to treat them."

"Got it."

Trevor started to walk off. "Oh, and just an FYI. They like to run."

I laughed. "Oh gosh, I feel a race coming on."

We rode in silence for a bit until we were off the main trail, cutting through one of the pastures. Steed seemed lost in thought, and I couldn't help but wonder if he was thinking about what Chloe had said.

"Today at the spa, Chloe told me her Christmas wish list."

He laughed. "She's been asking to write a letter to Santa Claus, but told me it wasn't ready for me to read it. Of course, I can hardly read what she writes anyway."

I chuckled.

"What was on it?" he asked.

I cleared my throat. "Well, some things you'll love, one you will hate."

His brows pinched together. "Really?"

Nodding, I giggled. "Yep. She said she wanted her own horse. A bed for Patches so she could sleep in her room with her."

Steed let out a roar of laughter.

I went on. "A Barbie dream house. Some books, other things like dresses and make-up."

"Make-up?" he gasped. "What the fuck does she need make-up for?"

My failed attempts to hide my smile only made him frown more. "Fuck," he said, his hand raking through his beautiful brown waves.

"Then she said she wanted a boyfriend. Preferably Timothy Knox."

Peeking over to watch his reaction, I thought he was going to blow the top of his head off.

"Boyfriend! Who the fuck is Timothy Knox?"

My cheeks ached from holding back laughter. "He's a classmate. Sweet little boy. He always pulls her chair out for her if he is near. And he always sits next to her at lunch."

Steed's eyes widened in horror. "W-what?"

I looked ahead of me. If I kept staring at Steed, I was sure to start laughing my ass off.

"You need to move him."

Lifting a brow, I asked, "Move him? Move him where?"

"Away from my daughter! To another class!"

"Steed, I'm the only kindergarten teacher. I can't have him moved. Besides, I wouldn't even if I could."

"Why not? The little bastard is going after our Chloe."

My breath seized in my throat.

Our Chloe.

Not wanting to make a big deal out of what he said, I ignored it. "They're five. It's harmless."

"It's not harmless if my daughter wants to be his girlfriend." He shook his head and brought Marley to a stop. "I'm going to be sick."

A small part of me felt sorry for him.

"Then I probably shouldn't tell you she asked for a kiss from him also."

Steed's face turned white, and he slid off of his horse. He stumbled for a few steps and dropped back onto his ass.

It shouldn't have, but damn, it turned me on seeing him react this way. I knew I was making a mistake sliding off my horse, but I was tired of playing it safe. Besides, it was obvious that Steed needed me.

CHAPTER 23

Paxton

Standing over Steed, I watched while he cradled his head in his hands.

"This is payback. Karma. My sin coming back to haunt me."

Sighing, I kicked at his boot. "Stop it. You're making a big deal out of nothing. I thought we were going to ride."

He glanced up at me. "Are you sure you can keep an eye on this little Timothy bastard?"

I grimaced. "Steed, I don't think you should be calling my students names like bastard and little prick."

He scoffed and stood up. I was about to say more but my voice caught in my throat. I was so taken by this man's beauty that I struggled to think straight, let alone speak. His blue eyes popped against the off-white cowboy hat. My eyes traveled down to the day-old scruff on his face. I wanted desperately to feel it against my skin.

Moving my gaze farther down, his tight blue T-shirt showed off his perfect broad chest and I swear you could see the faint outline of his six-pack abs. To say he had a nice body would be putting it light-ly. His body was amazing. It was clear the man worked out. A lot.

The tight Wrangler jeans and cowboy boots finished off the package. And what a freaking hot package. My mouth watered, but at the same time felt dry. My tongue zipped out and ran over my lips…anything to make my dry mouth feel wetter.

Steed took a few steps towards me, and I backed up until I bumped into Allure.

"You look like you've got something on your mind, Pax."

Oh, I do. You. Inside me. On top of me. Behind me. Making me scream out your name.

"I, um… I…um…"

I'd planned on telling Steed I was ready to take the next step to-day. I didn't think I could stand another moment with his burning hot body near me. I ached for his touch. Longed to have him do all the things he had been promising to do.

He lifted his hand and ran the back of it over my cheek, causing me to tremble. A slight lift to the corner of his mouth proved he was gauging my reactions. "Tell me, Pax. Tell me what you want."

I knew in my heart Steed meant every single word he had said about leaving, not coming home, being torn up about our child. His promise to never hurt me again. My stupid head was the one arguing with my heart.

I closed my eyes. I was tired of listening to my head. It was time to follow my heart.

Focusing only on him, I whispered, "You. I want you, Steed. More than anything."

His eyes lit up. "What are you saying?"

Pulling my lip in between my teeth, I inhaled a deep breath through my nose before letting it all out. "I want *you*, Steed." My voice sounded shaky, but not from fear…from desire. "I *need* you."

A slow, crooked smile appeared as he cupped my face with his hands. "Paxton, are you sure? Because I want you to be one hundred percent sure about this."

My heart was beating like crazy. My body ached with anticipation. Steed acted as if he was going to take me here and now. What? Was he thinking he would fuck me up against the damn horse?

The wetness between my legs grew. Shit. I'd be okay with that.

"Paxton?"

My eyes swung up to meet his. With a nod, I replied, "I'm sure."

His eyes closed and a look of relief washed over his face. I was positive it had been hard for him to keep his hands to himself these last few weeks. I loved him for doing it, though.

Steed's mouth pressed against mine in a heated kiss. My hands quickly found their way under his T-shirt, my fingers moving across his skin, over that perfect body of his.

He dropped both hands from my face and slipped one under my shirt. My head was spinning with desire. A part of me wanted his hand in my pants, not under my shirt. When he pushed my bra up and started playing with my already hard nipple, I pulled my mouth from his and gasped for air.

I was on fire and the pulling and tugging of my nipple only fueled it.

My body trembled against the rock-solid horse who had yet to budge. Steed's mouth was on my neck, kissing and licking. Building my body up and making me ache even more.

"Fucking hell, Pax. You drive me crazy."

The only thing I could do was let out a soft moan when he pushed my bra all the way up and started sucking on one nipple while pinching the other.

Fuck, I forgot how amazing he was at getting me worked up.

"Are you wet, Pax?" he asked while his tongue licked and flicked my nipple.

I needed help standing up, so I grabbed onto his shoulders. "You should find out…for yourself," I managed.

Steed's head popped up and our eyes met. "*Fuck*," he gulped.

With quick hands, he had my jeans undone and his hand down them. When his fingers brushed over my panties, I gasped. "Steed!"

He pushed my jeans down and dropped to his knees. My breath was coming faster now. *If this horse moves, I'm going to fall straight back on my ass.* Especially with my jeans around my ankles.

"Goddamn it, I want to taste you."

Watching him pull my panties down was the hottest thing I think I'd ever seen. I could see the anticipation on his face. There was no way I could spread my legs enough, but somehow he managed to lick up my entire core and flick my clit.

"Jesus!" I cried out. He stood and cupped my face, his eyes staring into mine.

"How long has it been, Paxton?"

I swallowed hard. Not sure if my answer would kill the mood or not. "Ten years."

His eyes widened in surprise. He slowly shook his head and pushed his finger inside of me. My sharp intake of air made him slow down.

"No. Don't. Please don't stop," I begged.

When he buried his face into my neck, I wrapped my arms around him. "Baby, I'm so sorry," he whispered.

I closed my eyes and let the feel of his finger moving take everything away.

"More," I said in a needy voice. I didn't care how it sounded. If I had the guts I would have told him to fuck me right here.

Steed slipped another finger in and hissed. "So fucking tight."

Oh God, it felt so good. My mind started to wonder. What was his sex life like with Kim? Did he enjoy being with her? Was it meaningless sex or did they connect? I couldn't help myself. I needed to know.

"How long has it been for you?" I asked with nothing but fear laced in my words. Steed stopped finger fucking me and drew his head back.

"A little over six years."

My heart dropped. "What?"

"The night we conceived Chloe was the last time I had sex with Kim. It was our...our wedding night."

His words both made me happy and hurt like hell. Knowing he had married another woman still hurt, no matter what the reasons were behind it all. But then, knowing he never had sex with her after that made my wounded heart feel a bit better. Their connection wasn't real. Nothing about their relationship was real except for sweet Chloe.

His soft lips ran over the edge of my jaw. His hot breath caused my heart to beat even faster. "It's always been you, Pax. Always you."

My hand gripped the back of his neck, pulling his mouth to mine. Our kiss was hungry...almost frantic. Steed's fingers moved again, building up my body to what I was sure was going to be the most explosive orgasm ever.

My hips rocked against his hand. Shit. I needed more.

I gripped his shirt, our tongues dancing erotically against each other. I broke the kiss long enough to pant out, "More." Steed pushed another finger in. The slight burn caught me off guard. I tensed, and he stopped.

"Don't stop!" I cried out.

"Jesus, Paxton. I need to fuck you."

His mouth was back on mine while his fingers worked me into a frenzy. Thrusting my hips faster I moaned into his mouth. My release building and building to the point where I *needed* to come.

My orgasm hit me so fast and hard it took my breath away. I choked out Steed's name. "Steed! Oh God!"

"That's it, baby. Fuck, I can feel you coming."

When they say it felt so good your eyes rolled to the back of your head…yeah. I was seeing freaking stars. A haze filled my head as my body trembled with nothing but pure pleasure.

If his fingers could do this to me, what would his mouth feel like? Or him inside me?

Another wave hit me just thinking about—

"Oh God! Steed, I'm coming again."

"Goddamn it, Paxton," Steed said, his voice so low and deep I knew he wanted the same thing as me.

"Need you. Steed, I need you inside of me. Please. Please…fuck me!"

It was right then that Allure decided she'd had enough. She starting to walk off. My jeans were around my ankles, and Steed was totally in a daze from me begging him to fuck me. I'd let my lust-filled mind speak for me, and it was clear Steed had not prepared himself for that. He let go of me while he stared.

"Steed!" I cried out as I stumbled back. It took him a few seconds to realize I was going down.

"Paxton!" I grabbed his T-shirt, and we both went down. With a loud thump we looked at each other and started laughing.

"Oh my God! I'm in the middle of the pasture half-naked!"

Laughing, Steed shook his head and gazed into my eyes. His beaming face faded. Our gaze deepened, and I didn't want to tell him the grass was itching the hell out of my ass. The moment was too beautiful.

"I've missed you so damn much," he said. "I want you to know that. There wasn't a single day that went by where I didn't think about you."

"I wish you would have come back."

His eyes closed, and he buried his face into my neck. "So do I."

Steed laid over me with his face pressed against my skin. I had no idea how long we had been laying there. "Steed. The horses?"

"They're fine."

"Well, um, my ass is itching so bad."

Lifting his head, that sexy crooked smile of his appeared. I could barely see his dimples through the scruff on his face. My stomach fluttered from the way he looked at me.

"Then we better get you up."

I giggled. "Please."

He stood, then picked me up like I weighed nothing. Bending, he lifted my panties up followed by my jeans. Watching him do something as simple as that had my libido kicked into overdrive. Again.

He buttoned my jeans. God, he was handsome as hell. I swear he got more handsome as the years passed. Chewing on my lip, I felt my cheeks heat.

Steed looked at me, his brows pinched together in question. "Why are you blushing, pumpkin?"

My lips pressed together, and I had no idea what to say. My naughty words from earlier were not something my students' parents would expect to come from the kindergarten teacher.

"I'm embarrassed," I answered honestly.

The smirk that moved across his face told me he knew exactly why I was embarrassed. Steed had always been a dirty talker. I was sure all the Parker boys were. The first time he made love to me he was sweet and gentle but didn't have a problem telling me my pussy was squeezing his cock. He drove me over the edge and we both came together our first time. It was sexy and sweet and...magical. I had known from that moment on no man would ever make me feel the way Steed did.

"A little bit of grass on your ass is nothing to be embarrassed about."

I lifted my brow and tilted my head. He knew that wasn't why.

With a chuckle, he put his hand on my cheek while he ran his thumb over my bottom lip. "Is it because you told me to fuck you?"

I opened my mouth and bit down on his thumb. His eyes turned darker and the grin turned to a full-blown smile. I whispered softly, "Yes. That's why."

"Do you still want me to fuck you?"

CHAPTER 24

Steed

Paxton's breath stalled and I waited with anticipation for her answer. Her cheeks were still flushed from her orgasms. My dick was so fucking hard, and I had been positive I was going to come right there in my pants when she came the second time.

"Yes."

My stomach dropped.

Thank fuck. Finally.

I would have waited forever for Paxton to be ready, but I wasn't going to lie to myself; it had been getting harder and harder to wait.

I grabbed her hand and whistled. Both horses glanced up and walked my way. "Damn, we've got two smart girls," I said with a chuckle.

"Steed?" Paxton asked with a soft voice.

I focused on her eyes, hating the fear in them. "Yeah, pumpkin?"

Her thumb came up to her mouth, and she started to chew on her nail. "Well, um... I'm... Shit." She dropped her hand and head at the same time. Staring down at the ground, she said, "I'm scared."

My finger lifted her chin until her beautiful eyes met mine. "I am too, Pax. I'm scared, nervous, excited, worried. Hell I have more emotions swirling around in my head than I've ever had. But you know what?"

"What?" she asked in the sweetest voice ever.

"Our love is worth it. The feelings between us are worth it. If you told me right now you wanted to go back and play Candyland with Chloe, I'd take you back to the house and kick your ass at it."

Covering her mouth, she giggled.

"I'd do anything for you, Pax. But it doesn't mean I'm not scared too."

Lifting on her toes, she kissed me. "I want this more than anything. I don't think I can wait a second longer."

I grinned. "Good. Now let's go. I've got the perfect place."

It didn't take Paxton long to figure out where we were going. I wanted to open the horses up in a fucking run just to get there. My dick was straining against my jeans still. All I kept hearing was Paxton moaning and saying my name, then telling me to fuck her. I wasn't going to last a minute inside her.

I brought my horse down to a walk as we came up to the trail.

"Steed, we're at the old house."

Smiling, I winked. "Shit, I haven't been here since the last time we were together. I have no idea what condition it's in."

Paxton made a face and we both laughed. We headed down the trail, and I pulled out my phone, texting Trevor.

Me: *Gramps' old cabin. What kind of shape is it in?*

Trevor: *Hell yeah! Finally getting laid. It's in great shape.*

Me: *It is?*

Trevor: *Yeah. Dad had it totally remodeled a few years back. Said he didn't want to see his dad's childhood home fall to the wayside.*

I wanted to lift my hands up to the heavens.

Trevor: *You do know I lost my virginity in that cabin.*

Me: *I think all of us lost our virginity in that cabin. It was the only place besides the barn to bring our dates where we wouldn't get caught.*

Trevor: *LOL! Those walls have seen a lot of fucking.*

Me: *And they're about to see more.*

Trevor: *HA! Finally, dude. Maybe now you won't be such a bitch.*

Me: *Fuck you, Trevor.*

Trevor: *The key is in a fake rock at the bottom left of the first step. Have fun!*

Me: *Got it. Thanks.*

"Who are you texting?" Paxton called out.

Glancing over my shoulder, I answered, "Trevor. He said the cabin's been remodeled."

"Really? Why?"

"Something about Dad not wanting to see his father's place of birth fall apart."

She smiled, and I gave Marley a small tug back on the reins.

"Should we tie them up?" Paxton asked looking at Allure and Marley.

There was a small creek that flowed behind the cabin that I knew they would both want to get to. "Nah, let them graze around here. They might want to get a drink. I don't think they'll wander too far."

She lifted her brow, clearly not sure about my decision to let the horses wander free.

"Trust me, pumpkin. They won't go far."

I took her hand and led her to the cabin, stopping to get the key from where Trevor said it would be. I glanced down and looked for a rock big enough that would hold the key. After picking up a couple, I found the fake rock then started up the stairs.

"So, you're not planning on this taking long if you think the horses won't go that far."

I glanced back at her and winked. "Trust me, I can make it last longer than the first time we were here."

She tried to hide her grin and failed.

The first time I brought Paxton here we were sixteen. It was our first time, and everything about that night was awkward. Neither of us knew what the fuck we were doing. Both of us were virgins. I'd gotten her off a few times with my hands and mouth; she'd done the same. But the moment I slipped inside her warm pussy, I had to bite on my cheek to keep from coming. I pumped all of five times and came so hard I almost passed out. My only saving grace was that Paxton had come right along with me.

Embarrassing as fuck. That shit better not happen tonight.

When we walked in, I switched on the light. We both let our gaze roam over the two-room cabin.

"Oh, my gosh. It's beautiful in here." She turned to me. "Did you plan for us to come here?"

I shook my head. "No! Not at all."

"Then what's with the fresh flowers on the table?"

Shrugging, I walked over to them. "Not sure. It doesn't look like anyone's been here for a while. Maybe they're fake."

Paxton leaned down and smelled the flowers. "They're real. Someone's been here at least within the last few days."

Heading into the bedroom, I turned on the light. The bed was made and looked like it hadn't been touched in weeks. There was a light covering of dust on the side table.

"Well, doesn't look like anyone's been staying here. Maybe Mom brings them for some reason?"

Paxton walked over to the fireplace and looked at all the photos. I guess when Dad remodeled he'd added a few family pictures. "There's a picture of us!" she gasped.

"What? Really?"

She peeked over her shoulder at me and grinned. "From high school. Looks like it was the Christmas of our senior year."

I couldn't help but smile. "Shit, we look so damn young."

Pointing to my older sister, Waylynn, Paxton said, "Waylynn is so beautiful. God I always wanted to be like her."

I jerked my head back. "Why?"

"Look at her. She's beautiful. Body to die for, and she wasn't afraid to go after what she wanted. Sometimes I wonder what would have happened if I had just gone after you."

We faced each other.

"Well, you're more beautiful than Waylynn, your body is fucking amazing, and we're done playing the *what if* game. You're here and I'm here, that's all that matters."

She nodded. "You're absolutely right. So. What do we do now?"

I tossed my head back and laughed. "Jesus, it feels like our first time all over again."

Her eyes searched my face while she chewed on her lip nervously. I reached up and pulled her lip out from her teeth.

"Except this time, I know what I'm doing," I added.

The way her mouth dropped slightly open had my dick pressing on my jeans, begging to come out and play. I took her hand in mine, lacing our fingers together and walked us to the bedroom. The queen-size bed was a nice upgrade from the twin mattress we first had sex on. Plus, knowing all my brothers had brought their firsts here and used that bed was not something I was looking forward to again.

When we walked into the room, I smiled and pulled her against me. The heat from her body drove me insane.

I laced my hand through her beautiful brown hair. I pulled slightly, causing her to let out a sharp intake of air and then moan. My lips moved across her neck with soft kisses.

"Steed," she whispered.

"I'm going to make love to you, Paxton. Then, I'm going to fuck the living shit out of you."

Her head dropped back. "Yes," she hissed.

"I've dreamed night after night about my cock buried balls deep inside you."

She swayed, and I grabbed her waist to steady her.

"I can't wait," she gasped as my lips moved to hers.

"First, I want to taste you."

CHAPTER 25

Paxton

I was dizzy with desire. All the dirty words Steed whispered against my skin had me so worked up I was sure all he would have to do is look at me down there, and I'd come.

"Let me make you come on my tongue, Pax."

Jesus. What is he doing to me?

"Yes. Okay. Right."

Hell, I couldn't even form a sentence.

He chuckled. The bastard. He knew he was driving me crazy. He also knew I was a sucker for his dirty talk.

Steed lifted my shirt over my head and tossed it to the floor, thanking God I'd worn my dark blue lace bra and panties and that I'd shaved and waxed all the important areas. I knew the time was getting close to when I would beg him to take me. I just didn't know when the time would present itself. Better to be prepared!

Reaching behind my back, he unclipped my bra and let it fall down my arms to the floor.

He swayed a little as he stared at my breasts. *Well, that's a nice confidence booster.*

I stood awkwardly, not knowing what to do while Steed stared at my chest.

"Is everything okay?" I asked shyly.

"Fucking perfect. Amazing. Jesus you're perfect, Pax."

My cheeks heated as I lifted his own shirt over his head. The itch in my fingertips to touch him was hard to ignore. Placing my hands on his chest, he inhaled sharply. I smiled, loving his reaction to my touch.

Letting my tongue glide over my lips, I leaned in and kissed his perfectly sculpted chest.

"Paxton, baby, I've missed you."

I lifted my eyes to meet his while I continued to kiss his chest, making my way down to his abs. I was hungry with lust and love for this man and that brought out something brazen in me. Plus, he had been so patient…the least I could do was give him a bit of attention first.

Dropping to my knees, I unfastened his belt, my shaking hands unbuttoning his jeans. His hands sunk into my hair and a small groan slipped from his lips when I unzipped and ran my fingers over the bulge in his briefs. I swung my eyes up and beamed when I saw the look of pure love on his face.

I pressed a light kiss right where his trail of hair led to the one thing my body was aching to have. "I know what I'm doing now as well."

"Fuuck," he said with a strained voice. I couldn't help but smile.

"Your boots?" I asked. He scrambled to kick his boots off. I tugged on his jeans and briefs and almost laughed when he helped pull them off and almost lost his balance. I could hear his breathing over my own and that did something to me. Knowing how much he was anticipating my touch made me feel sexier. Wanton. It drove my libido up even more.

His hard dick twitched against that perfect body of his.

Shit. I'd forgotten how big he was. I would need a few days to recover after today.

Cupping his balls with one hand, I wrapped my hand around his hard, thick shaft. The hiss from his lips urged me on, melting my nerves as his hand grabbed a handful of my hair, and he groaned.

My tongue moved lightly up his dick before I took him into my mouth. His pre cum caused me to moan in delight at the taste of him. *Oh, how I've missed Steed's taste…*

Steed's entire body jumped, and he cried out, "Fucking hell!"

I remembered what he liked me to do during a blowjob, and I quickly got to work sucking and licking him as if I was starved for him. My other hand gently worked his balls.

"Oh God, Paxton." He used his hands to still my head. His hips rocked into my mouth, and I loved hearing him moan.

Swirling my tongue around him I relished the taste of this man. Strong hands grabbed me and pulled me to a stop.

"I'm about to come in your mouth."

I grinned sheepishly. "Is that a bad thing?"

He was fighting for his breath. "Yes, I want to be inside you when I come."

"Oh," I whispered with a sly grin.

Steed's hands quickly went to work at getting my jeans and panties off while I kicked my boots off.

"Christ almighty. Paxton, I'm trying so damn hard to go slow."

I swallowed hard. "I don't want slow, Steed. I only want you."

His hands cupped my face before his lips pressed to mine. Backing me up to the bed, we crawled onto it, not breaking our kiss once as I laid down. He moved over me. I was positive my heart hadn't ever beat this hard. Not even our first time. I had been more nervous and scared about it hurting. Now…now I was melting with the heat between our bodies. Knowing what to expect drove me even more. Damn. I was so horny. I was soaked between my legs.

As if on cue, Steed's hand moved lightly down my body and between my legs. I spread them apart, panting with the need for him to touch me.

"Steed," I whispered against his lips when I pulled away for air. "I need to feel you. Please, it's been so long."

His fingers slipped inside, causing me to jump and lift my hips into his hand.

"You're so damn wet."

"Yes," I hissed.

Pressing his lips on my neck, he kissed me until he reached a nipple. Taking it into his mouth he sucked and pulled while his fingers quickly worked my orgasm up.

"Faster!" I cried out. I didn't care how needy and shaken my voice sounded. I was on the edge of the abyss, and I needed to fall over it. *Now.*

Steed's mouth moved to my other nipple. He gently bit down, and my back arched, my orgasm hitting so hard I cried out with the only word I could manage.

"Steed!"

Pleasure ripped through my body. Steed moved back up my body. His hands all over me as he squeezed my breast, blew hot breath on my nipple. I was a trembling mess.

The minute I started to free fall back down to reality he started his assault again.

"You're so damn beautiful, Paxton. Watching you come is one of my favorite things."

Fighting for words, I smiled and said the only thing that came to mind. "*Holy shit.*"

He winked. "I'm not done, pumpkin. You're so tight. I don't want to hurt you when I push inside of you."

"Not done?" I gasped.

He disappeared again. This time he buried his face between my legs and swiped his tongue over my sensitive clit.

"Fucking hell!" I cried out. My hands grabbed at the bedspread as I tried to lift my hips up. Steed's strong hands pushed my hips down while he moved his mouth ever so slowly over my hot pulsing core.

It wasn't going to take me long to come again. Hell, my body still felt the aftershocks from my other orgasm.

"Steed. Oh God. Oh God!" He slipped his fingers inside while his tongue worked magic on my sensitive nub. One move with both sent me over the edge.

My entire body went rigid as the orgasm burst through. Squeezing my eyes shut, I saw nothing but a pulsing light. My hands grabbed at Steed's hair, and I wasn't sure if I wanted to pull him in closer or push him away. He must have scissored his fingers because an instant sting mixed with my pleasure and caused me to jump. I was too far over the edge to care though. My hips bucked while at the same time I desperately tried to get away. I needed it to stop. It was the most intense orgasm I'd ever had in my life. I didn't care that I was crying out Steed's name. It felt fucking amazing.

He finally let me go and I laid on the bed feeling completely spent. My muscles lax and unable to move.

"Damn, baby. That was amazing to watch."

I opened my eyes to see his beautiful smiling face staring at me. My chest was still rising and falling as I tried to get my breath under control.

"I can't wait another second, Paxton. I need to be inside of you."

I nodded. "I need that too. Desperately."

Steed was over me, his lips against mine as he guided the head of his cock into me. I stiffened while he slowly entered.

"Are you okay?" he asked softly.

"Yes. Yes. I just need a second to adjust. It's been a long time."

The look in Steed's eyes made my chest tighten and my stomach dip. It was like his life depended on being inside of me. Right this very moment.

He pulled out some before pushing back in. We both moaned in delight.

"My God. You feel so fucking good," he spoke against my lips.

My fingers dug into his back as I arched, needing to feel him deeper.

"I can't control myself, Paxton."

Our eyes met. "Then don't."

CHAPTER 26

Steed

Holy fucking shit. I was in heaven. Paxton's pussy squeezing my cock was the most delicious feeling ever. I'd forgotten how amazing she was. How she made me feel when I was inside her. Nothing else in this world mattered but us. The only woman I'd ever loved was back in my arms and I was trying so hard not to let loose and fuck the living shit out of her.

"I can't control myself, Paxton."

Her eyes turned dark with desire. "Then don't."

It was a whisper, but it seemed like a shouted plea. I leaned up and grabbed her hips, pulling out and pushing back in harder.

"Fuck!" I cried out. Paxton grabbed at the bedspread, her face flushed with her earlier orgasms. When I looked down, I saw my cock moving in and out of her body. It was hot as hell, and I had to fight my orgasm off. No fucking way I was letting it end things that quick.

When I glanced back up, Paxton was on her elbows, watching our bodies become one. Her bottom lip caught between her teeth as she stared at my cock pounding into her over and over again.

Jesus, her watching was *hot*. *Where did my sweet, innocent Paxton go?* I fucking loved this older version of her. I sped up, the sounds of our bodies slapping together driving me closer and closer to my release.

Paxton dropped back down, her head thrashing from side to side.

"More! Steed, deeper!" she cried out as she met me thrust for thrust.

A sheen of sweat covered our bodies. Dropping down, I pulled her closer as I moved in and out. Her little moans and noises were like music to my ears. I wanted her to come again. To release when I did.

"I love you so much, Paxton. Christ, I've missed this."

Her eyes snapped open, and I was overcome with how blue they looked. I could see her love for me. No longer was there doubt or fear. No more pain and hurt. Only love.

"I…love…you," she panted.

"I will never leave you. Never!" I said while pressing my mouth to hers. The kiss was almost as amazing as the fucking.

Dragging her mouth from mine, her eyes seemed to spark as she cried out, "I'm going to come."

The feel of her pussy pulsing on my cock with her release was my undoing.

I pulled out and pushed back in fast and deep. A long deep grunt pulled from the deepest part of my throat as I called out, "Oh fuuck."

Her arms and legs wrapped around me, clinging to me for her life. Both of us let out small moans while we came together.

Filling her with my cum made my heart beat harder and my chest squeeze.

It wasn't until our bodies came to a stop that I realized what we had done. With my face buried in her neck, I was too fucking afraid to ruin the moment by pointing out we had just had sex without protection. No wonder if felt so fucking good.

Paxton's fingers moved lazily over my back while my cock still twitched inside her.

"That was the most amazing moment of my life," she softly said.

Drawing back, our eyes locked. "For me too."

Her gaze searched my face before landing back on mine. She chewed on the corner of her lip then said, "We didn't use protection."

My heart sank. "I know. I was so caught up in everything, I didn't think about it until right after. I'm sorry, Paxton."

I tried to read her but couldn't. She traced a finger over my stubble. "Neither one of us thought about it. But you should know… I'm not on the pill."

Ten years ago I'd have freaked the fuck out. Now, a small part of me hoped like hell I'd just gotten her pregnant. Another part of me, the greedy selfish bastard, hoped I hadn't so I could have her to myself for a bit longer.

"What happens happens. It changes nothing for me. I love you, and I want you to be a part of my life, Paxton. Forever."

Her eyes threatened to spill over with tears, but she was able to hold them back.

"Is it wrong a part of me wants it, but the other part doesn't?"

I grinned. "No, because I just thought the same damn thing."

She chuckled. Leaning down, I kissed her softly. Slowly. I could feel my dick coming back up, and I started to move again. Paxton moaned softly into my mouth.

"Do you want me to stop?" I asked. One time going without protection was one thing. Twice was just playing with fire.

"Could you pull out? I want you again."

Before I had a chance to answer, the door to the cabin opened and we both froze.

"Who is that?" Paxton mouthed.

With wide, surprised eyes, I mouthed back, "I have no clue."

I could hear movement. Whoever it was walked in, set something on the table, and made their way over to the sink.

Slowly pulling out of her, I felt my cum. Paxton must have felt it also because she sat up and peered down. I frantically looked around for something to clean her with. The red bandana caught my eye. It had something written on it, but I didn't pay attention when I grabbed it. I wiped off Paxton then cleaned myself off and threw it on the floor.

We quietly slipped off the bed and got dressed. It took everything out of me not to start laughing. It might have been one of the ranch hands coming to check things out if they saw the horses.

Then the person started humming.

Paxton stopped moving and covered her mouth. An expression of pure horror moved over her face.

Amelia!

CHAPTER 27

Steed

"Meli?" I mouthed.

Nodding her head, Paxton dropped her hands and pulled on her boots.

"Okay. Words…come to me!" Amelia said. I could faintly hear the sounds of her fingernails tapping against her keyboard.

Now it made sense. The flowers sitting on the table were Amelia's favorite. She had told me she had a hiding place for writing when she was struggling with a story. She must have meant the cabin.

"What do we do?" Paxton mouthed as she pulled the comforter off the bed and picked up the bandana and wrapped it all in a ball. I loved that she was trying to clean up.

Smiling, I took her hand in mine. She shook her head and pulled back when I tried to get her to walk with me out to the living area.

"Steed! No!" she whispered.

The typing stopped. I put my finger to my mouth to get Paxton to stop talking. She dropped the bedspread like it had burned her.

The typing started again as did the faint sound of music. I slowly opened the door to the bedroom. Amelia's back was facing us. Paxton tried to sneak out of the cabin without Amelia seeing us. I watched as she tiptoed over to the front door. Amelia caught sight of her and screamed, then jumped up. Which made Paxton scream and throw her body against the front door.

"It's just me!" Paxton screamed.

Amelia covered her chest with both hands. Her eyes jerked from Paxton to me, back to Paxton and finally back to me.

"Jesus, son of Mary! You scared the living piss out of me! What in the hell are you—" She stopped talking. A slow smile moved across her face.

"You slept together!" I glanced at Paxton. She wore a huge grin as her cheeks turned a beautiful shade of pink.

Amelia jumped up and down. "You slept together! Oh. To-the-M! To-the-*get it girl*-G!"

Covering her face in her hands, Paxton groaned. I walked over and pulled her into my arms. "We've been caught, pumpkin."

Amelia did a few spins, a fist pump, mumbled something about motivation and then stilled.

"Wait. You had sex in here? Please tell me you were finished when I walked in."

I wanted to laugh at the horrified look on her face as it all sank in. "Actually, we were gearing up for round two when you walked in."

Paxton hit me on the stomach while Amelia covered her mouth and stumbled back a few steps. She fake gagged…or maybe she gagged for real. I'm not sure.

"You were…when I… That's gross."

Paxton dropped her head and buried her face into my chest. "I'm so humiliated."

"Don't be, Pax. We didn't know anyone would be showing up."

"Why must you guys use this cabin as your fuck zone? Oh my God! I walked in on Trevor banging some whore on my work table a few months ago! He has a house on the ranch! You have a house. Why are you here in my happy place?"

"We were out riding and things got a little heated. I couldn't take Paxton back to my place because Mom's there with Chloe."

Amelia sighed. "Did you at least clean up?"

Paxton pushed off me. "We started to! Steed, get the bedspread and that little bandana."

I started for the bedroom, but Amelia stepped in front of me. "B-bandana?"

"Yeah," I said trying to walk around her.

"What about it?"

"I had to use it in a pinch."

Her eyes widened. "So you used it for blowing your nose?" She looked hopeful that I might agree with that.

I shook my head. "No, if you must know, when you walked in I was still buried balls deep inside Paxton."

"Oh God," Paxton said with a groan.

Amelia snarled her lip. "Gross."

"You're taking the conversation there, sis. I needed to wipe the cum off of us, and I saw the bandana on the side of the bed. I used it. I figured it was something Mom had picked up for decoration."

Horror moved over her face. "No! You didn't! Steed! Why didn't you walk into the bathroom and get a towel like any normal guy?"

"I panicked, Amelia! I was fucking my girlfriend less than three minutes before you walked in! What the hell was I supposed to do?"

She spun around and covered her mouth. "Too much information!"

"You were the one jumping all around saying how happy you were we had sex!"

"Um, maybe I'll just go in and get that stuff," Paxton said walking between us and into the bedroom.

"Steed! That was a gift from one of my readers! They made it for me because one of my characters in a book I wrote always carried a bandana."

Oh shit.

"Why in the hell did you have a gift from one of your readers on the side table in the cabin?"

"Because I thought it would look cute in here with all the furniture. And this is my writing cave, you asshole!"

Paxton came out of the bedroom carrying the bedspread. "Amelia, I'll take care of this and get it all cleaned. I'm sure it's…fine."

Pinching the bridge of her nose, she shook her head. "It has my brother's cum on it. Oh God." Covering her mouth, she gagged again, and I couldn't help but laugh.

I took Paxton's free hand in mine and pulled her towards the door. "Hey, you could put this whole scene in a book!"

I could practically feel the anger pouring off of her as she turned to me. She picked up a book and threw it at me. "Fuck you, Steed Parker!" Amelia screamed.

I lost it laughing while I ducked out of harm's way.

"Steed, that wasn't very nice," Paxton said, trying her best to hide her own laughter.

Glancing up, I couldn't help the lightness that crept into my chest as I watched Paxton sitting in the oversized chair with her legs tucked under her. Chloe was snuggled up, staring at the pages of the book Paxton was reading.

This was the life I had dreamed of for so many years. A family with Paxton. It had been a month since we had sex in the cabin. A month of pure fucking bliss. Every chance we had we were in bed together. Making up for lost time.

Damn, I loved making love to Paxton. It was the only time I ever felt completely relaxed. Contentment wasn't even the beginning of how I felt.

"Daddy? Are you going to get our turkey this year for Thanksgiving?"

My eyes drifted to my daughter's, and I smiled. "Uncle Tripp always shoots the Turkey for Thanksgiving."

"How come?" Chloe asked.

I shrugged. "Guess it's always been the tradition. Grandpa had him shoot his first turkey when he was about your age."

Her eyes widened as she jumped out of the chair and ran across the room to me. "Can I shoot a turkey with Uncle Tripp?"

With a chuckle, I nodded. "If you want to. I'm sure he would love that, but maybe next year when I can teach a little more about guns and how to safely use them."

Chloe spun around and faced Paxton. "Paxton, have you ever shot a deer?"

"I sure have. I was with your Daddy when I shot my first deer."

My mind drifted back to that day. Paxton sitting up in the deer stand with me, so serious about killing her first buck. I'd never been more proud than when she shot him, and he dropped straight to the ground. Perfect shot.

"Daddy! Daddy! I want to be like Paxton! Please can I shoot a deer?"

Laughing, I pulled her onto my lap and tickled her stomach. She kicked and laughed until I stopped. "You really want to shoot a deer, Chloe?"

Her big blue eyes looked into mine. "I want to be like Paxton when I grow up."

My heart melted and my gaze jerked up to see Paxton wiping a tear from her cheek. "She is pretty amazing, isn't she?" I asked not really expecting my daughter to answer.

"She is. I can't wait until she's my mommy."

We both smiled. This past month I hadn't pressured Paxton with our relationship. If it were up to me she'd be moved in, and my ring would be on her finger. But I knew she wanted to take things slower. We made sure we went out at least three times a week. Twice alone and once with Chloe.

Paxton's blue eyes stared into mine, and I replied, "Neither can I, pumpkin. Neither can I."

CHAPTER 28

Paxton

"One week off. You have no idea how much I need this week off."

Corina set her oversized bag down on one of the kid's desks as she dropped into the seat. It was the last day before our Thanksgiving break, and we had a half day. Next week we had the whole week off. It was a much-needed break for all of us.

"Hard to believe Thanksgiving is next week," I said.

She rolled her neck. "Thank God. I love my students, but I need a break from them and their parents. If one more mom tries to set me up on a date, I swear I'm going to blow a fuse."

I chuckled. "They mean well."

Lifting her brow, she asked, "They still snooping for information on you and Steed?"

"Gina is. Pretty much everyone else knows we're seeing each other."

"Speaking of, how are things going with you guys? I never see you anymore so I don't get the dirty low down."

"Dirty low down?"

Corina nodded. "Please. If he is anything like his twin brother, I'm sure the boy does dirty, dirty things to you when you're alone."

My cheeks heated. "Have you seen Mitchell again?"

Her smile faded and a look of hurt moved in so fast I might have missed it had I not been focused on her. "No, but I've gone out a few times with Tripp. At least he's interested."

She faked a laugh.

I leaned back. So Mitchell was honoring the brother code. Interesting. "How's it going? With Tripp?"

With a shrug, she replied, "It's okay. He loves politics and law and throws in a bit of ranching every now and then. Those seem to be the only three things he ever talks about."

"Why do you go out with him then?"

Chewing on her lip, she replied, "He's nice. Treats me with respect. And it keeps me from sitting home all alone watching Disney movies and daydreaming about my prince charming. I get the feeling he is looking for arm candy, especially since he wants to run for mayor someday."

"Have y'all slept together yet?"

She tossed her head back and let out a roar of laughter. "No. I informed him I wasn't the type of girl to spread my legs open like that. Besides, we aren't even remotely close to that in our relationship. If you can call it that."

I leaned forward. "And yet, you did with Mitchell. Spread your legs."

Her face was pained. "That was different. It was a moment of weakness, and I had been drinking. It was a mistake. *Clearly* he thinks so as well since he went radio silent afterwards."

Dragging in a deep breath, I blew it out. I needed to let her know about both Mitchell and Tripp liking her. "I'm pretty sure Mitchell likes you, Corina."

Her eyes grew wide, and I swore I saw confusion in her eyes. Then she laughed and said, "I doubt it."

"No, Corina, he does."

Her smile faded. "It was a one-night stand. Just like you said, Paxton. I'm over it."

I opened my mouth, but someone knocked on the door. Corina turned to look over her shoulder and I glanced up. Steed stood there with a beaming expression on his face.

Damn. He looked hot as hell. His black T-shirt showcased his ripped upper body perfectly. His cowboy hat was in his hand and his hair was a disheveled mess. I could imagine him running his hand through it as he worked on the ranch with Trevor. Letting my eyes travel down his body, I couldn't help but notice how his Wrangler jeans fit him perfectly. The icing on the cake were the cowboy boots I had given him so long ago. I loved that he still wore them. My lower stomach pooled with heat.

I wanted him. Now.

Jesus. Anytime this man is around I'm horny as hell.

Steed tilted his head and lifted a brow. I'm sure he noticed the way I was eye fucking him.

"Hey, Steed. How's it going?" Corina asked, standing and reaching for her bag.

I made a mental note to finish our conversation about Mitchell later.

"It's going good. How about you?"

She shrugged. "Same crap, different day."

He chuckled. "Tripp said you're heading back home for Thanksgiving?"

Corina paused. "Um. No. My parents are going on a cruise, and my older brother is going skiing with his fiancé. I'm planning a nice Marie Callender's turkey pot pie and *Cinderella*."

I stood. "What? Why didn't you tell me you were staying in town?"

Swinging the bag over her shoulder, she winked. "It's no big deal. I'm planning on catching up on some reading and work."

"You should come to our place for Thanksgiving, Corina. My mother cooks for a small army," Steed offered.

Corina laughed. "Your family *is* a small army. Thank you, but really, it's okay."

I rounded my desk and took her wrist. I knew Corina; she would hate being alone. "Please come. I know Melanie and John would love to have you. And Chloe adores you. Plus my parents will be there. Please."

Her eyes wouldn't meet mine. "I'm late for an appointment. We'll chat later about it, okay?"

I nodded and dropped her wrist. "Sure."

Corina kissed me on the cheek and headed towards the door. "You guys have fun today."

Steed watched as Corina made her way out of my classroom and down the hall. Turning back to me, he frowned. "Shit. Tripp is an asshole."

There was no way I could hold back my chuckle. "What makes you say that?"

"Because by the look on her face, she clearly told him she wasn't going home. He didn't pay attention. He never pays attention unless it has something to do with him."

My eyes focused on the doorway Corina had walked through moments ago. "I think she likes Mitchell. You know they spent a night together."

Steed's brows lifted. "No shit? When?"

"That night you took me home from Cord's bar. She was with Mitchell, and she told me they pretty much got lost in each other all night, which I might add is so unlike her. But Mitchell hasn't called or anything."

"That's because Tripp's laid claim."

"Laid claim? What is she, a cow? Does Tripp even like her?"

With a grim twist of his mouth, he replied, "Sorry. Bad choice of words. Anyway, I think he likes her. He seems to enjoy her company, and he does talk about her, but come to think of it, he seems to talk about her more when Mitchell's around."

"I wonder if Mitchell likes her."

Steed made his way over to me. With each step, my body grew hotter. "If he does, maybe he's confused? He actually felt something for a woman, and he doesn't know how to deal with it. Then add Tripp into the equation."

Rolling my eyes, I mumbled, "Men."

He stopped in front of me. "Ya know, when I first knocked and you looked at me, I could swear I saw a hungry look in your eyes."

I wiggled my eyebrows. "You saw right."

His hand slipped behind my neck, pulling me close. "What are you hungry for?"

"You."

"Chloe's with Amelia this afternoon."

My body trembled from the look of promise in his eyes. "I know. Auntie afternoon Amelia called it."

"Do you know what that means?"

"You're going to take me back to my place and have your wicked way with me?"

A crooked grin grew over his handsome face, and my knees wobbled. "As amazing as that sounds, no."

I pouted. Something one of my students would do, but it seemed to make Steed's eyes turn darker. Kind of like the other day when he stopped by my house and nearly ravaged me when I opened the door. He said it was my pigtails that got to him. I made a mental note to wear them more often.

"Amelia is keeping Chloe most of the day, so I made plans for this afternoon and evening."

My heart fluttered. An entire afternoon and evening alone with Steed. We'd been able to sneak in alone time over the last couple of months, but it had been a few weeks since our last…sleepover.

"I like the sounds of that, Mr. Parker."

"Grab your shit, let's go. The faster we start this date the faster my cock is inside of you."

I inhaled sharply. No matter how much he talked that way, it still shot a bolt of electricity right between my legs. If he slipped his hand in my panties, I had no doubt I'd be soaked for him.

"You're lucky no one heard that dirty mouth of yours."

He laughed. "Don't deny it. You like my dirty mouth."

My brows lifted, and my lower stomach pulled with an aching need. "Oh, I'm not denying it."

His eyes darkened. "I didn't think so."

I walked around my desk and grabbed some papers. Even though it was Thanksgiving break, I still needed to work on lesson plans. I nestled the paperwork into the Fry bag I talked myself into buying a few months back. Reaching for my purse, I turned and headed back to Steed.

"Did you really bring work home?" he asked.

I rolled my eyes. "I have to, or I'll get behind."

"You're a damn kindergarten teacher, Pax. You shouldn't be working so much outside of work."

Laughing, I hooked my arm around his. "Tell that to the higher ups who seem to love piling more work onto us."

As we moved through the classroom, my excitement grew. What did Steed have planned for us? More importantly, when would he make good on his promise to be inside of me?

We walked in silence. The only thing making any noise were my high heels clicking on the floor. I peeked up to see Steed smiling, and I longed to know what was making him wear his happy face.

I cleared my throat. "What are you thinking about?"

Turning to look at me, his smile grew bigger. "Us."

I couldn't stop my smile. "I like the sound of that. What about us?"

Steed pushed the door open, and we walked out into the cool fall breeze. I loved fall in Texas. The air smelled crisp and clean. Hints of spicy cinnamon and pumpkin wafted from certain stores or homes. Burning piles of leaves and sweaters always made me long for simpler days…sitting in bleachers and watching Steed play football was always a happy fall memory.

"How good we are together. How happy you make me and how I hope like hell I make you happy. The fact that Chloe loves the idea of us. It all makes me happy."

He reached for my hand and laced his fingers in mine.

"That makes me happy too."

We stopped at my car, and he turned me to face him. He placed his hand on the side of my face, and I couldn't help but lean into it.

"You make me so damn happy, Pax. I hope you know that."

"I do know that. And you make me beyond happy. I haven't been this happy in years."

Steed leaned down and brushed his lips over mine. "I have a feeling we're being watched by some nosy co-worker of yours or even a parent, so I'll behave. But later, my lips are going to be devouring that sweet soft mouth."

I swallowed hard, my heart beating harder. Opening my mouth, nothing came out but a small breath of air. Steed flashed his panty melting smile and kissed me softly, but way too quickly. "I'll follow you back to your place so you can drop your car off."

Nodding, I opened the door to my car and tossed my purse and bag in. Steed turned to leave, but I reached for his hand.

"Wait."

Steed faced me again, a slight look of concern on his face.

"I don't care what people see, what they think, or what they say. I love you and I never want either of us to hide that fact."

The concern melted away and his eyes lit up, causing my stomach to dip. He cupped my face within his hands, his eyes searching my face. "You're my everything, Paxton."

Those sweet simple words meant more than he could ever imagine. He leaned down and kissed me. It was one of those *knock my socks off* kisses. One that started out slow and sweet, but quickly turned passionate and needy. I grabbed his arms to steady myself because Steed was making my entire world wobble.

His tongue felt like it was everywhere. Over my lips, dancing with my own, exploring my mouth like he'd never kissed me before. It was a mind-blowing kiss. He hadn't even touched my body anywhere other than my face, and my core was pulsing.

When he finally pulled back, I dragged in a breath. My heart beat like crazy.

"You're my everything," I managed to whisper.

"Now maybe Gina will get the picture that I'm not interested in her."

I pinched my brows then looked over his shoulder. She was standing at the front entrance of the school with two other moms. Steed must have seen her when he turned to walk to his truck.

Focusing back on him, I snickered, "Let's hope."

CHAPTER 29

Steed

Paxton quickly changed into jeans and a long sleeve T-shirt when I told her to dress casual and warm. She packed an overnight bag at my request and bounced down the stairs, the smile on her face evidence of how happy she was. I loved seeing that light shine in her eyes.

"Ready!" she said. "Now, will you tell me where we're going?"

"Nope."

She playfully slapped me on the arm. "Brat. Why won't you tell me your plan?"

"Because it's a surprise. I thought you loved surprises."

Laughing, Paxton nodded. "I do!"

Taking her bag out of her hands, I winked. "All right, then let's get the show on the road."

First place on my lists of stops was the new store Paxton talked about checking out every time we passed it. Pulling up in front of the store, I parked. She instantly got excited.

"Oh, Steed! You brought me to the new little store! I've been dying to go in and see if I could find something for Chloe's room. It's so bare, and I was thinking we could redecorate it for Christmas."

I stilled, my heart pounding in my chest. This woman never ceased to amaze me. She never thought about herself, always others, and the fact that she was thinking about Chloe and making her happy made me fall in love with her even more. I didn't think it would be possible to love her any harder, but she kept proving me wrong.

Paxton's smile faded as she looked at me. "I mean, if you'd rather have Amelia or your mom plan something I totally understand."

Her words jerked me back to reality. "What? No! I want you to do what you want to the house. To Chloe's room. She'd love it if you decorated it."

The corners of her mouth rose again. "Okay, you worried me when you went still."

I took her hand and brought it to my lips. Kissing it gently, I said, "You amaze me. That's all."

Her eyes shined bright with happiness.

"Let's go shopping," I said, kissing her hand once more.

Two hours later I was walking out of the store with my arms loaded with bags.

"I can't believe we found all that stuff!" Paxton said with a fist pump. She opened the back door of my truck, and I started piling the bags on the seat.

"I can't believe we were in that store for two hours," I groaned then sighed.

Her hand moved across my back, causing my body to come to life, and my dick to do a little twitch in my pants. With a blushing expression, she uttered, "I promise I'll make it up to you later."

Turning to her, I grinned. "Want to shop some more?"

She laughed and lifted on her tiptoes to kiss me. After a quick peek, she asked, "Now what?"

"Now we head to the next location."

Paxton placed her hands on her hips and frowned. She looked so damn cute I had to fight the urge to take her into my arms and dry hump her.

"Trust me," I replied, placing a kiss on her lips.

"Always," she replied, making my heart soar.

After helping her into the truck, I walked around the front, slowing so I could send off a text.

Me: *How's it going?*

Mom: *All done! I have the basket packed and put it in your refrigerator. Trevor set everything else up with the help of Mitchell and Cord, but I'm afraid we can't pull Cord away from it.*

I laughed.

Me: *Tell him I'll kick his ass if he's not out of there by later this evening.*

Mom: *Watch your mouth, Steed Jonathan Parker*

When I glanced up, Paxton was staring at me through the driver's side window with a sexy grin.

I jumped into the truck and flashed her a quick grin. I loved how she reacted not only to my touch, but when I smiled at her.

"Who were you texting?" Paxton asked.

"Mom."

Her brow lifted. "Your mom? Is she in on something?"

I nodded. "Yep."

Dropping back in her seat, she chuckled. "So let me ask you something."

"Go for it, pumpkin."

"Did you arrange for the auntie day with Amelia and Chloe?"

Peeking at her, I winked. Her teeth sunk into her bottom lip while she stared.

"Keep looking at me like that, Paxton, and I'm going to pull over and drag you over here and sink you down onto me."

"That doesn't sound like a bad idea."

Lust raced through my body and went straight to my dick. *Damn, this girl makes me horny as hell. I can't get enough of her.*

"I'll give you one hint," I said as I pulled out onto the main road.

She scooted in her seat, and I could feel her eyes on me. "Okay! I'm ready for it."

"We're going to be eating."

When I glanced over to her, her finger was tapping on her lips like she was in deep thought. "An early dinner?"

"Maybe."

"Well, it was a half day at school today. You knew I would eat lunch early, so I'm going to guess that your mom prepared dinner for us, or she made us reservations somewhere." She shook her head. "No, no. I'm not dressed nice enough to go out to eat."

I laughed. "Why don't you sit back and relax. You'll find out soon enough."

She huffed. "The only way I can truly relax is if your hands are on my body."

My head snapped over to her. Jesus. She was looking at me with the sexiest grin. "Don't tempt me to pull over, Paxton."

Her hand covered her heart, and she gasped. "Me! Tempt you? I wouldn't think of it."

CHAPTER 30

Paxton

It didn't take long to figure out we were heading back to the ranch.

"So…we're going back to your place? What exactly were you planning on eating?"

He slammed on the brakes and threw the truck into park on the side of the street. Throwing the door open, I watched Steed get out of his truck and round the front.

Oh, shit. What did I do?

I unbuckled, knowing what that look in his eyes meant. Steed opened the door, took my hand and pulled me out of the truck.

"W-what are you doing?" I asked, my heart pounding, and my stomach pulling with the hope that he was going to take me right here.

"I'm going to fuck you because you're driving me crazy with the little comments you keep making."

I laughed nervously. "What if someone drives up?"

"They won't," he said as he unbuckled his jeans.

With shaking fingers, I did the same, kicking one of my boots off in the process so I could get my jeans down one leg. I knew how this looked. Pulling over, still dressed and dying to have him inside of me. But Steed didn't seem to be bothered so neither was I. This man did things to me. Made me crazy with desire and besides, I'd waited ten years to have him again.

Steed pushed his pants down, allowing his ample dick to spring out, and causing me to run my tongue over my lips. Reaching into his back pocket, he pulled out his wallet and fished out a condom.

My jeans were off one leg and I was practically panting with need as I watched Steed roll the condom on.

"Are you horny, Paxton?"

I nodded. "I have been since I saw you standing in the doorway of my classroom."

Two of his fingers slipped inside me, causing me to inhale sharply.

"You're always so ready for me, baby."

My hands went to his shoulders. "Yes. So ready."

Where did this version of me come from? The need to have Steed inside was so strong it almost scared me. I knew he wouldn't hurt me again. Still, it was a reminder of how much I loved this man and needed him in my world.

He grabbed my hips and lifted me like I weighed nothing. When I slowly sank down onto him, Steed let out a long low hissed, "Fuck yes."

My head dropped back as I adjusted to him stretching me. He was so big, and I could feel the aftermath of our love making in the ache between my legs for days after. And knowing it was caused by the man I loved made it that much better.

"I've been dying to be inside of you, Pax. I hate not having you in my bed every night."

Slowly, he started to move. I used my hands on his shoulders to help me meet his thrusts.

"Yes," I panted. It was hard to think, let alone speak. When Steed made love to me, I was lost to him heart and soul. Nothing else in this world mattered. It was simply me and him.

His kissed me and that triggered both of us. I couldn't get him deep enough. He couldn't get close enough. He started to move faster. Harder. Pulling out and pushing in so deep I fought to keep my moans in. After all, sound carries in the country.

"Son-of-a-bitch. I need to get deeper, baby," he whispered on my lips.

My chest was heaving as his mouth moved along my neck. I hated that we had layers of clothes separating us, yet at the same time it was hot as hell the way he took me against his truck. At three in the afternoon.

Yes. Hot. As. Hell.

"Paxton, baby, I need you to come. I can't hold off…any longer."

I didn't want him to stop. Steed inside of me was my favorite thing ever. Whether he was making slow sweet love to me, or fucking me.

It all felt so good.

He grabbed my ass and pounded into me harder. Deeper. And I fell. So fast and so hard I saw stars across my eyelids.

"I'm coming!" I cried out, not caring if my words traveled on the wind. Steed pushed in and let out the sexiest moan I'd ever heard. Maybe it was a grunt. I couldn't tell and I didn't care. It was laced with pleasure and lust. He dropped his mouth onto mine and kissed me as we both came.

When he finally stopped moving, we stood there for a few moments. Steed's forehead rested against mine, our breath labored.

"Why is every time with you so damn amazing?"

I chuckled. "I could ask you the same thing."

His blue eyes met mine. "You're amazing."

My heart melted. "You've already told me that."

"And I'll tell you every day at least once a day for the rest of our lives. I love you so much."

"I love you too."

When he finally pulled out of me, I whimpered. Then I realized he had just taken me up against his truck in the middle of a pasture where anyone could have driven up.

My face heated. I quickly got my jeans on as Steed took care of the condom.

When he walked back, he grinned from ear to ear. "You're blushing, Pax."

Covering my cheeks with my hands, I laughed. "We just had sex out in the open."

His hands landed on my hips, dragging me closer. Pressing his lips to mine, he whispered, "I can't control myself around you. Never could and pretty damn sure that will never change."

I beamed as I wrapped my arms around his neck and kissed him. A honking horn had us both drawing back, horror etched on our faces. Steed leaned back to look around his truck to see who was coming.

"Holy. Shit. That would have been awkward."

"What? Who is it?" I asked in a panicked voice.

Glancing at me, Steed laughed. "My dad."

"Your...dad?" I gasped with a strained voice.

"Yep!" He grabbed my hand and pulled me toward the approaching truck. I scanned both of us quickly to make sure everything was where it was supposed to be.

The Ford F-350 truck stopped right behind Steed's truck. Tripp was sitting in the passenger seat with a shit eating grin on his face.

They both got out and made their way over to us. "What's wrong? Something the matter with the truck?" John asked while reaching his hand out for Steed's.

"No, sir," Steed replied with a grin. "We were just stopped here. I had to take a piss."

Tripp looked at Steed and then me, but didn't utter a single word. I'm sure it was written all over my face.

I just had sex! Hot sex. Steamy hot sex.

John spoke with Steed about the financial books for the ranch while my thoughts wandered to a few minutes ago.

My eyes drifted to Tripp who was still standing there with that damn smile on his face. He totally knew what we had been up to. Thank goodness they hadn't driven up sooner.

"I told Rob you were itching to get up and fly next week. He said everything is up to date on the plane and to let him know which day you wanted the plane ready," John said.

I turned to them. "Fly?" I asked, confused.

Steed wove his fingers with mine. "Yeah, I have my pilot's license."

Steed flies planes? I knew his father had a pilot's license and he kept a pilot on his payroll, Rob Donovon.

But Steed is a pilot? I wasn't sure why that surprised me. He had mentioned wanting to fly back in high school.

He said it like it was no big deal. His father was giving him instructions to call Rob to let him know when he wanted to go up.

"Check out the back pasture while you're up there, will you?"

"Yeah, sure."

"Did you know he flew planes?" I asked Tripp.

He chuckled and nodded.

"Paxton, sweetheart, how are things at the school?" John asked, pulling my attention away from Tripp.

I lifted my hand and gave a thumbs-up. My nerves still rattled at how close he had come to catching us. "They're going good!"

"Chloe informed us last night that she wanted to be a teacher, like you."

I grinned like a silly fool. "She tells me that all the time. I adore her."

John gave me a loving smile. "She adores you, just like the rest of us." He glanced to Steed and winked. "All right, we were just coming over to tell Steed about the plane and that I need those numbers from last quarter when you get a chance. Y'all have a good day."

He leaned in and gave me a quick hug and kiss on the cheek. When he stepped back, he looked between us. "Behave now, you hear?"

My face heated. Tripp shook Steed's hand while laughing. "Yeah, y'all behave." He leaned in closer so John couldn't hear, even though he had already started back for the truck and probably wouldn't be able to anyway. "And you both have that 'just fucked' look on your faces. I'm guessing we nearly drove up on party time."

"Fuck you, Tripp," Steed quipped while giving him a playful push on his chest.

Walking backwards, Tripp threw up his hands in a defensive way. "Hey, I'm all for living in the moment!" He laughed hard and loud before slipping back into the truck.

When they turned around and headed back, I dropped my hands to my knees and dragged in a deep breath.

"That was close. Too close. Thank goodness your dad didn't drive up sooner."

Steed chuckled as he tugged me toward the passenger side of the truck. I opened the door and jumped in.

"He totally knew what we were doing."

My heart dropped, and my stomach twisted. "You think?"

"Hell yes. He isn't stupid. Besides, Tripp was right. You do have that 'just fucked' look on your face."

I buried my face in my hands and groaned. "Great. Just great. I'm never going to be able to look him in the face again!"

CHAPTER 31

Steed

Paxton stared out the window as I headed to my place. Every now and then she let out a sigh.

"Pax, stop worrying. I'm sure my parents know we're sleeping together. And the last time I checked, we were both twenty-eight years old."

Her head dropped back against the seat. "Ugh. I know, I know. I don't want your parents to think I'm a whore."

I parked, then turned off the truck and faced her. "Why in fuck's sake would they think that?"

She gave me a look that said I should know the answer to that question. "Steed, we had sex out in the open. For the whole world to see."

With a quick wink, I replied, "And it was hot as hell, admit it."

Her lower lip pulled in between her teeth. "I will admit it was hot. *Very* hot."

I flashed her a dimpled smile, and she practically melted in the seat. Damn, I loved this woman. "Come on, we're running behind schedule."

Paxton chuckled. "I didn't realize we were on a schedule. Was our little stop back there part of today's plan?"

"No. Our little love fest put us a bit behind, but I think we can make up the time."

She grinned and hopped out of the truck, not waiting for me to come around and get her door. We met in front of the truck, and I reached for her hand, guiding her into the house.

"So, you're a pilot?" she asked after we stepped through the front door.

"Yeah. I thought I told you. I took lessons in Oregon. Started out as a way to get my mind off..." My voice trailed off, and I stopped walking.

"Me?" she asked with sadness laced in her voice.

My heart wrenched, and I pulled her to me. "Yes, if I'm being honest. I'm sorry I was gone for so long."

A weak smile moved across her face. "I think we have established that. It's just that I hate..."

Lifting my hand, I brushed her hair back. "You hate what?"

Her eyes drifted down. I placed my finger on her chin and lifted them back to mine. "Pax, please tell me."

"I hate that we missed so much time together. That so many years were filled with sadness and anger." She shrugged. "The last few months have been so blissfully happy for me, I can't help but wonder what life would have been like had I not gotten—"

My finger moved to her lips. "Don't say that. This moment, right now with you, it's because of what happened ten years ago. We might have taken the long way, but we made it. We're together and nothing or no one will ever change that."

Her arms wrapped around my neck. "You're right!"

The love I felt for Paxton consumed my heart and soul, yet I fell in love with her a little more each day.

Taking her hand in mine, I pulled her towards the kitchen. "Come on. We're late."

Paxton grinned and let me guide her. We walked into the kitchen, and I smiled when I pulled the large basket out of the refrigerator.

"What's this?" she asked while walking over to me.

"Dinner," I responded. Her eyes lit up as they darted from the basket to me. I held my breath, waiting for her reaction.

"You had a picnic basket made up for dinner? Are we going on a picnic?"

I loved the excitement in her voice. One of Paxton's favorite things to do when we dated was to go on picnics. I'd talk Waylynn into packing us a lunch, and I'd surprise Paxton with different locations. I was almost positive one of those picnics was when we conceived our child.

"We are," I replied with a wink.

Paxton's face lit up like Christmas morning. I swore I could get drunk with happiness simply by watching her smile.

"Did Waylynn come in to make us dinner?" she asked with a chuckle.

"Not this time. Mom did it all. She was over the moon when I told her my plans."

She lifted a brow. "Dang, had I known your mom was in on this little secret date I would have pumped her for information."

Taking the large basket, I huffed. "All you would have had to do is bat those pretty eyes at her, and she would have caved. I think my mother is as happy as we are that we're together."

I took her hand in mine, and we headed back out to my truck.

"My mother is too. She's started asking questions again about why we broke up."

A slow heavy feeling settled into my chest. "Do you think you'll ever tell your parents?"

Paxton was silent for a few seconds before she answered me. "I think I will, when the time feels right. It hasn't yet."

Stopping at the passenger door, I faced her. "You don't have to tell them if you don't want."

Chewing on her lip, she nodded. "I feel guilty keeping it from them, but over the years it's been hard enough to think about, let alone tell them, and the longer I wait, the harder it is."

I placed my hand on the side of her face. "Pax," I breathed before lightly kissing her lips.

She grabbed my T-shirt as if she needed to steady herself. "My broken heart is nearly healed, Steed. But I think there is always going to be a void there. An ache that won't really ever go away because of our loss."

My eyes closed as my own ache seemed to throb a tad bit harder. Gazing into her eyes, I nodded. "I know. I feel the same way."

For a few moments we were lost in each other's eyes before Paxton smiled. "Let's go have a picnic. I'm starving."

I kissed her nose and held the door open for her. After putting the picnic basket into the backseat, I made my way to the driver's side and hopped in. I was hoping like hell Cord would be gone by the time we got there.

As we neared the picnic site my nerves started to rattle. I had no idea why I was so nervous. It wasn't like I hadn't just fucked her against the side of my truck.

No, that was exactly it. I'd been acting like a horny damn teenager for the last few months. I needed to shower her with love and affection. I needed Paxton to know it wasn't about the sex. Not that the sex wasn't fucking fantastic, but it was also something so much deeper.

Our love.

Paxton gasped as we drove up to the elaborate setup I had planned and my brothers had executed.

Holy shit. They didn't do this all on their own, did they?

The large blanket was laid out with a bunch of different sized pillows tossed on it. There was a bucket of ice sitting off to the side that should be holding the expensive-ass champagne in it. In the middle of the blanket was a bouquet of Paxton's favorite flowers, peonies.

Hung up a few feet in front of the blanket was a white sheet strung up by twine.

"Steed!" Paxton gasped as she threw the door to the truck open and headed to our setup.

I grinned when I saw the old, wooden box I had found in the barn; Paxton would love it. It held the brown bags filled with popcorn for the movie later.

Paxton hands were over her mouth. Her eyes glistened as she took it all in.

Her eyes captured mine. "You did this?"

I took a quick look around. "Well, I planned it all out, spent an entire day drawing it to perfection so Trevor would get it right. Cord and Mitchell helped too." Laughing, I shook my head. "They got it spot on."

She threw her body into mine. "It's perfect! Amazing! Beautiful!"

Wrapping my arms around her, I held her close. "There isn't anything I wouldn't do to make you happy, Paxton."

We stood there for a few minutes, simply holding each other. I was pretty sure Paxton was crying, but I knew they were happy tears. When she finally pulled back, our eyes locked. "You are the most amazing man I've ever met. This is so romantic, Steed."

I wiggled my eyebrows. "Wait until you see the movie I picked out."

She let out a chuckle. "Please tell me it's not porn!"

Laughing, I bent down and picked up the picnic basket I had set down earlier. "No! Well, unless Trevor switched out the movies which I could totally see him doing."

"So could I!" Paxton added with a shake of her head.

"Let's eat," I said as I guided her onto the blanket. I set everything out for dinner, making a mental note to check the DVD as soon as I got a chance to sneak over there.

Damn Trevor.

CHAPTER 320

Paxton

The moment I saw the picnic area set up, my breath caught in my chest and a warmth spread through my body. Steed had remembered how much I loved picnics. My cheeks heated thinking back to past picnics…

"Steed, this is all so amazing. I have to say though, with age comes better picnics!"

He laughed while taking out the plastic plates and silverware. My heart was beating faster simply from watching him. I loved how he took so much care planning this day. From shopping at a store I had been longing to go to, to setting up the perfect picnic. Right down to the movie later.

"Mom's fried chicken. Your favorite."

As if on cue, my stomach growled, and we both let out a chuckle.

"Fresh fruit. Yogurt dip, the kind Waylynn makes. I had to call her and ask for the recipe. Chloe helped make it last night for our 'special date' as she kept calling it."

I smiled as my chest fluttered. "She's so precious, Steed. You've done an amazing job raising her so far."

He stopped what he was doing and focused on me. "She loves you, Paxton. When we were mixing up the dip last night, she told me her biggest hope was for you to be her mommy."

My vision started to blur as happiness coursed through my body. "What…what did you say to her?"

"That I wanted that too. More than anything."

His words overwhelmed me with joy. I couldn't help but grin like a silly fool. "I want that too. I love her also, Steed, as if she was my own daughter."

Steed wiped my tears away with his thumb. "Thank you for loving her, Pax. You're an incredible woman, and I'm so thankful to know that you're in Chloe's life."

Oh dear.

My heart was hammering in my chest. A mixture of excitement, happiness, and fear swirled together. I longed for the day when Chloe called me something other than Paxton. Or when she came to me for advice. It also scared the crap out of me.

Steed had made it very clear that Chloe's mom was completely out of the picture. Would Chloe grow to resent me? Think I was the reason her mother gave her up?

"Stop overthinking whatever it is you're overthinking, Pax."

My head snapped up. "Huh?"

Steed poured a glass of champagne and handed it to me.

"You're overthinking something. I can see it on your face."

I gave him a weak grin. "You don't think Chloe will ever resent me, do you?"

He pulled his head back in surprise. "What on earth for?"

With a half shrug, I replied, "I don't know. Maybe she'll think I'm the reason her mother gave her up?"

Steed reached for my hands. The way his thumb slid over the top of my hand made my skin feel on fire.

"Paxton, Kim never wanted Chloe, and it wasn't hard for Chloe to figure out her mother didn't love her as much as I did. First, she wanted me because she knew my heart belonged to someone else. Then she wanted money. Chloe was an accident she never wanted, but used as a pawn in her twisted game. She's not going to resent you because she never truly knew what a loving mother was. We weren't ever a family. We were a nightmare. I'm so ..."

His voice cracked, and he had to clear it before going on. "I'm so glad Chloe is away from her."

"Me too," I murmured.

Steed shook his head and cleared his throat. "If I had only come back home sooner."

"No more what ifs. We have to both stop doing that. It's the past, and we need to focus on the future."

He flashed me a brilliant grin that made me dizzy and had me forgetting what we were even talking about.

Steed and I were soon lost in conversation as we ate the fried chicken and fruit. He talked about the ranch, I talked about the kids at school. We laughed about Trevor and discussed Corina. It felt as if there wasn't a ten-year void at all. We fit into each other's worlds so perfectly. It was fate.

"Do you think I should invite Corina for Thanksgiving? I'm not sure if Tripp would mind or not," I asked while I waited for Steed to take out what he said was the ultimate dessert.

"I'm not really sure what is going on between her and Tripp. He likes her, but I think he likes her because he knows Mitchell likes her."

With a frown, I exhaled a frustrated breath. "I think Corina really likes Mitchell. I mean, she slept with him and Corina is not that kind of girl. At all."

Steed opened the container lids off of two pieces of apple pie.

"Oh my goodness. Please tell me that's your mom's. Please."

Laughing, he nodded. "She made it just for you."

My mouth was watering as I stared down at the yummy pie. Steed handed me a fork, and we both dug in. I let out a moan as I took my first bite. "So good."

"Yeah, it is."

Stretching my legs out, I set my fork down. "But I'm stuffed and I want to save room for popcorn!"

"We're going to go for a ride next."

I lifted my brow. "Mr. Parker, please tell me you are talking about a ride in your truck."

He chuckled and looked at his watch. "No, our ride should be arriving here any minute."

Now I was intrigued.

"Back to Corina. I think you should invite her. I'd hate to think she was all alone on Thanksgiving and clearly Tripp isn't going to invite her."

"I don't want to cause problems between your brothers."

"Honestly, I have no idea what's going on. I was surprised Tripp missed the fact that the girl he is dating wasn't leaving town. Regardless if it is casual dating or not."

"I don't think they are serious," I replied, feeling a heaviness in my heart. I really needed to sit and talk to my best friend.

"Then invite her. Who gives a shit what's going on between Tripp and Mitchell? Why should Corina be alone?"

Hearing a whistle coming from behind us, I turned to see Trevor leading Lady and Allure. Focusing on Steed, I grinned as I chuckled. "*That* kind of riding!"

He stood and winked as he helped me up. "Unless you'd rather do the other kind of riding your dirty mind was thinking of."

"I find that statement coming from you rather funny."

Steed laughed and led us to the horses.

"Didn't even hear you pull up, Trev," Steed said, reaching his hand out to shake his brother's.

"I'm stealthy like that," he replied with a sweet smile. "I'll meet you at sundown in the spot?"

Running his hands over his horse, Steed responded with a nod then answered, "Yeah. That sounds good."

"The spot?" I asked with my head tilted.

"Don't worry your pretty little head, Paxton," Trevor said. "My brother's got everything well planned out."

"I see that," I said with a huge grin. Steed helped me get up onto Allure. Even though I was capable of getting on a horse by myself, I liked having him help me. I'd missed that attention from a man.

Trevor lifted his hand and called out over his shoulder, "You kids have fun! Remember, practice safe sex!"

"Shut the hell up, Trevor. You asshole!" Steed shouted at his retreating brother.

Some things never changed, especially the way the Parker brothers interacted with each other. One minute they would be the best of friends, the next they were telling each other to fuck off. I rolled my eyes and let out a giggle as I gave Allure a small squeeze to get her going.

We rode next to each other in silence for the longest time. I loved being out on the ranch. I always had. The peacefulness was good for my soul. The sound of nature worked its way into my mind, relaxing me along with the easy stride Allure was keeping next to Lady.

"Penny for your thoughts."

Steed's warm voice penetrated my thoughts. I turned my head and we smiled at each other. "Just how peaceful it is out here. I love it so much."

"So do I."

"Did you enjoy living in Oregon?" I asked.

With a harsh laugh, he shook his head. "Hated it. Every single minute. Had I not met Kim I'm positive I would have been back home sooner. Probably after school."

I nodded. The thought made me feel sick. Steed only went out with Kim because Joe's mother spread false things about our relationship to Melanie. My body shook with anger.

No. No looking back, Paxton. Only to the future.

And what an amazing future it would be.

CHAPTER 33

Steed

My heart soared hearing Paxton say how much she loved the ranch. Spending the day with her like this was something I wanted to do more often. Having her near me made me happier. I always felt so light on my feet with her around me.

"So, where are we going? This spot of yours?"

Smiling, I replied, "It's actually *our* spot. We've been there a number of times. We were just in my truck."

She gasped. "The lookout?"

I nodded. "I thought we could watch the sunset."

Her eyes lit up, leaving me breathless. Paxton was never hard to please. She enjoyed the simplest of things and appreciated them. Unlike Kim. They were two complete opposites. Having Paxton in Chloe's life was going to be so good for her.

"I love that idea," Paxton softly said.

"We better pick it up some, or we'll miss it."

We set off in a trot, heading toward the spot where I had originally given her the promise ring, which I noticed she had started wearing again.

Sliding off my horse, I walked up to Paxton's and helped her down. She wrapped her arms around my neck, and we were soon lost in a kiss.

My body warmed as I deepened our connection. My hand slid under her shirt to feel her warm skin against mine.

When we both pulled back for air, I leaned my forehead against hers. "You make me feel so alive."

Her arms tightened around me. "I'm so glad you gave me a ride home that night."

Wrapping her tightly, I picked her up and held her for a few seconds. God, how I loved this woman. I set her down and brushed a stray hair away from her face.

"Come on. Help with the blanket."

Her brows lifted. "Blanket?"

I laced my fingers with hers and walked to the side of Lady where Trevor had packed what I asked him to.

"And wine," I added with a smirk.

"Why, Mr. Parker, aren't you the romantic one."

"Well, I figured wine, old blanket, sunset. I couldn't ask for a better scene to make love to you."

Her lips parted before a slow smile slipped over her beautiful face. My heart hammered like it always did before I made love to her. The need to have her body against mine was growing by the second. My fingers ached to touch her and make her call out my name.

"Steed," she softly breathed.

I handed her the wine and pointed to her side saddle. "Glasses are in yours. Will you grab them, and I'll lay out the blanket?"

She nodded and did as I asked.

Finding the perfect spot would be key. We were at one of the highest points on the ranch. It over looked the Frio river below and the vast hill country. It was one of my favorite spots on the ranch. Paxton and I used to come here often. I couldn't count on my hands how many times I made love to her in the back of my truck at this location. Under the stars, under the sun, in the rain. The memories coursed through my mind, making my body heat.

After laying out the blanket, I motioned for her to sit. When her hand touched mine I felt her love zip through my body.

"This is all so wonderful. I've had such an amazing day today."

A warmth filled my chest. "So have I."

Pulling her over to me, she sat between my legs, her head resting on my chest as we looked out over the hill country. A warm contentment settled in my chest. This woman was my life. Everything I ever wanted or needed was in my arms, and I had no intentions of ever letting her go.

"This has always been one of my favorite spots," she said while her hands moved lazily over my legs, and she melted into my body.

"Mine too."

She tilted her head and looked up at me. Her eyes danced with joy. "I haven't been this happy in a long time. Thank you."

Heat raced through my veins as my body ached to be closer to her. "I'm going to spend the rest of my life showing you how happy you make me, Pax."

Her skin flushed, and her smile left me dizzy and breathless.

I guided her gently down on the blanket, our gaze never breaking. Slowly moving my hands down her jeans, I pulled her boots off one at a time. The way she was staring had my heart racing.

"When we were apart, Pax, I felt so lost. Every little thing I saw reminded me of you. Not a day went by when I didn't think about you. The only thing that kept me going was Chloe."

Paxton's hand came up to the side of my face. Her eyes were a window into my own soul. I knew she had felt the same way.

"I will never be lost again because when I'm with you…" I paused as I pulled her jeans and panties down and off her legs. I licked my lips as I ran my fingers along her soft beautiful skin. Her body trembled, and I couldn't help my smile. I spoke again after getting my emotions in check. "When I'm with you, I feel whole. And so utterly happy I want to shout it from the highest place I can find."

She smiled as she reached for my T-shirt and pulled it over my head. I followed her lead, pulling her up and removing her shirt. My fingers traced along her bra and her body erupted in goosebumps. I slid my hand behind her and unclasped her bra in one quick movement.

"You're a little too good at that Mr. Parker," she said with a stern look.

"Well you see, I had this hot girlfriend in high school, and I used to take her bra off all the time. She had the most perfect set of tits that I needed them in my hands all the time. Practice made perfect, I guess."

She playfully pushed me away with a totally fake stern look. I stood and kicked off my boots and took off my own jeans. Her brows lifted and her lips pressed tightly together as I stood before her naked.

"You better hope your daddy doesn't come driving up."

Lowering my body, I pulled her to me, causing her to let out a small scream. "I paid Trevor hefty to not let anyone near until the sun dips below those hills."

"Is that so? What were you planning on doing up here with me?" she asked. Her nose scrunching up in the most adorable way.

"Isn't it obvious, Paxton? I'm going to make love to my girl as the sun sets."

Her smile faded and her eyes glistened. "That's the same thing you said to me the first time we were up here."

Running my nose over her jaw line, I lifted my head and kissed her forehead. "I know. I remember."

Her arms wrapped around my neck, pulling me closer to her body. I could feel the heat between her legs as she drew me close.

"Baby, I need to get a condom," I spoke against her lips.

She nodded, letting go of me. Turning, I grabbed my jeans and fished one out my wallet—only one left, but that was all I needed.

I tore it open, quickly covered my dick, and moved back over her. I teased her entrance with my tip while pressing my lips to hers.

Paxton wrapped her arms around me, pulling me to her. The kiss deepened, and I pushed a little further in before pulling back out. I reached my hand down and slipped two fingers inside.

"Fuck… You're so wet, baby."

Her eyes closed and she lifted her hips, silently begging me to enter her body.

I brought my hand back up and rested on my elbows, both hands cradling her head. Our gazes locked, and I slowly pushed into her.

"Steed," she gasped as we became one. I let out a soft moan and stayed perfectly still for a few moments…needing to feel her pussy throbbing around me.

Christ, this is perfection.

Neither one of us had to say a word. We were both lost within each other. I slowly pulled out and pushed back in, causing Paxton to dig her nails into my back.

My lips moved across her neck softly and slowly before I kissed the soft skin under her ear. "Paxton Monroe. You are my life. The only woman I will ever love."

CHAPTER 34

Paxton

My body was spent. Two rounds of amazing sex with Steed and countless orgasms today, and I was a puddle of mushy happiness. We laid on the blanket, our bodies tangled up with one another, as we stared out at the beautiful view in front of us.

"How do you feel?" Steed asked while his fingertips moved lightly across my arm.

"Amazing. Wonderful. Marvelous. Fantastic. Satisfied. Relaxed."

The rumble in his chest from his laughter moved through my body. I had never felt so elated in my life.

"I'm glad you feel all of that."

"And more," I added. "So much more."

Our heads turned to each other. The love in Steed's eyes warmed my heart. He gently traced his fingertip over my face, lips, and jaw. Everywhere he touched I was on fire. Not to mention it sent my stomach into a frenzy of twists and turns.

"I like the more part the best," he softly said.

Reaching down, he wove his fingers with mine. The sun was sinking farther down the sky.

"May I ask you something, Pax?"

"Of course you can," I answered as I looked at him.

"The tattoo on your foot, when did you get it?"

Glancing down at the scrolled tattoo that read "Let It Be", I drew in a deep breath and blew it out.

"I got it after my last counseling session. I picked that phrase because it had finally hit me that what I really needed to do was let go. That I couldn't let my sadness and anger control my life. I needed to let it be. Go the way fate was taking me and know that it would all work out someday."

Steed sat up and ran his finger over the tattoo before glancing back at me. "I love you. I love your strength, your faith, and your kind soul. You're amazing."

Smiling, I sat up and placed my hand on the side of his face. "Thank you for that."

His hand cupped the back of my neck, drawing me closer to him. The kiss was soft and gentle. It was the perfect way to end this part of the evening.

"We should get dressed before Trevor shows up."

He nodded, but the disappointment in his eyes was evident.

"Yeah, I guess you're right."

We both stood and silently got dressed. Then we settled back on the blanket, me between his legs with my head resting against his solid chest. The sun was touching the hills and turning the sky the most beautiful colors. Pinks and reds spread across the horizon in beautiful wisps of clouds. It was stunning.

The sound of two vehicles pulling up had us both turning.

"Who's driving your truck?" I asked as Steed stood and helped me up.

A wide smile curled his mouth. "Mitchell. He's got Chloe."

"Chloe?" I asked with my own grin.

"Yeah, she's going to join us for movie night. I thought she might like to do that with us."

Oh. My. Gosh. This man. Swoon-a-thon going on here.

The way he loved his daughter did crazy things to my heart. I fell even more in love with him knowing he wanted to make Chloe a part of our day.

"That sounds amazing!"

I took his hand in mine and kissed the back of it. "Steed, Chloe is very much a part of our relationship and in no way do I resent anything about that. It warms my heart to see you with Chloe and know how much you love her. She is a part of my heart now too, and I'd give my last breath for her."

Steed's eyes widened in surprise before they filled with tears. He opened his mouth to say something, but instead of speaking, he closed his eyes and slowly shook his head before catching my gaze.

"I love you so fucking much." He pulled my body against his and pressed his mouth to mine. The trucks stopped, and I had thought he would let me go, especially knowing Chloe was here. But he didn't. He held me tighter and kissed me deeper. By the time he was done I was dizzy and had to hold onto his arms to steady myself.

"Wow," I breathed.

He grinned. "I want her to see what true love is."

Oh lord. There goes my heart again.

"Daddy! Paxton!" Chloe said as she ran up to us. Instead of hugging just Steed, her little arms wrapped around both of us. We dropped to her level at the same time. I couldn't help but smile when I saw how happy she looked, a grin spread wide across her face.

"I had the best day with Aunt Meli and then Uncle Mitchell picked me up and took me for ice cream! But it wasn't at the store!"

Steed pulled his head back with a surprised expression. "It wasn't? Where was it?" he asked as he glanced up to Mitchell.

"It was this farm house. Daddy! They made the ice cream and asked me what kind I wanted and if I wanted anything in it!"

"What did you get?" I asked.

Chloe smiled. "Chocolate with strawberries cause that's your favorite, Paxton. And I want to be just like you and grow up to marry a cowboy like my daddy!"

I was overcome with emotion, and it took every ounce of strength I had not to cry.

Taking her hands in mine, I replied, "I love that plan, Chloe. So very much."

Steed pulled her to him, making her squeal in delight. "Let me help your uncles, then I have a surprise for my two favorite girls. But no more talk of you growing up."

Chloe kissed him on the cheek, then reached for my hand. My heart fluttered, and I had to put my other hand over my stomach to calm the butterflies. This sweet little girl held a piece of my heart so strongly I was almost brought to tears.

I knew Chloe had never had a real mother figure in her life, and I was going to do everything in my power to be there for her, always.

"Did you and Daddy have fun on your day together?" Chloe asked.

Gazing down at her big blue eyes, I smiled. "We did. Your daddy is very romantic."

She nodded. "He likes sunsets and always says they remind him of his special spot on the ranch. Is this his special spot? Is that why he brought you here?"

My eyes swept over to where Steed was helping Mitchell and Trevor put Allure into the trailer. I felt breathless watching him. "Yes, Chloe Cat. Your daddy used to bring me here all the time. It was kind of our spot."

When I glanced back down at her, she had a dreamy expression on her face. "I hope I can marry a boy someday who is like my daddy."

Dropping down to meet her eye to eye, I pulled her in for a hug. "Me too, baby girl."

When she leaned back, her little eyes looked deep into mine. "I love you, Paxton."

I almost fell on my ass. Her words hit me square in the chest and dug themselves deep within my heart, and I was positive they would stay buried deeply forever. Lifting my hand to the side of her sweet little face, I let out a shaky breath. "Oh, Chloe. I love you too."

Her little arms wrapped around my neck and she whispered, "I pray each night you'll be my mommy. I hope God hears me."

Closing my eyes, I struggled to keep the tears back. "I pray for the same thing, Chloe."

"Does he hear us?"

I'd never in my life experienced this feeling before. A love so pure and real it would forever own my heart. "I *know* he hears us."

When she pulled back, I opened my eyes to see Steed standing behind Chloe. The way he stared at me made my chest squeeze, and my heart take a dive straight to my stomach. I prayed I hadn't said anything I shouldn't have, but I wanted to be honest with Chloe. Dropping to his knees, Steed wrapped us both in his arms and slid his hand behind my neck. Pulling me closer, he kissed my lips.

"I love you both."

Chloe giggled. "Kiss me, Daddy! Kiss me!"

Jumping up, Steed picked up Chloe and kissed her with a quick peck on the mouth then kissed her cheek.

"Give me some of that loving!" Mitchell said as he took Chloe and started flying her around like a plane. She laughed and cried out as Mitchell traded her off to Trevor.

I smiled as I watched three of the Parker brothers totally get lost in the love of one little girl. And oh how easy it was to get lost in Chloe's love.

CHAPTER 35

Paxton

Chloe and I snuggled up to Steed as we watched *Brother Bear*. The temperature had dropped some so we had two quilts pulled over us. I was munching on popcorn and so was Steed.

When Chloe found out she was part of Steed's special day with me I thought she was going to burst from happiness. She got to pick out the movies, and so far we had watched *Frozen*, to which Steed knew the words to every song. I wasn't sure if I was impressed or turned on. No. I knew I was for sure turned on.

And now *Brother Bear* was playing. I couldn't believe how engrossed I was in the movie. Steed bumped my arm, and I nodded, not wanting to miss anything.

"Pax, Chloe's asleep."

Pulling my eyes from the movie, I saw that Chloe was snuggled up into the side of Steed.

Lucky little thing.

I smiled. "I'm so completely jealous of her right now it's unreal."

He grinned. "You could stay the night, you know."

I let my smile fade some. "I don't want Chloe to know I'm staying the night."

"You could sneak out before morning and go into the guest bedroom."

My teeth dug into my lip as I thought about it. "Is that why you had me pack a bag?"

He nodded.

Bouncing my eyes back and forth from Chloe to Steed, I muttered, "I don't know."

Steed jutted his lip out to pout. "Please? Spend the night with me. I want to sleep with you in my arms."

Focusing on Chloe, I took a deep breath. "Okay, but we have to be careful. I don't want her knowing I'm sleeping with her dad. It might be weird for her."

With a nod, Steed grabbed the back of my neck and pulled me in for a quick peck on the lips. "Come on. Let's head back to my place."

"What about all of this?" I asked as I stood and Steed carefully picked up Chloe without waking her.

"Trevor will get it. Trust me, he got paid hefty for helping me with all of this. Besides, he's working at the bar tonight. If I know Trevor, he'll bring a girl back here and fuck her."

I snarled. "Nice."

Steed chuckled and shrugged the best he could while carrying Chloe to his truck. "Just keeping it real."

"Uh-huh. Well, I was perfectly fine not knowing that bit of information."

After slipping Chloe into the back seat, Steed quietly shut the door and grabbed me. His hands were all over me. In my hair, caressing my breasts and finally under my shirt. "God it's been so fucking hard to keep my hands off you. I want to bury myself inside of you and stay there all night."

My chest heaved as I fought to get air. His words sent heat immediately to my throbbing center. No matter how many times we were together, the need for more was always there.

"I think that sounds like a plan," I breathed back.

After Steed had put Chloe to bed, he grabbed my hand and dragged me downstairs to the master bedroom. We shed our clothes like it had been weeks since we were together. The desire was thick in the room, and I wondered how long sex with Steed would be like this. Would we ever get tired of each other? Would the need to have him inside me lessen over time?

His lips were all over me. My mouth, neck, nipples, stomach, inside of my thigh. I dug my fingers into his hair and pulled him close to the pulsing ache between my legs.

"Ohmygawd…Steed. I want you."

And before I knew it, Steed's mouth was over my hot center, and I was covering my mouth to bury my cries of passion.

A sweet darkness swept over me as I floated on a cloud of utter bliss. I barely felt him moving over me. The sound of a condom ripping open brought me back down to earth. I was still reeling from my orgasm when Steed pushed inside of me. His slow lovemaking from earlier was gone. He was desperate for me, and I loved every second of it.

"That's it baby. Fuuck. That feels so good."

My hips met his thrust for thrust. The buildup of another orgasm was right at the edge.

"Goddamn it, Paxton. Baby, I need you to come."

Just as my release let loose, so did Steed's. His mouth clamped over mine, taking in my moans of pleasure.

Then the knock on the door had us both stilling.

Shit. I prayed like hell he had locked the door.

Steed pulled out of me and ripped the condom off so fast it was unreal. I rolled over and off the bed, hitting the floor with a small thump.

"You can...Pax? Where did you go?"

"Down here!" I whispered.

Steed walked around the bed and looked down at me. "What in the fuck are you doing on the floor?"

"Daddy?"

The door to his bedroom opened, and Steed grabbed the sheet and wrapped it around him.

"Hey, pumpkin. What's...um... What's...ah."

I covered my mouth with my hand to keep from laughing. Steed was totally flustered.

"Why do you have your sheet wrapped around you, Daddy?"

"I um... I couldn't find my sleeping pants, baby. What's going on? Why are you out of bed?"

The bed moved, and I pictured Chloe crawling up on it. "I can't sleep. Daddy, we need to talk."

My heart dropped. That sounded serious...and cute as well.

"Um, okay, pumpkin. Want to go to your room and talk?"

"No. This is okay here."

I smiled and dropped my head. I was so going to be busted. And I was completely naked.

Shit!

The bed dropped more as Steed sat down.

NO! I need clothes. A blanket. I need out of this room!

"You sure you don't want to go back up to your room?"

"I'm sure."

I sighed internally.

"What's on your mind, pumpkin?"

"Paxton."

I froze and my breath stilled.

Oh. No. She hates me!

"What about Paxton?"

"Daddy, I really want her to be my mommy. Why can't you marry her?"

A huge smile moved across my face. I spied one of Steed's T-shirts. Reaching for it, I carefully slipped it on.

"I can marry her."

"Well, why don't you?"

I covered my mouth with my hand. *Oh, how I love this little girl.* I could see it in her eyes how much she longed for a mother. Amelia told me how Chloe talked about me and asked a million and one questions each time.

"It's not that simple, baby."

"How come? Don't you love her?"

"I love her very much. But when the time comes for me to ask her, I want to make it special. And that means planning."

She giggled. "Like how you planned her special day today?"

"Yes! Exactly like that."

Steed's bed was tall enough for me to sit up without my head showing. Pulling my knees to my chest, I tried to still my racing heart.

"Daddy?"

"Yes, pumpkin?"

"Will Paxton want to give me a baby brother or sister?"

Tears streamed down my face. It was in that moment that it all made sense. Everything that happened ten years ago…right up until this moment. This little girl was meant to be in our world. She was destined to be in *my* world and even though she wasn't my child, I would love her like she was.

"I know she will want to."

"Will she love her baby more than me?"

Burying my hands in my face, I silently sobbed. It took every-thing not to jump up and pull her into my arms. I wanted to reassure her I would always love her no matter how many kids Steed and I had together.

"Oh, Chloe, no. She would love you both equally."

"But…but I'm not really her baby."

My face was soaked with tears as I dropped my head back against the bed.

"That doesn't matter, Chloe. Paxton loves you so much, and I know there is nothing more that she wants than to have you as a daughter. Just because you didn't grow in her belly doesn't mean that she won't love you like I do. She wants to be your mommy as much as you want her to be."

A silence lingered, and I held my breath.

"I can't wait to call her mommy. She's the prettiest girl in town, Daddy."

Steed laughed. "I know she is. And she's mine."

Chloe laughed. "Silly, Daddy. She's *ours*."

And there it was. I slowly fell to my side and laid in a fetal position, happiness swirling around me as I tried to hold back sobs. I couldn't believe a few months back my heart had a black void in it. Now...now it was overflowing with so much love and happiness I was completely overwhelmed.

"That's right, Chloe. She's ours. Now let's get you up to bed."

Five minutes later Steed walked back into his bedroom. I was sitting on his bed with my knees pulled to my chest, sobbing like an idiot.

Fear hit Steed's face as he rushed to me. "Christ. Please tell me those are happy tears."

I nodded. "V-very...h-happy...t-t-tears!"

He laughed and pulled me up in front of him. His thumbs attempted to wipe away my endless tears.

The way his blue eyes searched my face before he chuckled and those dimples peeked out from his unshaven face caused my knees to go weak.

Reaching into his pocket, Steed pulled out a small little band. "Chloe thought the reason I wasn't asking you to marry me was because I didn't have a ring."

Drifting my gaze to the band, I grinned. "So she gave you one?"

He chuckled as he lifted my hand up. He slipped the band next to the promise ring I wore on my left hand. "I'll just leave this here for right now."

Burying my face into his chest, I broke down crying. Again.

"Shhh…baby, it's okay. Please don't cry."

Before I knew it, we were on the bed, and I was snuggled into Steed's side. Contentment wrapped around me like a perfectly fitted glove.

Pressing his lips to my forehead, Steed whispered, "Sleep, baby. Get some sleep."

CHAPTER 36

Steed

I walked into my father's office and stopped when I saw Trevor shaking his head and cursing.

"What's wrong?" I asked.

"Fucking hogs got in the north pasture and tore it to shit."

I panicked. "What? When?"

"Must have been yesterday. It almost looks like a damn pattern."

My hand clutched my chest as I fell back into one of the chairs in front of my father's desk. "Thank fuck," I breathed.

"What?" my father asked, giving me a confused look. "What in the hell do we have to be thankful for, Steed? I don't want that many hogs on our ranch."

Before I had a chance to say anything, Chloe came running into the office. "Granddaddy! I'm ready for our date!"

My father all but melted into a puddle when Chloe jumped into his arms.

"Our movie date! It's time?" he asked with a huge grin.

"Yep! Grammy's ready, so come on!" Chloe grabbed his hand and pulled at him. "Come on! Come on! We don't want to be late."

Glancing back at us, Dad smiled. "We'll figure this out tomorrow."

"You want me to go plow up the rest of the field?" Trevor asked.

"Why don't we go tomorrow and take a closer look?" I suggested.

"That sounds good. Excuse me boys, I've got a date with my granddaughter."

Trevor and I stood and watched Chloe drag Dad out of his office. He stopped to grab his cowboy hat off the hat rack before he was tugged out the door.

"Damn, she's cute as hell, Steed. She's got Dad and Mom wrapped around her finger. Not to mention Mitchell, Cord, and Amelia. Tripp's never around long enough."

I laughed. "Yeah, she has us all wrapped around her finger."

Trevor slapped my back. "That's the gods honest truth right there. All right, I'm calling it a damn day and taking the rest of the afternoon off. You still going flying?"

"Yeah. Hey Trev, before you leave let me ask you something."

He stopped and motioned for me to talk with a jerk of his head. "Has Tripp mentioned anything to you about Corina?"

He shrugged. "Not really. I mean I know he called dibs on her and that pissed Mitchell off, but then I'm pretty sure Mitchell and Corina hooked up the night you came to the bar to chase off the accountant. I mean as the night went on they were all over each other and Mitchell took her home. Or she took him home. I don't know."

"You ever tell Tripp about it?"

He shook his head. "Nah. That shit's between them. If you ask me though, Tripp's only dating her because he knows Mitchell has a thing for her. Which is fucking weird cause I didn't think either one of them were looking for a relationship."

I scrubbed my hand over my rough chin. "Yeah, well something's going on. Paxton wants to invite Corina over for Thanksgiving, and I told her she should. Tripp didn't bother to."

"Why not? No sense in the poor girl being home alone. And I thought Tripp said she was going out of town?"

I shrugged. "I guess he misunderstood her. Plus, I don't think they're *that* serious with this whole dating. I think it's more of a causal thing."

"Then invite her. What harm could come of it?"

Nodding, I agreed. "Yeah, I'll make sure Paxton does."

"Make sure I do what?"

We both turned. Paxton stood in the doorway dressed in jeans, converse sneakers, and a light blue sweater that made her eyes stand out all the way across the room.

"Invite Corina for Thanksgiving."

She smiled. "I didn't have to. I guess Tripp realized she wasn't leaving and he invited her."

Trevor slapped my arm and winked. "There ya go. I'm out of here. Later y'all."

I followed him and stopped in front of Paxton.

"Hey," I said, kissing her on the lips.

"Hey. Your mom said you were back here. So what's the emergency? You broke me away from helping my mother decided between Antique White, Simple White, or Dover White."

With a chuckle, I replied, "Sounds like I saved you."

"You did! I was about to pull my hair out. Who knew there were so many shades of white!"

I took her in my arms. "Do you want to go up in the plane with me?"

Her eyes lit up like the Fourth of July. "Seriously? I'd love to! Are you just flying around for fun?"

"Yeah, but Dad needs me to check out a few things as well."

She did a little jump and clapped her hands. "How exciting! The last time I was up in a plane was when your dad took us to see the Christmas lights that one year."

"That's right. You haven't been anywhere? No vacations or anything?"

She shrugged. "Nope."

Hell, I was going to have to fix that little problem. I made a mental note to plan a trip for us. Maybe over spring break or something.

Placing my hand on her hips, I motioned for her to walk out of the office. "Come on. Let's go. Rob is waiting for me."

My father had a hanger and a small runway adjacent to the ranch. He'd bought the property years ago when he was going for his own pilot's license. He knew he would want to keep a plane here since the closet airport was a couple hours away in San Antonio.

The drive over to the hanger was filled with Paxton talking about what she was making for Thanksgiving. She had a cooking date planned the day before with my mother, Amelia, and Chloe. My heart ached when my sister Waylynn called. I could hear in her voice that she wanted to come home. But her asshole husband Jack had some fucking fundraiser and he needed Waylynn there. I swear the asshole was keeping her away from her family. I'd flown out twice with Chloe to visit my older sister. I could see the longing in Waylynn's eyes for a child of her own. Dickhead wasn't ready.

"Your dad got a new plane?" Paxton asked, pulling me from my thoughts.

"Yeah. He bought it about a year ago. It seats six."

Looking over at me, Paxton wore a nervous expression, wringing her hands in her lap.

"You okay?" I asked.

"I think so. You're sure you know how to fly it?"

' I reached for her hand. "I wouldn't take you up in this plane if I wasn't sure I could fly it. I've flown bigger planes before."

Her brows lifted. "Really? That's kind of hot."

Drawing my head back, I stared at her. "That turns you on?"

She nodded and chewed her bottom lip.

"Well, let's see how you feel after we land," I said.

Nervously giggling, she nodded.

Jumping out of the truck, I waved to Rob as I jogged around to open Paxton's door. With her hand in mine, we headed to the plane. I hadn't been the least bit nervous taking her up, but now anxiety swirled in the pit of my stomach.

CHAPTER 37

Paxton

I had to admit this was amazing. My hands still shook a bit, but Steed really did know what he was doing. We flew around, and he pointed out different places.

"Everything looks so different from up here!" I said into the microphone that hung from the giant headphones I wore.

"It really does. It's amazing. I want to take you up during sunset. It's beautiful."

I smiled, loving the excitement in Steed's voice. He really enjoyed this, and I loved being a part of it. "I'd love that. Would you take Chloe up too?"

"Hell yeah! She's already seen the sun setting over the Pacific Ocean numerous times."

The urge to ask him if Kim ever went up gnawed at the back of my mind. I wasn't sure why; I hardly ever thought of that dreadful woman.

My internal battle with the question volleyed back and forth before I finally caved. "Did Kim ever go up with y'all?"

He laughed. "Hell no. She was never interested, and I never in-vited her."

A small part of me fist pumped internally. "Is that your parents' place?" I asked.

"Yep. I'll fly over the guest house."

"When are you going to stop calling it that?" I asked with a chuckle. "It's your house now."

"Yeah, I know. It feels weird living there, though. I've talked to my parents about paying something for living there. At first they said no, but finally came around when I said I would move into town. I never would…but they don't know that. Damn place is huge though."

Now it was my turn to laugh. It was a huge house. I imagined it filled with more kids. Lots of noise, a few dogs. Maybe even a cat or two. Chloe's conversation with Steed a couple nights ago took center stage in my mind. I was soon staring out the window and not even paying attention to what was there. Steed turned the plane so all I could see was blue sky.

"Look over here. The cows."

I leaned over to see out his side of the plane. "Where are the cows?" I asked.

"Hold on. There're coming up."

Stretching my neck more, I was beginning to feel a little nause-ous, and I wasn't sure if it was because Steed was tipping the plane or if it was from lunch.

"Can you straighten the plane out? I'm feeling sick."

"Yeah, let me make this one turn." He straightened out the plane then pointed out my window. "Take a peek out your window, and you'll see it."

I did as he asked, while my hand came up to my mouth. I fo-cused on the plowed pasture out the window. The black dirt was a sharp contrast to the brown grass.

The words MARRY ME were spelled out across the pasture. I wasn't sure how long I stared at it, but now it was moving behind the plane. I tried to keep looking before it was finally gone from my view. When I turned back to Steed, he was holding an open ring box that contained a beautiful princess cut diamond, along with a brilliant smile covering his beautiful face.

"I lost our love once before. I vow never to lose it again. Paxton Lynn Monroe, will you do me the honor of becoming my wife?"

The nausea in my stomach was instantly replaced by butterflies circling deep in my belly. My hands shook as I brought them to my mouth again. Steed was proposing. He was asking me to be his wife in the most romantic way I could ever have imagined. Tears pricked the back of my eyes as I tried to find my voice.

My chest felt light, my heart floating on a cloud of utter bliss, while my body trembled with pure happiness.

Dropping my hands, I smiled and nodded. "Yes! Yes, I'll marry you!"

His smile grew even wider, and the threat of his own tears were evident in the glistening of his eyes.

"I love you, Pax."

My mouth rose up at the corners even bigger. "You have to land this plane, Steed, because all I want is to throw myself into your arms. Oh, and I love you too!"

He laughed. "Does that mean you want to wait until we land for me to put the ring on?"

"Yes! Hurry! Land!"

He snapped the ring box shut, took the plane off auto pilot, and got busy with getting us back to the ground safely. My leg bounced the entire time as he lined the plane up with the runway. I glanced every other second to the ring box. Peeking at Steed, I was positive his expression of happiness matched mine.

We landed and I let out the breath I didn't know I had been holding. The moment the plane came to a stop, I unbuckled and so did Steed. My arms wrapped around his neck, and I let my emotions free.

He held onto me tightly as he whispered, "You've made me the happiest man alive, Pax."

Through my unlady-like sniffles, I replied, "You've made me the happiest woman alive!"

He pulled back and ran the back of his hand down the side of my cheek before opening the ring box again.

I got a good look at it and gasped. "Oh my God." Lifting my eyes to meet his, I asked, "Is that…"

He nodded. "The ring you pointed to the day we picked up my mother's necklace. Yes."

My heart hammered, the memory coming back.

"It will only take a second to run in and pick up the necklace my father bought for Mom's birthday."

I nodded and let the warm rays from the sunroof him me. It was the summer before our senior year. Steed and I had been down at the river all morning with friends, but the one hundred degree temperatures drove Steed and me to leave.

Pulling up to the jewelry store, Steed parked and rushed over to my side of the truck to open my door. He smiled and my stomach did that silly dip it always did whenever he flashed that sexy grin.

We stepped inside, and as Steed walked up to the saleslady, I wandered around the store. I soon found myself in front of the engagement rings staring at the most breathtaking ring I'd ever seen.

"Want to see it?"

My eyes snapped up to see Judy Pinhouse. Her daddy owned the jewelry store.

With a quick glance at Steed, I noticed he was in a deep conversation with Mr. Pinhouse.

I shrugged. "Sure! Why not."

Judy giggled as she unlocked the glass door and reached in. She placed a blue velvet pad in front of me and set the ring on it.

"It's a princess cut diamond that my daddy personally designed. It's one of my favorites."

Picking it up, I smiled. "It's beautiful."

"Yeah, the girl who gets this will be lucky."

I nodded. "She sure will."

My body came to life as I felt him next to me. "Whatcha looking at?" Steed asked as Mr. Pinhouse walked over.

"Aw, you're admiring the princess cut I designed."

"It's beautiful. I love it so much."

He smiled, glanced over to Steed, and gave him a wink. "She's got good taste."

Steed's arm wrapped around my waist, and he looked at me with so much love. I was sort of freaking out inside as his eyes searched mine. I didn't want to give him the wrong idea. After all, we were only seniors in high school.

"Well, Judy and I were just having fun looking at rings. This one caught my eye. It's truly stunning."

Mr. Pinhouse thanked me as I handed the ring back. "I'm glad you liked it, Paxton."

Liked it? I loved it.

Steed's voice pulled me from the memory. "After you told Mr. Pinhouse you loved the ring, I went back later that day and worked out a plan with him to buy it. After working on the ranch that summer and doing some extra work for Dad and Pete Moss, I earned enough to buy it a few days before Christmas."

I covered my mouth as shock and realization hit me.

"You've had this ring since our senior year of high school?"

He nodded as he gazed into my eyes. "I've never let go of the dream to marry you, Pax. Never."

Focusing on the ring, he took it out of the box and slipped it on my finger. "It's always been you. It will forever be you."

I threw myself at his body again, which was hard to do in the small cockpit of this plane.

"It's beautiful! This is beautiful!" I uttered as he pulled me close.

"Now let me take you home so I can make love to you."

Drawing back, I wiped my tears away and chuckled. "I like that plan."

I laid contently in Steed's arms and stared out the large picture window in his bedroom, my fingers moving mindlessly over his chest. Every now and then I would look at the beautiful ring on my finger and a rush of overwhelming happiness would hit me. Steed's soft breathing told me he was sleeping.

This moment couldn't have been any more wonderful. Everything about it was perfect.

Then a wave of nausea rushed through me. I quickly sat up, jolting Steed awake. My hand covered my mouth, and I flew out of bed to rush to the bathroom. Dropping to the ground before the toilet, I threw up.

Wave after wave hit me, and it took me a moment to realize Steed was behind me, holding my hair back. After I had nothing left to throw up, dry heaves decided to make their appearance.

Finally, it stopped.

My stomach muscles ached, and my throat felt raw.

I groaned, and Steed handed me a hot washcloth. It felt so good when I pressed my face into it. Standing, I turned to see him leaning against the doorframe of the bathroom. The pleased expression he wore made my brows pinch together.

"I'm glad to see me getting sick has made you happy."

He slowly shook his head before he pushed off and stepped close. Placing his hand over my stomach, I inhaled sharply. I didn't want to get overly excited, but now I knew why he had been standing there with a goofy grin on his face.

"You don't think?" I asked.

He shrugged. "It only takes one time."

My hand covered his. Had we conceived a child that day at the cabin? The same cabin where we made love for the first time? The thought alone was so damn romantic it made my body tremble.

Steed lowered his mouth to mine, kissing me gently. His soft kisses moved to my jaw, along my neck, and to that sensitive area under my ear. "If you're pregnant, do you realize what that means?"

My head dropped back as his lips moved back across my neck. "W-what? Does that mean?"

"We made this little miracle at the cabin, where we first made love."

I grinned. "I thought the same thing only moments ago."

His hands slipped behind my neck, pulling me close.

"You know what we have to do right now?"

With a giggle, I replied, "Drive into town for a pregnancy test?"

"Fuck yes!"

He pulled back, turned, and raced into the bedroom. "Paxton! Get dressed!"

Following his lead, I rushed to the bedroom and got dressed. I glanced at Steed and his eyes sparkled and gleamed. I was positive mine did the same. My chest felt light and even though I was still a bit nauseous, nothing could bring me down from this high.

Slipping my Converse shoes back on, Steed nearly toppled me when he grabbed my arm. "Come on, let's go!"

I laughed. "Steed! Let me get my shoes on."

He swept up my remaining shoe then grabbed me and cradled me in his arms. "You're going entirely too slow, Pax."

I couldn't contain the happiness that bubbled out as Steed carried me to his truck. Gone were the two scared teenagers from ten years ago…

Setting me in the seat, Steed placed his hand on the side of my face and flashed me a sexy grin. I knew what he was thinking. Both of us were excited, yet afraid to get our hopes up.

My hand covered his. "No matter what happens, that day will always be special."

Leaning in, he softly kissed my lips then added, "Yes, it will."

CHAPTER 38

Steed

My pulse raced as I pulled into the local drug store. Throwing my truck into park, I practically shouted, "Hold on! I'll get your door!"

I jumped out and ran to Paxton's side. She sat in the passenger seat with a wide grin. Opening the door, I reached in and scooped her up into my arms. Letting out a small yelp, she laughed.

"Steed, what in the world are you doing?"

"What? I want to you help you out of the truck."

Narrowing her eyes at me, she shook her head. "I'm not incapable of getting out of the truck. Besides, we don't know if I'm…" She looked around and whispered, "Pregnant."

"Why are you whispering?" I asked, setting her down.

"Because there is a lot at stake if I am."

My brow lifted. "Such as?"

"My job? Do you have any idea how they would frown at their kindergarten teacher being knocked up out of wedlock?"

"Fuck them!" I shouted as she slapped her hand over my mouth.

"Steed Jonathon Parker!"

I drew her into my chest. "Jesus, Pax. You calling me by my full name in that tone turns me on. Will you dress up like the naughty teacher, and I'll be your bad boy student?"

Humor crossed her face.

"Paxton, how are you?"

The voice behind me made her expression drop, and she immediately jumped away from me.

"Mr. Hines. H-how are you?"

Glancing over my shoulder, I flashed a grin at the school principal—who also happened to be Paxton's boss.

"I'm doing well. Ready for some turkey tomorrow. How about you?"

Paxton rubbed her stomach and let out a nervous chuckle. "Yes. Turkey and dressing. All that yummy food. *So* ready."

I was positive he had no clue who I was, even though Mitchell and I had him for our eighth grade teacher, and we singlehandedly killed three class pets by accident that year. I remember him sending a letter home to my father stating that if we killed another class pet we were going to have to finish out eighth grade in in-school suspension.

"Mr. Hines, this is…" Paxton paused, her cheeks turning pink as she glanced down at her ring.

"Paxton's fiancé. Steed Parker," I said.

He grimaced, and then anger shot across his face.

Oh, yeah. It was safe to say he remembered who I was.

"Steed Parker. Kill any turtles lately?"

Paxton's smile dropped and a look of utter horror replaced it.

I let out a nervous chuckle. "No, sir. I put those days behind me years ago."

He huffed, then focused back on Paxton. "Enjoy your time off, Paxton."

"Um, you too, sir."

He walked away…right into the drugstore.

Paxton hit my chest, hard. "Shit! He went into the drugstore, Steed."

"So?" I asked as I grabbed her hand and headed to the door.

"We can't buy a pregnancy test with my boss in there."

I laughed and shook my head. "Then we'll mingle until he leaves."

Paxton stopped walking. "Mingle? Steed, we're not at a party!"

"You know what I mean."

We walked into the store and sure enough, the old goat was right there asking the young girl behind the counter where the orange flavored Metamucil would be. Leaning down to Paxton, I uttered, "I could have gone my whole life without hearing that."

Covering her mouth, she pulled me deeper into the drugstore. After walking up and down each aisle and grabbing random things, we found ourselves in *that* aisle. The aisle you paid your older brother and sister to go down and buy condoms.

"I'm nervous," she said.

"He left!" I yelled, making my way to the pregnancy tests. I stopped dead in my tracks. Paxton's parents walked by the aisle and then stopped.

"Hey kids! What are you doing here?"

Paxton hit me on the back. More like punched me. Here we were, standing in the middle of the aisle that just happened to contain not only the pregnancy tests, but an array of condoms. A thought hit me. If Paxton was pregnant, that meant no…more…condoms.

"We're not buying condoms I can tell you that!" I shot out. Why I said it, I had no fucking clue.

Paxton glared at me, wearing a horrified expression. "Oh my God. You didn't," she whispered harshly before hitting me in the back again.

From the look on her father's face, I realized I had some serious ass kissing to do.

Always quick on her feet, Paxton turned back to her parents. "Hey Mom and Dad, we were going to get something for Steed's allergies."

When I glanced past the Monroes, I saw the display of allergy medicine.

April, Paxton's mom, smiled while David, her father, continued to glare.

"Oh my! Oh my goodness! Paxton!" her mother cried out.

Jumping back in surprise, Paxton shouted, "What?"

April rushed up to her daughter and grabbed her hand. "He did it!"

My eyes drifted down to the engagement ring.

"Oh, Steed, when you came over the other day to ask for Paxton's hand in marriage I had no idea you were going to ask so soon!" April said, tears building in her eyes.

David's glare turned into a slow smile. "Congratulations, son! Did you do it like you planned? In the plane?"

"Wait, y'all knew?" Paxton asked.

Both of her parents laughed. "Yes! Of course. Steed has always been such a gentleman."

David grunted under his breath, and I gave him a weak grin.

"He took us out to lunch a few weeks back to ask for your hand in marriage. Then he told us how he planned to ask."

Trying to smile and ignore the fact that we were standing in front of the condoms and pregnancy tests, my eyes caught Paxton's. She was struggling to hold back her tears, and I wondered if she would be successful in doing so.

I winked, and she let out a nervous giggle. "Well, I see y'all are good secret keepers."

Her mother and father wrapped her up in a loving embrace.

"Well, we only came in to grab aspirin. Your father had a headache from helping me prepare all the pies for tomorrow. It was so sweet of your parents to invite us over, Steed."

"Mom's excited and so is Dad. He keeps going on about show-ing you his new fishing rod, David."

Paxton's father let out a roar of laughter. It seemed like the whole condom thing was slowly disappearing. "John always did love his fishing."

"I'm excited to see Chloe again. Paxton mentioned bringing her over to play with our cat."

I rolled my eyes and sighed. "Yes. Little stinker has been beg-ging for one."

Both April and David chuckled before April took her husband by the arm and gave him a tug. "We need to get going. We'll see you kids tomorrow. Steed let your mother know if she needs anything to give me a call."

"I will, April. Thank you."

As I watched them wander off, we slowly walked to the allergy display. I picked up box after box and pretended to read them while Paxton stretched up on her toes to watch her parents.

"They're gone! Come on!"

We spun around and rushed to the tests. My eyes glanced over them. What in the hell? Why were there so many different brands? And why in the hell did our small-town pharmacy carry them all?

"Which one?" I asked in a hushed voice.

"I don't care. Grab one of each! Let's just go before someone else see us," Paxton replied in a hushed tone as she reached for the First Response. She grabbed two.

I grabbed six of Clearblue brand only to have Paxton gawk at me.

"Six?"

"Well, we want to be sure."

She giggled. "I think two is enough."

Shrugging, I put four back and then reached for two of the EPT tests. Paxton grabbed one that simply read Pregnancy Test. The last one was Fact Plus. I grabbed two of those and added it to the pile of tests in my hands.

"That should be good," Paxton stated with a smile.

"You sure? What if they don't work?"

"Whatcha doing?" The voice came from behind, causing both of us to let out a scream. My first instinct was to discard the six boxes of pregnancy tests I had in my hand. I watched as they all dropped at our feet.

My sister Amelia peered at the boxes and then snapped her head back up to us. Her look of shock quickly turned to pure excitement.

"Oh! My! Freaking! Hell!" she shouted.

Paxton and I both replied with a quick, "Shh!"

Dropping down, I gathered the tests back up.

"You're pregnant?" Amelia asked. Then she screamed. Loudly. "Holy fuck! And you're engaged?" She grabbed Paxton's left hand, causing her to drop two of her tests.

Paxton giggled, beaming with happiness. "Yes! Steed asked me earlier today in the most romantic way ever."

Amelia's eyes landed on me, and she wiped a tear away. "I'm so happy. Does Chloe know?"

I shook my head. "Not yet."

Covering her mouth with her hands, Amelia shook her head. "I'm so happy, y'all… I think I'm going to cry!"

I rolled my eyes. "I love you, sis, but we really need to get the fuck out of here before someone else walks up and—"

"Jesus, is it national buy your condoms day?"

Groaning, I dropped my head at the sound of my brother Cord's voice.

"Why the hell are you in this aisle, Amelia?" he asked in an angry voice.

"Oh fuck off, Cord. I'm an adult and if I want to buy condoms, I'll buy condoms."

Paxton turned to me. I knew she wanted out of there just as much as I did, and here we were, listening to Cord and Amelia argue whether she was allowed to have sex or not.

"I'm twenty-two years old, Cord. I've been fucking guys for a few years now."

"Oh, come on!" I said. Cord looked like he was about to blow a gasket.

"Meli, so help me God, if I ever find out who you've slept with I'm going to beat their ass so bad…"

"Listen, as much as I'd love to stay here and listen to y'all, we need to leave," I said as I started to push between the two of them.

Cord's hand grabbed my shoulder, stopping me. He stared down at the tests, then back at me. "Why do you have pregnancy tests in your arms?"

His eyes swung over to Paxton, and it dawned on him. "Holy. Shit. Are y'all?"

"They don't know yet! That's why they're here, Cord!" Amelia said as she jumped up and down and pretended to clap her hands.

Cord looked back at me. "Dude! This is fucking amazing. Come on, let's go!"

Both him and Amelia turned on their heels and headed down the aisle. "Oh wait!" Amelia said as she rushed back and grabbed a box of condoms.

I wanted to throw up in my mouth when she held up the extra-large and said, "Here's to hoping!"

"Grab me a box of those, Meli!" Cord said.

Amelia laughed. "Are you sure you don't need extra small?"

"Just get me the extra-large. Super extra if they have them," he said tossing his head back in laughter.

"Is this really happening right now?" Paxton asked.

"I don't know what bothers me more. The fact that they think they're going with us or that my brother just asked my baby sister to grab him a box of condoms."

Paxton laughed as we followed Amelia and Cord to the check out, both of them still arguing about whether Amelia was old enough for sex.

CHAPTER 39

Paxton

Somehow Cord and Amelia were standing in the middle of Steed's living room, staring at me with wide hopeful eyes.

"Y'all, not to sound like a total ass, but we were kind of thinking this would be a private moment," Steed said, his arms crossed over his chest and one brow lifted.

Amelia and Cord turned to each other with questioning looks, then lost it laughing. Turning back to us, Amelia stated, "Seriously? We see you with boxes of pregnancy tests, and you expect us to walk away and pretend like we don't know. Not happening, Parker."

"It's cruel if you make us leave now. We're in too deep," Cord added.

I rolled my eyes and let out a long sigh. "They can stay, but you're not coming into the bathroom with me. Only Steed is, and you have to give us a few minutes to process the results."

They nodded their heads as if they were my kindergarten students. I tried hard not to let the flicker of amusement in my eyes show. I had to admit, this was a complete one-eighty from the last time I held a pregnancy test in my hands.

"Let's go, Paxton. You two stay," Steed said as he pointed to both of them.

"Do you at least have booze?" Cord called out.

"Help yourself to whatever you find, bro."

My pulse quickened as we drew closer to Steed's room. Once we walked in, I froze.

Stopping, he turned to look at me. "Baby, what's wrong? Are you okay?"

Chewing on my lip, I said, "I need a second. It's hit me all of sudden. I might be pregnant. How did I not realize I was late?"

Steed took my hand and led me over to the bed. "Pax, I didn't think about it either. Maybe deep down inside we *did* notice but chose to ignore it for whatever reason."

I took in a deep breath and exhaled. "I think you're right. Maybe the fear of what would happen? Being disappointed? I don't know."

"Well, we can sit here and analyze it, or we can see if you are."

With a wide smile, I agreed. "You're right. So? You ready to find out?"

His eyes filled with excitement. "Never been more ready."

We both stood. My stomach was in knots. I wasn't going to try and fool myself that I wasn't excited. And I knew by Steed's reaction, he was as well. It was a far cry from ten years ago when we were two young, scared teenagers.

When we walked into the bathroom, Steed laid all the tests out, and I couldn't help but laugh at how crazy it was for us to buy so many.

"Damn, I guess we bought a lot."

I agreed. "We did buy a lot. I guess you could say we were excited?"

Steed laughed. "A little."

For both of us, it was like the first time finding out if we would be parents. And yet it wasn't a do-over, because I knew we would never forget our first child. But this time around I had a sneaking suspicion that Steed wasn't upset that we had forgotten protection. Deep down I knew whatever was meant to be would happen. We would both be happy, whatever the outcome.

Amazing what a little bit of growing up and life lessons will teach you.

I picked up the First Response test, and Steed picked up the EPT test.

"I say we open one of each brand."

"I'm not sure I have that much pee," I cackled.

Steed ripped open the tests and set them on the counter while I turned on the water and leaned my head in, drinking it straight from the faucet.

After five minutes of drinking tap water, I stood up and covered my stomach. "Eww. I made myself sick drinking so much water."

With a laugh, Steed sat on the toilet and pulled me onto his lap so that I was straddling him. He lifted his brows, and I could feel his dick hardening under me.

"You in the mood to fool around?" he asked with a wink.

Lifting my brows, I shook my head and *tsked*. "Your brother and sister are out in the living room!"

"You could be quiet. Besides, you have to practice for when you move in."

My head drew back to look at him better. "Move in?"

"Yeah. At some point, Pax, I'm going to need you in my bed every night."

"What about Chloe? What would we say about me moving in and us not being married?"

He smiled. "Looks like it's a quickie marriage, especially if you're pregnant."

Wrapping my arms around his neck, I rubbed against him. The friction caused by his hard one and my jeans were driving me a little crazy.

Digging his fingers into my waist, Steed pushed up, causing a moan to slip out by mistake. He smiled and slowly shook his head.

God the feel of him and the layers of clothes between us was driving me insane. "I want more," I panted as I pressed my lips to his.

"Fuck yes," he murmured.

Jumping off him, I quickly kicked off my Converse sneakers and jeans. Steed simply pulled his jeans down and his long, hard dick sprang free. I licked my lips and pushed him back down on the toilet.

Quickly straddling him, I smiled and asked, "Should we use a condom?"

"If you're not pregnant, do you want to wait?"

I shrugged. "I want to feel you and let things happen how they're supposed to happen."

"Fate," he said softly while running his finger along my jaw line.

"Fate," I replied with a huskier voice than I intended. My libido was taking over. Steed's dick was inches from me, and I wanted it.

He reached down and slipped his fingers inside me. A look of pure satisfaction moved over his face as he closed his eyes.

"*Fuuck*." He groaned out then positioned himself at my entrance. Slowly sinking down on him, I dropped my head back and bit my lip to keep from moaning in utter delight. Once I had him all the way in, I let my body adjust to him.

"Jesus… I'm filling you to the fucking core, baby."

I nodded and brought my head up, meeting his eyes with mine.

"Move, Paxton, or I'm going to take over."

Amusement danced in his eyes as I started to move. In and out so slow until even I couldn't take it any longer. Things turned fast and hard quick. I lifted up and slammed down on Steed. Each time I felt him hitting a spot that made my toes curl.

"It's not…going to be… long!" I panted.

"Hurry, baby. I need to feel you come around my cock."

I covered my mouth with my hand. Eyes widening, my orgasm burst free and rushed through my body.

Steed's body shuddered, and he grabbed me, pulling me to him as he came with me. His body trembled as he filled me with his hot cum. The thought of it nearly had me coming again.

I slowed down and sat on him. Feeling him twitch inside of me was freaking amazing. Sex with this man would never get old.

"You know," he said with a naughty grin plastered on his face. "Any other couple would have waited to see if they were pregnant before they had the celebratory fuck."

"We're not any other couple," I playfully said with a wink.

"No, we are not."

The knock on the door caused me to jump. "Well?" Amelia asked.

"I'm waiting to pee."

When the handle rattled, I panicked. "I locked it," Steed said before lifting me off of him and grabbing a towel to wipe his cum off me.

"Drink water, and hurry!" she called through the door.

"Stop being so bossy, Meli. If I remember right, you weren't even invited!" Steed said.

We could hear her huff. "All I know is you better not be fucking in there."

"They're fucking?" Cord asked on the other side of the door.

Steed buttoned his pants and said, "There's a window. We could sneak out."

"I heard that!" Amelia cried out.

CHAPTER 40

Paxton

I sat on the counter while Steed ran the water in both sinks, the tub, *and* the shower. Pee was nowhere to be found.

"It's because of Amelia and Cord. I can't perform under stress!" I cried out while burying my face in my hands.

"Want to fuck again?" Steed asked.

Lifting my head, I stared at him. He flashed me that dimple, causing me to laugh.

Then, it hit me.

I jumped off the counter. "I have to pee."

"I'm ready!" Steed shouted as he got ready to hand me the tests. We had a system down we were sure would work. He'd hand me a test and have the next in his hand ready to go.

"Okay, let's go!"

"Jesus, Pax, I'm impressed you can stop and start your pee like that."

"Me too!" I chuckled.

After I peed on six tests, I wiped, flushed, and washed my hands. Steed turned off the shower and tub, and I turned off the faucets. We turned our backs to the tests, laced our fingers together and waited.

Taking in a long shaky breath, I looked at Steed. "Should we turn around?"

He shook his head but squeezed my hand. "Wait."

Facing me, he cupped my face within his hand. "No matter what it says, I love you, and I'll always love you. And if we're not, it just means we're not ready for that step yet. If we are then we've been so blessed the last few months."

I nodded. "R-right."

His eyes searched my face. "I don't want you to be disappointed."

A warm feeling moved into my chest. He was worried about me and how this would affect me. "I love you and just when I think I couldn't possibly love you more, you prove me wrong. I won't lie and say I'm not emotional. I'm thinking about the baby we lost. I'm scared I'll lose another baby. I'm excited. I'm a plethora of emotions. Disappointed won't be one of them. Fate. Remember?"

He kissed my mouth softly and with so much love I swore I could feel it pouring into my body.

Drawing back, he asked, "Ready?"

I sighed deeply and answered, "Ready."

"On three."

I nodded.

"One. Two. Three."

We both turned, and my eyes swept across the tests.

"Fuck, is that a yes or a no?" Steed asked, staring at one of them.

I picked the first one up. *Pregnant*. Then I picked up the next one. It read the same thing. *Pregnant*.

"This is two lines! We have two lines!" Steed cried out. "Pregnant! It says pregnant!"

Tears were burning my eyes as I tried not to get emotional. Steed dropped the tests, grabbed me, and picked me up in his arms.

"We're having a baby! We're having a baby!" he said while squeezing me.

He quickly put me down. "Shit! I squeezed you!"

Laughing, I wiped my tears away. "It's okay. I'm sure the baby is nice and safe in there."

Steed took a step closer and threaded his fingers in my hair, the palms of his hands on my face.

"We're having a baby, Pax."

I half-cackled, half-cried.

Wow.

The last few months we had come full circle. My heart felt like it was floating in my chest.

"Crazy three months, huh?" I said while he pressed his forehead to mine.

"The best three months of my life," he answered softly.

"We better go tell Amelia and Cord," I said with a giggle.

The moment we walked into the living room, they both jumped up. Cord almost looked sick, and I knew memories of ten years ago were floating about in his mind.

"So? Am I getting another niece or nephew?" Amelia asked.

I remained quiet, letting Steed tell them.

Squeezing my hand, he chuckled. "Yes, you're going to be an aunt again."

Amelia jumped up and down and Cord rushed over to me. He picked me up in his arms and spun me around. "Holy fucking shit! You two make my head spin! You hate him, you love him, you get engaged! You get pregnant!"

"It's like a romance book!" Amelia shouted as Steed pulled back from her hug.

"Are you happy?" they both asked at the same time.

"Yes!" I answered.

"Hell yes, I'm happy!" Steed replied.

"How far along do you think you are?"

"Well, I'm almost positive I know when we conceived."

Amelia covered her heart with her hand. "How romantic! When?"

I couldn't help it, I busted out laughing and so did Steed. "October."

Amelia glanced back and forth between us and then a horrified look moved over her face. "My cabin?"

Steed nodded. "Hey, did I ever give you that bandana back, Meli?"

Thanksgiving Day

Melanie and my mother quickly moved about the kitchen. I couldn't help but smile as I watched them talk and laugh. I also couldn't help the small amount of guilt I had for insisting my mother not talk to me about Melanie or any of the Parkers. She eventually stopped spending time with Melanie and that broke my heart. They had been the best of friends and the reason I met Steed at such an early age. Our families had traveled together. Vacations, Sea World, Six Flags, and Steed and I were always joined at the hip. Then one day…we fell in love.

Melanie placed a dish of stuffing on the island and stopped to look at me.

"Paxton, are you feeling okay?"

My eyes lifted from the yummy cornbread stuffing to meet hers. "Yes! Why do you ask?"

She shrugged, then tilted her head. "You seem flushed."

Lifting my hands to my cheeks, I smiled. "I feel fine. Just thinking of how we used to spend our family vacations together."

Melanie smiled. "That was fun. But still, you seem a bit off. You're sure you're okay? All that cooking last night got to you, didn't it?"

"No! I loved it!" I answered as Chloe climbed up on the stool next to me.

"Paxton spent the night in the guest room," Chloe busted out as my mother and Melanie looked at Chloe, then me. Little stinker ratted me out.

I had told Steed I didn't think I should stay, but he wanted to celebrate the baby and since I had the cooking party with his family yesterday afternoon, Steed said he needed to be with me. Who was I to say no?

"Is that so?" my mother asked with a huge smile.

"Yep. Aunt Meli stayed too."

I grinned. Ha! Take that! Steed only had to pay her two hundred dollars for that little favor.

"Yep, but poor Paxton was throwing up this morning before Daddy took her back home. Daddy had to pull over, and she got sick again. Ain't that right, Paxton?"

"*Isn't* that right. Ain't isn't a word, Chloe Cat," I said, attempting to keep my voice still and unaffected.

She snapped her fingers and peered up. "Darn it. Why don't I ever remember that?"

A quick survey of the area, and I saw Amelia. I went to call for her when my mother said, "Not feeling good, huh?"

Don't. Look. In. Her. Face.

"Yeah, I'm sure it was something I ate last night."

Melanie leaned over and said, "Chloe, sweetheart, will you go find Uncle Trevor? I need him to do me a favor. He's around here somewhere."

Chloe's eyes lit up. "Okay, Grammy! I'll go find him."

Watching her run off, I slid off the stool. A voice stopped me.

"Stay, Paxton Lynn Monroe."

Shit.

I took in a deep breath and blew it. *Act normal. Just be yourself,* I chanted to myself.

"Did y'all need help?" I asked with a fake grin.

They both shook their heads. Melanie crossed her arms and stared. "I knew it! Didn't I tell you a few weeks ago, April!"

Huh?

"Um…you knew what?" I asked as my gaze swung between the two of them.

"You called it, Melanie."

"What are we talking about?" I asked.

Raising her eyebrow, my mother said, "Maybe she doesn't know."

"I don't know what?" I asked.

"Oh…that could be."

They turned and started cooking again. I was about to ask them what in the hell they were talking about when I felt Steed's arms wrap around me. He gently placed his hands over my stomach and kissed my neck.

"How are you feeling?" he asked in a soft voice.

"Okay," I stated, looking suspiciously at our mothers. "I think they know," I whispered.

Steed chuckled. "They couldn't possibly."

Spinning around, I motioned to go outside. Once we were off the porch, I started to tell him what Chloe had said and what their reaction was followed by the whole *I don't think she knows*.

Steed ran his fingers through his hair. "You think Amelia or Cord said something?"

I shook my head. "No. They promised, and I believe they won't spill."

Next thing I knew, Steed was spinning us around. "They're looking out the window. They totally know."

"Shit. Do you think they'll keep it a secret? And how? How do they know?"

"Amelia said you're glowing."

I chuckled. "I am not."

He cupped my face in his soft, warm hands. "You are."

"It could be because I'm engaged to be married to the love of my life."

His eyes closed, and I knew he was attempting to get his emotions in check. When he opened them, he looked directly into my eyes. "I know this isn't a do-over. I know we lost a precious child, and there will always be this void in my heart, but a part of me thinks I'm the luckiest son-of-a-bitch for getting this second chance with you. I would have been happy with just you saying yes to marrying me. But a baby. Pax, I'm so over the fucking moon it's not even funny. I feel like God is giving me another chance to get this right. When I found out about Chloe, I wasn't happy."

Sadness moved across his face. "I was angry, and I hated Kim for getting pregnant. But then I realized what was at stake. There was no way I was going to lose another baby."

I shook my head. "Steed, you never have to explain your love for Chloe. Ever. Everything happened for a reason, and I'm so happy to have her in my life. I can't wait to see her face when we tell her tonight at dinner we're going to get married."

The corners of his mouth raised, and I was blown over by that smile. We had decided to wait and announce the engagement, even though everyone knew. Chloe didn't, and Steed wanted her with the family when she found out.

"I can't wait either."

He glanced back and chuckled. "Want to have fun with them?"

I lifted a brow. "What did you have in mind?"

Dropping to his knees, he cupped his hands at my stomach and started talking to the baby.

"Hey little one. Your two nosy grandmas are spying on me and Mommy."

My fingers ran through his dark thick hair. Happiness blossomed in my chest with Steed talking to our child.

"Oh yeah, one more thing. Go easy on Mommy with the whole morning sickness thing."

I chuckled.

He gazed up at me. "Are they still watching?"

Trying to peek without them seeing me, I covered my mouth and turned away. Melanie and my mother had been hugging each other and jumping up and down.

"What?" he asked standing up and looking. "You think they're happy?"

"I'd say they were a little happy."

CHAPTER 41

Steed

To say this Thanksgiving was both the best and weirdest would be an understatement. I was bursting at the seams to tell Chloe about marrying Paxton. My mother and April had calmed down when Paxton and I walked back into the house. I guess they were waiting on us to tell them, because neither of them said a thing. We decided we were going to make them sweat it out for a few weeks, or at least until one of them broke down and asked us.

Then you had the whole Tripp, Mitchell, and Corina thing. Tripp had invited Corina over, and she had accepted. Mitchell couldn't keep his eyes off of her, and she did everything she could to avoid looking at him. Even my mother noticed it.

"What's going on between Mitchell and Tripp's Corina?" she had asked.

With a shrug, I told her she needed to ask Mitchell. No way I was getting dragged into it. But I also couldn't help but notice how she called Corina "Tripp's friend." I was sure it was because of the way he'd introduced her.

"Mom, Dad, this is my friend, Corina. She's from Chicago and her parents are out of town so she had nowhere to go."

The look on Corina's face was utter embarrassment, and I was waiting for Paxton to kick Tripp in the balls. She didn't need to. Corina did it for her with her own introduction when she made it clear she was friends with Paxton.

"Mr. and Mrs. Parker, thank you for the invite. Paxton's told me so many wonderful things about you both."

My mother tilted her head. "You know Paxton?"

Corina wore a huge smile. "We went to college together, and she asked me to move here to fill the first grade teacher's position."

Glaring at Tripp first, my mother then grinned when she looked back at Corina. "Well, we're so happy you could join us, Corina."

"Okay, everyone! Dinner is served!" my mother called out from the kitchen. Walking into the formal dining room, my stomach dropped as I watched Paxton help Chloe set a bowl of mashed potatoes on the table. Chloe stood on a wooden chair, and Paxton handed her the bowl and showed her where to put it. She then high fived Chloe and pulled her in for a hug. She was going to make an amazing mother. She already was for Chloe, and she had no idea. Chloe was no longer my daughter, but *ours*.

Tripp took a centerpiece from Corina and kissed her lightly on the cheek. Corina had been placing flower centerpieces along the massive pecan table my father had built years ago. It seated twenty when you put the two sleeves in. Dad had said he needed a large table for when all his kids got married.

Chloe tugged on my shirt. "Daddy, I want to sit between you and Paxton. Is that okay?"

I lifted her up and kissed her cheek, making her giggle. "Of course it is, pumpkin!"

When I put her down, she ran over to Tripp. "Uncle Tripp! Next year I get to shoot the turkey with you!"

Tripp dropped to Chloe's level and flashed her a wide grin. "I think that sounds amazing! I had to shoot two this year! I could have used your help."

Chloe snapped her fingers and said, "Dang it."

Tripp laughed and pulled her ponytail before giving her a quick kiss on the tip of her nose. Corina stood off to the side and observed it all. One glance around and I noticed Mitchell at the opposite end of the table.

My mother cleared her throat as she carried out the turkey. "Okay, all the food is on the table, but we have one announcement."

Pulling out my phone, I sent a quick text before looking back up at my mother.

"Steed?"

Standing, I reached behind Chloe and motioned for Paxton to stand. We held hands, and I felt her engagement ring. She'd taken it off before Chloe got home last night and slipped it back on just now.

"Paxton and I would like to announce we're getting married."

Chloe jumped up in her chair and focused on me. Tears filled her eyes. She turned and looked at Paxton. Holding up the ring, Paxton showed it to Chloe. My heart was in my throat as my daughter wrapped her arms tightly around Paxton. I wasn't surprised she had fallen in love with her so fast. Especially with as much time as we had all been spending together. When Chloe pulled back, she was sobbing.

That surprised me. Full. On. Sobbing.

"Does this mean...you're my mommy... now? Oh, please say yes! Please, Paxton."

It didn't take long for Paxton's eyes to water, but somehow she held it together. She nodded, until she could find the words. "Yes, Chloe Cat. I'm going to be your mommy."

Chloe cried even harder and turned to me, throwing herself into a hug. I wasn't sure how to handle her reaction. I knew she would be happy, but I didn't think she would have a meltdown. It made me realize how much my daughter had been longing for a mother figure. She finally let go of me. I used my thumbs to wipe her tears away, my heart aching at the sight of my daughter's tears. Happy or not, they killed me.

"Pumpkin, I don't want you to cry."

She nodded. "I'm just so happy, Daddy. This is the happiest day of my life."

A few chuckles echoed in the room. One quick glance showed my sister Amelia crying. Corina was also dabbing at the corners of her eyes, trying her best not to let her tears fall. Across the table my mother was smiling, but a few tears trickled down her face. My father leaned over and wiped them away before taking her hand in his and kissing the back of it. April was also crying, while David held her to his side.

My heart felt like it had seized in my chest. We were home, and my daughter was surrounded by the most amazing people on the planet. I was blessed to have such a family in my life.

The doorbell rang. Clearing the frog from my throat, I stated, "That would be my second surprise."

Peeking at Paxton, she winked.

"Who…who is it, Daddy?" Chloe asked, wiping the snot from her nose on her shirt.

I held up my finger and said, "Hold on. Everyone hold that thought!"

Rushing out of the formal dining room, I opened the front door. I put my finger to my mouth, but my sister Waylynn tackle-hugged me.

"I've missed you so much," she said against my neck.

Squeezing her tight, I picked her up and spun her before putting her back down. "I've missed you. Come on. Mom is going to freak the fuck out."

With her hand in mine, I led her to the dining room. "Look who I found at the door."

Everyone turned and shocked expressions spread over their faces, except for Paxton's. She'd been in on the plan to get Waylynn here.

My mother stood. She covered her mouth and shook her head.

Next to stand was my father. "Waylynn?" he said with his voice shaking.

"Fucking hell! You're home!" Amelia cried out as she ran up and threw herself at Waylynn.

Chloe finally realized it was Waylynn and jumped off the chair and rushed over. I stepped back and let everyone take their turn giving our oldest sibling a welcome home hug and kiss.

Making my way to Paxton, she grinned. "When something amazing happens, I say it's the best day of my life. At this rate, I'm going to have hundreds of best days!"

"I had no idea Chloe was going to break down like that."

Paxton looked at me warmly. "It was beautiful. Raw and real. I don't think I've ever been so moved."

Leaning in, I whispered, "Wait until she finds out about the baby!"

CHAPTER 42

Paxton

I walked around the classroom and glanced at all the pictures the kids were coloring. The assignment was to draw one of their Christmas wishes. I was supposed to call it "winter break," but I couldn't bring myself to be politically correct right now. I was too happy.

As I strolled through the classroom I smiled. If Christmas break was anything like Thanksgiving break, there would be lots of laughter and a few tears of joy.

Waylynn had stayed only two days, much to her family's disappointment. She needed to return back to New York to be with her husband for some charity event that Saturday night. Waylynn, Chloe, Amelia, and I all spent Friday in San Antonio. Shopping and getting our nails and toes done. It had been a blast, and Chloe had fallen in love with her Aunt Waylynn, but there was something in Waylynn's eyes, the false smile she wore, that had me talking to Steed about it. She didn't seem happy and even Amelia had noticed it.

One of the kids coughing pulled me from my thoughts.

Stopping at Timmy's desk, I glanced at his drawing and attempted to keep my chuckle in. It was a picture of him holding Chloe's hand. My heart warmed. Poor kid. He had no clue Steed would never let that wish come true.

I had to cover my mouth to keep from laughing at what he was going to do when I told him about this.

Walking around the room, I stopped and glanced over Chloe's shoulder. She was deep in thought as her crayon moved over the paper. It was a picture of an open field. The ranch, I was guessing.

Chloe was on a horse with a huge smile on her face and Steed and I were off to the side. My breath caught in my throat. She had drawn me with a bigger belly and Steed's hand over the small round bump. My belly was colored half pink and half blue. I took a few steps back before I regained my composure.

There is no way she knows.

Steed and I hadn't told anyone I was pregnant. Except for Amelia, Cord, and our mothers. And we hadn't actually told our mothers officially. No one else knew. On Christmas day we were going to make the announcement.

I took another step and peeked at the drawing. Yep, I looked pregnant in it. Why was it half pink and half blue? Then it hit me.

Oh. Lord. She was hoping for twins.

Twins.

I spun around and tried to keep my body from shaking. Why hadn't I thought about twins? My breathing picked up and I closed my eyes.

Deep breath in. Deep breath out. In. Out.

Twins? Oh, Lord.

"Ms. Monroe, are you okay?"

Snapping my eyes open, I looked at little Ricky. "Um…yes. I'm fine."

My classroom phone started to ring. I made my way over to it and pushed the thought of twins far from my mind. Very far.

"This is kinder!" I said with a cheerful voice.

"Um...Paxton, I'm sending Mrs. Haas to your classroom. I need you to come down to the office."

Mrs. Haas, the vice principal? That couldn't be good.

My heart started to race as I watched the door to my classroom open and Mrs. Haas walked in. She gave me a smile but her eyes told me something was very wrong.

"Sure, Mrs. Haas walked in so I'm on my way."

Hanging up, I called out, "Shave and a haircut."

"Two bits!" the class said as one.

All eyes were on me. "Class, I have to run to the office, but Mrs. Haas is here to keep everyone working on their projects. I want you to continue drawing, and when I get back, we'll chat about them. Then it's story time."

The kids nodded; some responded with *yes ma'ams*. Making my way past Mrs. Haas, she grabbed my wrist and pulled me outside the classroom.

"I feel you need a warning about what you're walking into."

Swallowing hard, I said, "Okay."

Did the school find out I was pregnant? There was no way... unless someone saw me buying the test or someone at the doctor's office spilled the beans.

No, that wasn't it. What if Chloe voiced her thoughts about a baby. Shit!

"Chloe's mother is in the office...making a scene."

I stared at her, unsure I had heard correctly. My hands covered my mouth and dread hit the pit of my stomach. "What?"

"I've already called Steed, but he didn't answer. I remembered from Chloe's paperwork that the mother was not allowed any contact, so I looked it up and I was right. I'm so sorry, Paxton. We didn't know what else to do. I wasn't sure y'all wanted a scene with the police."

Dropping my hands to my sides, I took in a deep breath. "No, you did the right thing. I'll be right back."

She nodded and went back to my classroom, disappearing on the other side of the door.

I should have been more freaked out, but a part of me was beyond pissed off that that woman had the nerve to show her face at Chloe's school. I took off at a fast pace down the hall, my high heels clicking on the tile floor and my heart pounding in my ears.

Walking into the office, Marge, the receptionist, pointed to the conference room Mr. Hines used.

"Marge, call Mitchell and tell him what's going on. If you can't get a hold of him, call the police."

"Oh, okay. Sure…right."

I wasn't sure where in the hell I was getting my balls from, but I pushed the door open and walked in like I freaking owned the room.

There she sat. The woman who had been married to Steed. Who birthed his child. She was beautiful. Her blonde hair was pulled into a neat bun. Her perfectly done make-up was a tad on the heavy side, but she was able to pull it off. Blood red nails tapped on the conference table but paused when I walked in. Her eyes moved over me as hate oozed off her body.

"Kim," I said with a curt nod.

Her eyes squinted then opened wide. She was surprised I had used her first name. She also recognized me. Steed had told me he carried a picture of me in his wallet, and she had found it and had threatened to burn it.

"You must be the whore who my husband pined over all those years."

Mr. Hines stood and I held up my hand for him to calm down.

"I don't know why you're here, but you need to leave before I tell the office to call the police."

She lifted a brow. "You're not even going to respond to me calling you a whore?"

"You were served with a restraining order to say away from Chloe."

Kim stood, trying to intimidate me. "She's my daughter, so back the fuck off, slut."

"That will be enough of the name calling! I'm having Marge call the police."

Mr. Hines stormed out of the conference room. I knew they didn't want to cause a scene, but a parent with a restraining order at the school should have been an immediate phone call to police. That was something I intended on taking up with Mr. Hines. For now, though, I had a bitch to deal with.

Leaning my hands on the table, I stared her in the eyes. "Let me remind you about how you signed over all of your parental rights to Chloe. You have *no* rights to her. None."

Her eye twitched. "He lied to me. The moment I found out that asshole was back in Texas and living on his rich daddy's plantation, I took the first flight out. I want him back, and I want Chloe back. I've changed my mind."

I snickered. "First off you twit, it's a ranch, not a plantation. This isn't *Gone with the Wind*. Second, he doesn't want you and neither does Chloe."

"We'll see. I have no intentions of leaving."

This woman had made Steed and Chloe's life a miserable hell all those years. Now that she saw money again, her delusional mind thought she could walk back into their lives as if nothing had happened.

"You know, we used to fuck like rabbits. All the time. It was especially good when I was pregnant. Steed would rub my stomach while pounding in and out of me telling me how excited he was for the baby."

Even though I knew it was a lie it caused a sharp pain in my chest.

What. A. Bitch.

"I wonder...*Paxton*... Does he fuck you from behind? It seemed to be his favorite position."

I'd had enough of this crazy ass lunatic. Walking around the conference table, I made my way towards her. My reaction caught her off guard, and she started to back up.

"Probably because he couldn't stand to see your face."

She gasped and jerked back like I had slapped her.

"Listen here and listen good, *Kim*." I dragged her name out like she had mine. "He was never yours, he'll never be yours, and if you so much as step within seeing distance of either him or Chloe, I will make sure the rest of your life is spent in prison."

As she stood before me speechless, I felt my lady balls growing.

A slow smile moved over my face. "Did I mention my future brother-in-law is a top law enforcement officer for the State of Texas? I don't know how things are done up in Oregon, but here in Texas things are handled on a more...personal level. Family comes first. Don't. *Fuck*. With. *My*. Family."

Her eyes widened. "Are you threatening me?"

"I don't make threats, Kim. You can bet your fake tits and eyelashes that every single word I say is set in stone. I love Steed and Chloe, and I'd risk my entire life for their happiness. So I suggest you get your skinny ass out of the state of Texas and never come back. Because if you do...I will personally kick your ass all the way to your jail cell."

I heard the door open and close about halfway through all of that, sure it had been Mr. Hines. I was mentally prepared to get fired, but it was worth it. There was no way this bitch was going to come back into Chloe and Steed's life if I had anything to say about it.

Pushing her shoulders back, she glared. "This is so not worth it. *They're* not worth it. Good luck, sweetheart."

Grabbing her purse, she stepped around me and stopped. A smirk crossed over her face. "Is that Steed's ring on your finger?"

I smiled. "Yes. And I'll let you in on another little secret, I'm also carrying his child."

Her mouth went slack and anger filled her eyes. Then she laughed. "Oh, Jesus Christ. That's perfect! Didn't take him long to knock you up. Well, I guess there is no use trying this avenue. Maybe I'll find an oil billionaire here in Texas." She rolled her eyes and huffed. "What a waste of seven years. I hope you enjoy the stretch marks the little fucker will leave behind. That little brat changed my body, and I'll never get it back to the way it was before I popped her out. Nothing but a waste."

Her words stunned me into silence. She pushed past me and walked out the door. I couldn't move. Feeling sick to my stomach, I took in a deep slow breath.

"I cannot believe she said that." Mr. Hines stood there with a horrified look.

With my hand on my stomach, I barely said, "She's more vile than I ever imagined."

I realized slowly that he had overheard me saying I was pregnant. Our eyes met and he nodded. "Well talk after the break, Paxton."

Shit. She just cost me my job. No. I had when I opened my big mouth and told her I was pregnant.

The only thing I could do was nod. "I…I better get back to my classroom."

Feeling numb, I headed out of the conference room and through the office. Mitchell and Steed rushed through the front door of the school, causing me to stop.

"She's gone," I said. I was all of sudden so tired. Exhausted, really. The only energy I seemed to have left was quickly fading.

Steed studied me, his eyes roaming over my body. "Are you okay?"

"Do you know what kind of a car she was driving?" Mitchell asked.

Shaking my head, I whispered, "No."

"It was a BMW. I wrote down the license plate," Marge said.

"Great! I'm going to run it and find her. This bitch is going to jail for violating her restraining order."

Steed never took his eyes off of me, but said to Mitchell, "Good. I want her in jail, with a clear message to never step foot in Texas again."

I forced a smile. "I'm pretty sure I got the message to her."

The room started to feel like it was rocking back and forth.

"Steed, I'm not feeling very well."

CHAPTER 43

Steed

Walking into the room, I fisted my hands when I saw Kim sitting at the table. Mitchell shut the door and stood off to the side.

"You had me fucking arrested?" Kim shouted.

I grinned. "You broke the law. Of course you were going to get arrested."

Her eyes flickered back and forth between Mitchell and me. "You did this on purpose."

"No, *you* did this. You gave up any right you had to Chloe. I got a restraining order against your ass, and you ignored it."

"You illegally got it."

Laughing, I shook my head. "Think whatever you want, Kim. I'm only going to tell you this once. If you ever set foot back in the state of Texas, I'll make sure you rot in jail."

Her brow lifted. "And how exactly would you do that?"

Placing my hands on the table, I leaned closer. "My parents are one of the richest families in Texas. My brother is a Texas Ranger. If you doubt for one moment that I couldn't make your life a living hell, you're crazy."

Her throat bobbed as she swallowed hard.

"After you spend the evening here in this nice jail of ours, I expect your ass to be on the next plane out of the state. Don't test me, Kim. I've put up with your shit for too long."

Her eyes narrowed into two thin slits. "I cannot even begin to tell you how much I hate you."

I moved closer, causing her to lean back. "Back at ya, Kim."

After I poured a mug of coffee, I ran my fingers through my hair and stared out the kitchen window. A heaviness filled my chest, and I tried like hell to push it away. My mind had been racing all afternoon and evening. It had taken everything out of me not to lose my shit on Kim.

I couldn't believe she had the fucking nerve to go to Chloe's school. Did she really think they would just hand her over? Of course she did. She never once dropped off Chloe or picked her up from day care. Kim had no idea how any of it worked because she left it all up to me. The one time she took Chloe to a playdate she forgot to pick her up, and they had to call me to come get her.

I was glad Mitchell had her arrested. I wish I could be a fly on the wall when she was sitting in that cell tonight. Chuckling, I shook my head and rubbed the back of my neck. What an idiot.

"Hey, how's Paxton?" Amelia asked while walking into my kitchen.

"I didn't even hear you come in."

She grinned. "Yeah, I kind of snuck in. I wasn't sure if you would be sleeping or not."

The tension in my neck increased, and I found myself rubbing it again.

"Paxton's doing good. The doctor stopped by and assured us that everything was fine with the baby, but it was best if Paxton took the next few days to rest."

"That's good the baby is okay," she replied.

"Yeah. It's really good. Luckily, she'll only miss half a day of school with it being Christmas break and all."

Her arms wrapped around her body. "That's true."

Making her way over to me, she smiled and grabbed a mug. She poured herself a cup of coffee and asked, "Do you want to sit on the back porch?"

I shrugged. "Sure. Why not."

After we made our way to the porch, we sat in silence for a few minutes. The sounds of nature always calmed me. Why didn't I sit out here more often? I made a mental note to sit out here each evening with Paxton.

"Paxton move in yet?"

"She's going to during the break, but she's pretty much staying here all the time."

"What does Chloe think about it?"

I smiled. "Paxton and I talked to her about it. Chloe doesn't seem to be bothered by it at all."

"Things will be easier when you're married, I'm sure."

Taking a sip of coffee, I nodded.

"Speaking of married, have y'all picked a date?"

"The sooner the better. Paxton's worried about her job. Today her boss overheard her tell Kim she was pregnant. He told her they would talk after the break."

Amelia's brows lifted. "Really? For Christ's sake, this isn't the fifties. Lots of people have kids outside of marriage."

"Not kindergarten teachers in small town Texas."

"Then get married over the break. She'll have the baby in July. Sure folks will gossip but who gives a flying shit what people think."

"I don't."

"Good! Steed, when people started to find out I wrote romance books, tongues were wagging like crazy in this town. I thought Daddy was going to fly through the roof when the teller at the bank mentioned I wrote porn books. You just let them get it out of their system. They'll gossip in their weekly bunko groups and Wednesday church meetings and then they move on to next week's gossip. It's a cycle."

"You're right."

"Of course I am. But…besides stopping by to check on Paxton, I had an idea. Well, actually it was Waylynn's idea. I just got off the phone with her."

Oh hell. When my two sisters got their minds together it usually spelled trouble. Twice Amelia and Waylynn had been on the verge of being tossed in jail when Amelia went to New York to visit her. Waylynn's jackass husband tried to ban Waylynn from seeing Amelia, and she pretty much told him to go fuck himself.

"Do I want to know?"

"Yes, I think you do. When Waylynn was in town over Thanksgiving and we all went to get our nails done, Paxton mentioned she always dreamed of a winter wedding around Christmas. The lights and holiday cheer made it the perfect time to get married."

"Yes, she has mentioned that before."

"Well then! Okay!"

I narrowed my eyes at my baby sister. "Well then, what?"

"You'll get married. On Christmas Eve!"

Staring at her like she was insane, I let out a roar of laughter. "Because it would be so easy to plan a wedding in…" I looked at my watch. "Five days."

A smile moved across her face that actually frightened me. "Do you trust me and Waylynn?"

"Of course I do. No, wait!" I held up my hand. "Trust you with what?"

"Planning your wedding. We can surprise Paxton. Think about it, Steed. You both want to be married, neither of you want the stress of that right now so how perfect will it be to have it all planned out for you? That way the two of you can concentrate on the baby, and Chloe, and your relationship!"

I leaned back in my chair and let the idea settle in some. "Where would we have it?"

"Here. On the ranch at Mom and Dad's place. I already talked to April and David to make sure they would be okay with that. They were thrilled with the idea, and April is beyond thrilled to be helping."

That made my heart soar. "Christmas Eve you say?" I asked with a grin.

"Yep. I already checked the weather, and it looks to be beautiful."

"Is Waylynn gonna fly down for it?"

Her smile faltered. "Um, she was coming home for Christmas anyway. Jack had a business meeting in London he was going to and told her it would be best if she stayed home for this trip."

"Fucker," I mumbled.

"Yeah. He is. That's a story for another day," Amelia added.

Leaning forward, I rested my arms on my knees. The more I thought about it, the better it sounded. Paxton would be mine. My wife. Chloe's mom. A no-stress wedding. She'd already brought up going to the justice of the peace and making it official, so I knew she wouldn't be upset.

With a tilt of my head, I smiled at my sister. "Let's do it."

Amelia set her coffee cup down and started to jump around. "Oh my gosh, Steed! I promise you won't regret it! I swear we'll make it so special for the three of you!"

Standing, I pulled my sister into my arms. I loved that she had included Chloe in that statement. "I know you will, Meli. I'm just glad the whole family will be here for Christmas."

"For your wedding too," she whispered.

"Hey, Amelia."

We both pulled away to see Paxton standing there.

"Why are you up? You should be resting," I said.

She flashed me a sexy grin. "The doctor said everything was fine. I'm sure it was the stress of the situation that made me feel ill. I feel amazing and very rested."

Amelia clapped. "Then, you wouldn't mind playing dress up with me would you?"

Paxton narrowed her eyes at my sister. "Huh?"

"I've got this dinner I have to go to and a friend of Waylynn's sent some dresses down to try on. What fun is it to try on designer gowns by yourself? I'll even bring them over here so Steed doesn't freak out."

I watched as Paxton's eyes lit up. "Oh! That would be fun. Especially since I won't be able to do that in a few months." Paxton rubbed her belly.

"Great! I'll run up to the house and grab them and then be right back."

Paxton nodded. "Okay, that gives me time to grab something to eat."

That was my cue. Rushing to her, I asked, "What do you want to eat, pumpkin? I'll fix it."

Her blue eyes filled with tears, and I was surprised when she wrapped her arms around me. "I'm so sorry you and Chloe had to deal with that awful woman."

"Hey, look at me."

She did.

"What she dished out to you was bad. Yeah, she was curt with both of us, but she wasn't that much of a monster. I shielded Chloe from a lot. She was trying to hurt you, and she succeeded. Don't let her even cross your mind ever again."

With a nod, she swallowed hard. "I hate that I let her affect me like she did. I was just so thrown off by her hate."

Anger toward Kim pulsed through my body. I fucking hated her. Hated that she had gotten to Paxton. At the same time, I was so relieved Chloe hadn't seen her.

Placing my hand on the side of her cheek, I leaned in and softly kissed her. "She'll never bother you or Chloe again. I swear to God."

She smiled while placing her hand over mine. "I know. Thank you for reassuring me though."

With a wink, I replied, "Come on. Let's get you some food."

CHAPTER 44

Paxton

Something was going on. I caught on to it the other day when Amelia had me trying on beautiful gowns from her friend in New York.

It wasn't a total loss on me that they were all white. Every. Single. One. Different shades of white. My mother would have been in her glory.

Or the fact that they were all *my* size. I chuckled thinking back to Amelia commenting with, "It's crazy she sent them all in your size!"

Amelia and I were close to the same size, but my breasts were a bit larger than hers.

Chloe came running into the library. "Paxton! It's Christmas Eve and Grammy just called to tell Daddy that Cord was on his way with Aunt Waylynn! She's here again!"

I drew Chloe into my arms and kissed her on the forehead. "That is so amazing! I'm so glad she is home again!"

"Yep, and Grammy said we're all going and getting our hair done!"

My smile faltered. Huh?

"Our hair done?"

She nodded. "Yep. And I know a secret. A big secret. B. I. G. I can spell, ya know."

I grinned. "Yes, I happen to know your teacher."

Looking at me with a confused expression, she busted out laughing. "You're so funny! But...my secret is huge." Chloe held her arms out as far as she could spread them.

Narrowing one eye at her, I asked, "Is that so? Who is the secret about?"

With a giggle, she covered her mouth. "You!"

My stomach dropped. Everything was starting to make sense.

The dresses. The way Steed was so nervous this morning. The private phone call he took where I overheard him saying he would pay twice the amount if they could make it happen on Christmas Eve. Now the hair.

"Grammy said you had to get your nails done, so we all had to get them done. As a way to..." She looked up in thought. "Right...as a way to throw you off she said!"

Oh, how I loved my little non-secret keeper.

"Chloe, is your Daddy planning on something big happening today?"

She shook her head. "Oh no, it's tonight! And after tonight, I get to call you Mommy." Jumping off my lap, she ran out of the room before she stopped and looked back at me. "See how good of a secret keeper I am! I didn't even tell you that you that the big secret was you and Daddy gettin' married today!"

And like that, she spun around and rushed out the door. I jumped up.

Married?

Today?

My heart started racing, and I couldn't help the smile that spread across my face.

I grabbed my phone and sent a text off to two different people.

Me: *How is Chicago?*

It didn't take Corina long to reply.

Corina: *Chicago?*

Grinning, I typed out my reply.

Me: *Yes…Chicago. You did fly home yesterday right?*

She didn't answer. Corina couldn't lie. It wasn't in her DNA to lie. Not even a white lie. A fib. Nothing. She was literally incapable of lying.

Next text.

Me: *Merry Christmas Eve! Hey…do you and Dad want to go look at lights tonight?*

My mother's reply was almost instant.

Mom: *What?! Lights?*

I covered my mouth to keep from laughing. *Oh. This is fun.*

Me: *What? It would be fun. We haven't done it in years, and I bet Chloe would love it!*

Mom: *Maybe we could go tomorrow or the next night. To-night's not good for us.*

Lifting my brow, I hit her number. *Let's up the pressure some.*

Her voicemail started after two rings. Oh my gosh, my mother sent me to voicemail.

Me: *You sent me to voicemail, Mom!*

Mom: *I'm in a meeting. Can't talk.*

Me: *What kind of meeting?*

Mom: *About the new town square.*

I frowned. *Shit.* That made sense. My mother was on the com-mittee to improve downtown Oak Springs, to get it growing even more than it was. Our little town had always been a bit of a tourist town with the Frio River and quaint stores.

Cord's popular bar proved that more could be done with the town square, and the committee wanted it to grow even more. New plans were now being laid to bring in new businesses and make it more of a tourist town. We already had people coming in for the Frio River; we just needed ways to keep them around, make them spend their money.

Me: *Okay. Well, maybe I'll take one of the horses out. Steed's gone, and it's just me and Chloe. We can pack a picnic or something.*

Mom: *NO! Her Grammy has plans to take y'all to get your hair done. Didn't you hear? Waylynn is in town, and you know how that girl likes to primp.*

Me: *I'm not in the mood for that.*

The phone rang, and I nearly jumped out of my skin.

"Hey, Mom."

"Paxton, please do me a favor."

"Okay," I replied, trying to sound normal.

"Go to the hair thing with Melanie. She's really looking forward to spending time with her girls."

"Mom, I know."

"Well, I'm just saying. With you and Chloe now in her life and Waylynn coming in, she's just happy."

"No, Mom. I know."

There was silence on her end before she finally spoke. "You know what?"

"The wedding. Chloe spilled the beans."

She muffled the phone and said something to someone, then came back on the line. "Don't move. We're on our way over."

When I heard a dial tone, I jerked the phone from my head and peered at it. She'd hung up on me!

Little did I know that an hour later our house would be full of people I loved. People who had worked so hard to keep this a surprise only to have an almost six-year-old rat them out.

Waylynn had flown in last night, much to my surprise. Corina had never left and had been staying at the main house where she, Waylynn, and Amelia had a sleep over last night. I wasn't going to lie, my feelings were a little bruised I hadn't gotten to be a part of it, but Corina said it was mainly a wedding planning night.

I was being primped big time. Melanie's best friend owned the hair salon and spa in town and was buffing my nails while Amelia painted my toes.

Waylynn pulled and twisted my hair while my mother and Melanie argued about the dress I should wear. Amelia had narrowed it down to the top three I had liked.

"Shouldn't I be the one to pick? I mean, since I know about the wedding and all?"

Amelia glanced over her shoulder. "Mom, seriously, Paxton should pick out her dress. I highly doubt Dad and David are arguing over what Steed's gonna wear."

They both frowned. I had already known which one it would be. Once I started to figure out what in the world was going on, I had secretly hoped the Rene Ruiz gown had made the cut. The gowns I had tried on the other night though were all amazing, but that one made me feel like a princess.

I also noticed the Oscar De La Renta was hanging up as well. When I took a peek at the $10,000 price tag I laughed my ass off. But Amelia loved it. I did too, but I loved the much less pricey Rene Ruiz even more.

After what seemed like hours, it was time for me to pick the dress.

Walking up to the one I had picked, I smiled.

"I knew you would pick the Rene Ruiz. It's classic and breathtaking on you," Amelia said with a huge grin. "Okay, everyone out except for Paxton, Corina, and Chloe."

Chloe's eyes lit up like Christmas morning. "I get to stay?"

"Of course you do, Chloe Cat. I need my two maids of honor to help me get dressed."

You would have thought I had given her the world.

I caught Melanie's stare and smiled. She returned it and mouthed, "Thank you."

With a simple nod, I watched as everyone left the room.

I'm getting married. Holy. Shit.

Placing my hand over my stomach, I breathed in and out a few times to calm my nerves. It was finally happening.

Taking Chloe's hand, I led her over to the window seat.

"How are you feeling about today, Chloe Cat?" I asked. I had told Corina I wanted to a few minutes to talk to Chloe without everyone in the room. She was making herself busy as she pretended to mess with my dress.

"Me?"

"Yes, you. Today isn't just a big day for your daddy and me. It's a big day for you too. I want to make sure you're as happy as we are."

Chloe's smile grew from ear to ear.

"You know how happy you are right before Santa comes? Or the tooth fairy?"

With a chuckle, I nodded. "Yes."

"Well, I'm so much more happy! I've been asking God for a long time for a mommy who loved me and my daddy."

My heart ached.

"I love you so much, Chloe Cat. And I love your daddy. You both make me so very happy. Don't ever forget that, okay?"

She nodded. "I won't."

I slid off the bench and knelt so I could look her in the eyes. "Is there anything you want to ask me before I marry your daddy and become your mommy?"

Chloe's eyes darted over to my dress. "Can I have your dress when you're done with it? It would be perfect to play princess in."

Laughing, I pulled her into my arms. "Yes! Consider it yours, Princess Chloe."

"Okay, let's get your mommy dressed," Corina said as she made her way over to us with the dress. My heart dropped, and my stomach started to flutter. Chloe must have noticed my nerves.

She took my hand. "Don't worry, you'll look like a princess too. I promise."

Kissing her on the cheek, I replied, "Thank you, Chloe Cat!"

I dropped my robe to the ground to reveal the white lace panties and matching bra. I wouldn't need the bra, but with Chloe in the room, Corina and I thought it best not to flash her my boobs.

Chloe's mouth rose into a wide smile. "Wow! My dad's gonna be happy!"

Corina and I were stunned before we lost it laughing.

Corina took the embellished strapless dress and nodded. Facing away from Chloe, who was now standing on the bed, I unclasped the bra and let it drop to the floor. Holding up my arms, Corina carefully slipped the dress over my head.

"Careful, careful!" Chloe chanted from behind, making sure my hair was safe. That had been her self-assigned job.

When the dress slipped on, Corina zipped it up and all three of us gasped. The strapless neckline was stunning. It looked old-fashioned, yet had a modern flair as well. The color was a creamy white.

"You are stunning," Corina whispered.

"You're a princess!" Chloe said with her hands over her cheeks.

Corina handed me a long box. "This is from me. It's your some-thing blue."

She put on a diamond necklace that held one blue sapphire stone in the middle. My fingers moved lightly over it as I attempted not to cry.

"It's...gorgeous."

Her eyes gazed into mine. "It's my grandmother's. Someday you'll be putting it on my neck when I get married."

Turning to her, I drew her in for a hug. "Corina! It's perfect. And it serves as my something borrowed as well!"

She laughed. "I didn't even think about that. Yes! It does."

Chloe stood in front of me. "You look like a princess," she said again as she stared up in awe.

I placed my hand on the side of her sweet little face. "Thank you, Chloe Cat."

"This is my gift to you! It's your something new. Well, it's from me and Daddy."

My heart soared as I took the box from her and opened it to find the most beautiful diamond earrings.

"Chloe! These are the most beautiful earrings I've ever seen."

She beamed. "I picked them out! Daddy said I had expensive taste."

Leaning down, I chuckled as I kissed her on the cheek.

Corina opened the door, letting everyone in. My mother walked up to me and started crying.

"Oh, Momma don't cry. You'll make me cry!"

"You look beautiful, sweetheart. Steed is going to pass out when he sees you."

"You're biased," I replied with a wink.

Reaching into her pocket, she pulled out a Bible and handkerchief. "I carried this down the aisle with your father. Your grandmother carried it, and your great-grandmother as well. It's your something old."

My hands shook as I took the Bible and handkerchief. At this rate, my face would be covered in my black mascara soon.

She kissed me on the cheek, and then it was Melanie's turn. She tried to speak, but broke down crying. Turning, she walked over to Amelia who pulled her into her arms.

"We better get going. It's time," Waylynn said.

Everyone started to pile back out of the room except for Corina and Chloe. Waylynn grinned. "You ready?"

I nodded.

When she turned to leave, I called out for her. "Hey, Waylynn?"

Glancing back at me, she said, "Yeah?"

"How did y'all do this? Plan all of this so quickly?"

She walked back to me and took my hands in hers. "That day at the spa when you said you wanted a winter wedding…we all knew we had to make it happen. I started making plans right then and there. To say I was excited y'all were back together is an understatement."

My heart skipped a beat. I was so blessed to have such amazing women in my life.

"Well, thank you. To you and Amelia for doing this. You'll never know what it means to me."

Kissing my cheek, she softly said, "It was my pleasure. I never got to plan my own wedding…so this was fun for me."

Her eyes seemed so sad.

"I'm so sorry."

With a shrug, the sadness was gone, replaced by excitement.

"Let's do this!" she cried out as Chloe started jumping, her curls going everywhere. She started to run out of the room when she stopped and turned back to us. "Oh no! I left Patches tied up in Daddy's office!"

My eyes widened in shock. "What? Chloe, why is your pet goat tied up?"

"In your Daddy's office?" Waylynn added.

Placing her hands on her hips, her little head tilted, she looked at us like we were idiots. "He's walking me down the aisle."

I couldn't help but laugh. Glancing over to a still stunned Waylynn, I said, "We better get one of the guys to go get Patches."

She faced me, her jaw dropped open. "You want the goat in the wedding?"

Peeking over to Chloe, I smiled and answered, "Of course. He's a part of the family."

CHAPTER 45

Steed

I stood under the arch and waited not-so-patiently for Paxton to appear. My parents and Paxton's had gone all out for this quickly pulled together wedding. It appeared like it had been months in the making. Everything was beautiful. The flowers, the cakes. It was everything I could see Paxton picking out. I was glad we had decided to keep it to close family and friends only. It made things easier when it came to planning.

Cord stood next to me. He was my best man and the one who won the straw drawing. Having four other brothers is hard when it comes time to pick a best man. Chloe had come up with the whole "drawing straws" idea, and my brothers loved the idea. Damn kids at heart...all four of them.

The music started playing, and I first saw my sweet little Chloe. Then Patches. *What in the hell?* She wore a huge smile as she skipped down the aisle while Patches trotted next to her. I couldn't help but laugh. The damn goat was in our wedding. We were never going to get Chloe to fall asleep tonight with all this excitement on top of it being Christmas Eve.

"Damn, Steed. She almost makes me want to have a kid," Cord said with a chuckle.

I glanced over to him. "A kid, huh?"

He frowned. "I said *almost*. The goat isn't helping."

Corina came next. I peeked over to Tripp. He was smiling, but one look at Mitchell and I knew which one of them was more captivated by her.

Mitchell.

The way he stared was a far cry from the way Tripp looked at Corina. I looked back, holding my breath as I stared at the back door.

When the wedding march started and everyone stood, I slowly exhaled only to have my breath taken again when Paxton walked through the door with her father. I heard gasps from the small group of friends and family.

"She's beautiful," I whispered as a smile spread over my face.

The simple cream colored gown hugged her body, and I couldn't help but let my eyes roam. They lingered a little more on her stomach before I dragged them back up and her blue eyes caught mine.

I shook my head slowly. I wanted to pinch myself.

Holy shit. She was mine. She was finally mine.

As Paxton and I walked around and talked to the guests, I could tell she was getting tired. So was Chloe who had stuck to our side like glue. She'd already started calling Paxton "Mommy," and every time she did, Paxton's face lit up.

Thank God it was mostly family, plus some friends from each side and a few of my father's closest business partners. Other than

that, it had been a small wedding and reception. We had made it
around to everyone in no time at all.

Somehow Amelia had found someone who was willing to make
a wedding cake last minute. It was decorated in white and soft blue.
The same blue as Chloe and Corina's dresses. Don't ask me how
they pulled that shit off.

Paxton leaned against me and sighed. "You tired?" I asked.

"A little," she said, then yawned.

"We cut the cake, we said hello and thanks for coming. I think
it's time to leave. Besides, look at Chloe."

Her eyes swung over to our daughter, and she laughed. Chloe
was sitting at a table, her head perched up with her hands, sound
asleep.

"That poor little thing. We promised her a movie too. We should
probably start making our way out of here."

I nodded in agreement. "Let's find our parents and let them
know we're ready to go."

Paxton laced her fingers with mine while we searched for our
folks. They were sitting inside talking to some old friends.

"Mom, Dad, I think we're going to take off. Paxton is tired and
poor little Chloe is passed out."

They all stood. Each of them took turns kissing us on the cheeks
and congratulating us.

"We'll make the announcement that y'all are leaving."

"Plans for a honeymoon?" Karen Alright, one of my parents'
friends, asked while taking a sip of wine.

"Not right now. We're going to go to Ireland during spring
break."

"Ireland?" she asked with lifted brows.

"Yes, Paxton's always wanted to go there so that's where we are
heading. Tonight we are taking our daughter home and watching
Miracle on 34th Street."

"How wonderful!" Karen said.

Forty-five minutes later, we were finally leaving. Chloe was asleep in my arms as we walked past everyone cheering out "Mr. and Mrs. Parker!" I gently put my sleeping beauty in the backseat of my truck, helped my beautiful wife in, and tucked her dress safely inside.

A quick wave to everyone, and I jumped into the truck and headed to our place on the other side of the ranch.

Paxton dropped her head back. "As much as I loved our wedding, I would have been just as happy eloping. I'm exhausted and I didn't even plan anything!"

I laughed.

We were soon back at the house, changed, and sitting on the sofa eating popcorn and watching the movie Paxton said we had to make a family tradition each Christmas Eve. I couldn't believe how fucking happy I was. As much as I wanted to sink myself into my wife and stay lost in her all night, this felt perfect.

Chloe sat in the middle, entranced with the movie. She had asked earlier if Paxton was going to sleep in my room with me and a part of me was bothered we had been lying to her. We told her yes, and she smiled big and stated that we were now officially a real family. I didn't want to ask why she felt like Paxton sleeping in the same room meant we were a family. I was going to ignore it. Ignorance was blissful.

When it was time to put her to bed so Santa could come, Paxton tucked her in like she had been doing the last few weeks, while I turned on her nightlight and grabbed her favorite doll and stuffed animal.

Our normal routine had changed a bit when Paxton moved in. I used to be the one to tuck her in. That job was given to her new mommy. Which I was fine with. Then it was prayers, a small story with her doll and giraffe and then lights out.

"Ready for prayers?" Paxton asked while kissing Chloe on the forehead.

"Yes!"

Closing her eyes, Chloe started her prayers, which were exactly the same every night…with a few changes when need be.

"Please bless my teacher Paxton. Please bless all my friends. Please bless, Sam, Bill, Lady, Allure, Marley, Little Bill, Harley, Chip, Milo, Buddy, all the goats especially Patches cause he's my goat granddaddy gave me, and all the cows and all the wildlife in the whole wide world. Please bless my Grammy and Granddaddy and my new Gran and Pops. That's what they want to be called 'cause I asked them and tonight I can officially call 'em that."

My eyes lifted to Paxton's. We both smiled, and she quickly wiped a tear away.

"Please bless all my aunts and uncles. There's too many to name."

That part always made me laugh since she pretty much just named four horses, two cats, and two dogs along with half the damn ranch animals in her prayers.

"And please bless Daddy and my new mommy. It's Paxton, God. I know that might confuse you 'cause she's my teacher too."

My heart felt light. A happiness so overwhelming hit me in the chest that I had to force myself not to cry. One look at Paxton told me she felt the same way.

"And one more thing God. Please bring me a baby brother or sister. Amen."

Paxton and I glanced over at each other, and she smiled. We had already talked about telling Chloe first before announcing it to the whole family tomorrow. It would make it more special for Chloe, Paxton had said.

I leaned over and kissed my daughter's cheek. "Pumpkin, God has already answered your prayer."

With a look of wonderment, she asked, "Which one, Daddy?"

Peeking over to Paxton, she took Chloe's hand and put it on her stomach. "I've got a baby growing in my tummy, Chloe Cat. A little baby brother or sister."

Chloe sat up. She had been so emotional when we announced we were getting married, I wasn't sure what she would do with this news. Her eyes filled with tears, and I held my breath. I hated seeing her cry.

"Is it true? Daddy, is it true Mommy has my baby brother in there?"

I nodded. "It is. Does that make you happy?"

She jumped up and threw her arms around me. "Thank you for bringing us home, Daddy. Thank you!"

I held her tightly and squeezed my eyes. "Oh, baby. I love you."

When she pulled back, her tears were streaming. "I love you too."

She turned to Paxton and wrapped her little arms around her neck.

"I love you so much, Mommy! Thank you for loving me and giving me a baby brother! Thank you so…much."

Chloe was now sobbing and so was Paxton. Each of them held onto each other as if their lives depended on it.

"Oh, Chloe Cat. I love you so much too!"

When my girls finally stopped crying, Chloe climbed back under the covers, folded her hands in prayer and smiled. "P.S. Dear God, thank you for going so fast on the baby brother. And thank you for helping Daddy find my mommy. He'd been looking a long time. His eyes aren't sad anymore thanks to Mommy's love."

Air rushed into my lungs. I stared at Chloe as she took her doll and stuffed goat and snuggled with them. "I better get to sleep or Santa won't come."

Paxton and I slowly stood. Both of us in a silent shock. I was positive that had affected Paxton as much as it did me.

We each kissed Chloe goodnight.

"Night, pumpkin," I whispered against her forehead.

"N-night."

Brushing her hair from her face, Paxton kissed her on the cheek. "Goodnight my sweet Chloe Cat."

She smiled and mumbled something before drifting off to sleep.

Taking Paxton's hand in mine, I led her out of the bedroom, down the hall and stairs, and straight to our bedroom. When I shut the door, we faced each other.

"That was the most amazing moment of my life," I said.

She nodded and wiped a tear away. "I thought the same thing."

My hand slipped behind her head, and I drew her to me. Gently kissing her lips, I softly spoke against them.

"I'm going to make love to you now, Pax."

"What about Santa coming and leaving all the gifts?" she asked.

With a wink, I said, "Even Santa takes time to enjoy the milk and cookies left out."

Paxton laughed and hit me on the chest. "You're bad."

"Not yet, baby."

Lifting her shirt over her head, I dropped it to the ground.

"I'm going to kiss every inch of your body as I whisper, 'Mrs. Steed Parker,' against your creamy skin."

"Steed." She gasped a needy breath.

Undoing her bra, I pulled it from her arms and threw it onto the T-shirt. Grabbing the waist of her sweats, I pulled them…along with her panties…slowly down and off her legs until she stood in front of me naked. Twice in the last few hours I had gotten to undress her. The first time left with me blue balls as I stared at my wife in her wedding gown and then those lace panties. It took everything out of me not to make love to her then.

I pressed my lips under her belly button while her hands combed through my hair, and she let out a soft whimper.

"You are my life, Mrs. Steed Parker. The reason I breathe. My heart beats right along with yours, and I can't imagine a world without you in it."

Dropping my forehead to her stomach, I took in a deep breath.

"You're everything I've ever wanted." Lifting my eyes to hers I smiled. "Our love was never lost because it stayed with me… always."

She dug her teeth into her lip, trying to hold back her emotions as I kissed her stomach. Our child was in there and that knowledge about knocked me over.

"I'd lay my life down for you and our kids."

Standing, I cupped her face in my hands and brushed her tears with my thumbs. My lips brushed over hers.

"My life."

Smiling against my lips, she replied, "My love."

EPILOGUE

Paxton

Three months later

Sitting on the blanket, I leaned my head against Steed's chest as we looked out at the Atlantic Ocean. So much had changed since we got married. The main thing was my job. After Mr. Hines found out I was pregnant, I thought for sure he would fire me. But with Steed and I getting married over Christmas, the news of me being pregnant didn't seem to be an issue anymore. Even though it was obvious I had conceived before the wedding, Mr. Hines choose to ignore that little fact. Maybe our little town was growing with the times?

I was pulled from my thoughts by Steed's hands, caressing the small baby bump that had popped out in the last few weeks. Last month we had the sonogram that told us the sex of our baby. I wasn't going to lie; we both breathed a sigh of relief to know we were only having one. Although, Chloe thought twins would have been super fun.

For her.

"How's my son doing today?" Steed asked, his hot breath trailing down my neck and giving me a warm sensation against the cold breeze coming off the Atlantic.

"He's doing good. I think I'm finally past the morning sickness. Thank God."

Steed's soft lips kissed my neck, shooting a throbbing pain between my legs.

"Mmm... If you keep doing that, I'm going to need some relief."

A low growl came from his throat.

"Fucking hell, Pax. My dick is rock-hard now."

I laughed. "Well, we have time before dinner."

We were sitting outside the breathtaking little house we had rented for the week. It had been cold in Ireland, but not too cold. During the nights it got colder, but we didn't care. We had been too busy in bed heating things up to notice how cold it was outside. The days had warmed nicely and had actually gotten up into the high fifties. For us, it was beautiful weather coming from an already hot Texas.

"Shall we go inside?" he asked.

Nodding, I pushed off him and waited for him to stand and offer me his hand. That was Steed. So considerate and kind. He always put me and Chloe first, no matter what he did.

After he lifted me up and slid his arm around my waist, we started to walk into the house. The same warmth I'd come to expect settled within my chest. My body tingled with the knowledge my husband was about to make love to me. Nothing else on earth was more amazing than Steed and me together.

He led me into the bedroom and flashed me those dimples, making my knees go weak. He gently brushed the back of his hand down my cheek and my body trembled. Other woman craved food during pregnancy, I craved my husband's touch. It both thrilled me and calmed me at once.

"You look beautiful, Pax," he whispered while his eyes roamed my face. The intensity caused my lower stomach to pull, and at the same time, my heart to melt at his sweet words.

My hair had been in a pony to keep the wind from lashing it around, but I was sure it was a crazy mess nonetheless. I didn't have an ounce of makeup on. We'd been lazy that day and decided not to sightsee but to enjoy the amazing ocean view we had instead. I'd thrown on Steed's sweat pants and one of his sweatshirts that hung off of me. At best, I probably looked like I had just woken up from a good night's sleep.

"I'm a mess," I stated with a chuckle.

He shook his head. "I've never seen you look more beautiful. Your wind tossed hair and flushed cheeks... I could stare at you all day and never get tired of the view."

My stomach dipped. "How do you do it?" I asked, wrapping my arms around his neck.

"Do what?"

"Make me feel like I'm the most beautiful woman in the world."

He looked at me like I had said the craziest thing ever, but it was true. Steed had a way of making both me and our daughter feel like we were his everything. The very air he breathed. The last few months were the best of my life. Steed worked the ranch during the day with his father and Cord, and the moment Chloe and I pulled up from school, he was there, wearing a smile and waiting to dish out amazing hugs and kisses for both of us.

I soon found myself giddy with excitement as we drove down the long drive to the house, wondering what surprise he would have in store for us. For Chloe, it was always something with the animals. A new book, or piggyback ride where he acted like a stallion. For me, it was something as simple as a single rose and a kiss, to a heart shaped locket with our family portrait in it. Each day he offered us something.

He spoiled us with love, and I couldn't imagine I could be any happier.

"Pax, you *are* the most beautiful woman in the world."

My eyes filled with tears as I realized that every day this man made me feel special. That my happiness grew each time he smiled at me, kissed me, held me in his arms, or whispered how much he loved me.

I loved this man more than I loved anything. He was the reason I breathed.

"Make love to me, Steed," I softly spoke as he slipped his hand around my neck and pulled my lips to his.

"It would be my pleasure."

Sneak Peek of

Love Profound

Amelia

Nervous as fuck.

That was me as I found myself about to step into the room where one of my romance books was being recorded for the audio-book version. My agent, Allysa, had mentioned it was in the process of being recorded, and we weren't far from where it was happening. I asked if I could sneak a peek and was shocked when she made a phone call and said we could.

The first thing I noticed was the drop-dead gorgeous guy in the booth who was bringing my words to life. His dark blonde hair appeared disheveled, probably from his hand sliding through it. He glanced up and his blue eyes met mine.

Well hello there, James.

I had to wipe the drool from the sides of my mouth. James was the hero in my book, and this beautiful piece of hotness in front of the microphone fit my character's description almost perfectly. Pure-ly a coincidence I was sure, but nonetheless, it made my insides melt a little bit more.

My pulse raced, and my stomach dipped. Jesus. The man had a voice that could talk the panties off of any woman. Shit. My readers were going to love this one. Hell, *I* was entranced, and it was my own book.

"We'll finish this chapter and then give you a chance to meet Liam."

My mind quickly thought of Liam Hemsworth. *Yummy.*

A few moments later, Liam walked into the control room. I swallowed hard as I took him in.

Tall. Check.

Built like a Greek God. Check, check.

Handsome as all get out. Check-a-dee, check, check.

Liam walked up to me and extended his hand. "Amelia, so nice to meet you."

Find your voice for Christ's sake, Amelia. "Liam, the pleasure is all mine. You're Australian?"

He smiled and I was pretty positive I heard angels singing. It should be illegal for a man to smile at a woman like that. "I am."

I nodded. "How long have you lived in the US?"

"Four years now."

I nodded again. Shit. All I could do was nod.

"Well, thank you for bringing a voice to my James. From the sound of it you're doing a great job."

Liam leaned in close and whispered, "He's a bit of a dirty bloke isn't he?"

My cheeks heated instantly. "Yes. He is."

Drawing back, he winked. "You're from Texas?"

I nodded and tried to get the sound of his sexy voice out of my mind. "I am. Ever been there?"

He laughed. "No. I'd love to though."

I didn't say anything to that…mostly because I was fighting the urge to tell him he could come home with me.

"You should visit some time."

Wait, what? Why in the hell did I say that?

His megawatt smile nearly had me stumbling backwards. "I'd love to… Amelia."

Oh. My. God.

Say my name again! Say it again!

My teeth sunk into my lip, and I was pretty sure I was going to leave indentations from how hard I was biting.

"We better let Liam get back to work. They're on a schedule," Allysa said while glancing between Liam and me.

"Oh, yes right. Well, it was nice meeting you, Liam."

He took my hand and shook it. When I turned to follow Allysa out, I felt a hand on my arm, pulling me to a stop.

"Join me for bevvies this evening," a husky voice spoke against my ear.

My eyes scanned the room. No one was paying attention to Liam and me. We had fallen behind everyone. Turning to him, I lifted a brow. "What in the heck is a bevvie?"

He chuckled. "Join me for a beer later?"

I chewed on the corner of my lip. I had no idea why I said that. Digging into my oversized purse, I found a card in the little pocket and handed it to Liam. "I'd love to. Here's my card. It has my cell on it."

Spinning on my heels, I walked out the door with a huge smile.

Well, my trip just took a turn toward fun.

Love Profound coming September 2017.

PLAYLIST

Contains Spoilers

Adam Sanders – "Thunder"
After Steed left Paxton for Oregon

Mat Kearney – "Air I Breathe"
Steed returning to Texas

Kacey Musgraves – "Keep it to Yourself"
Paxton in the classroom after open house and seeing Steed

Jackie Lee – "Getting Over You"
Steed seeing Paxton again after returning home

Chris Bandi – "Man Enough Now"
Steed and Paxton dancing at Cord's Place

Britney Spears – "Womanizer"
Paxton and Corina seeing the Paxton brothers at the carnival set up

Selena Gomez – "Nobody"
Steed and Paxton the night she shows him the velvet bag

328

Rascal Flatts – "Yours If You Want It"
Steed and Paxton first night back together

Dan + Shay – "How Not To"
Steed and Paxton horseback riding

Dierks Bentley – "Black"
Steed and Paxton make love in the cabin

Josh Turner – "Hometown Girl"
Steed's surprise day with Paxton

Brad Paisley – "She's Everything"
Steed and Paxton at the lookout

Chris Lane – "For Her"
Steed asking Paxton to marry him

Rascal Flatts – "The Day Before You"
Steed and Paxton getting married

As with every book, I couldn't do this without the people who help me! From my beta readers, to the editors, formatter, and the readers who pick up my books on release day. THANK YOU!